THE
BEAUTIFUL
POSSIBLE

Praise for *The Beautiful Possible*

"Poetic and deeply moving, *The Beautiful Possible* is an artfully woven story of love and loss, of spirituality and desire, of the stories that make us who we are and the stories we tell ourselves. Gottlieb's debut is beautifully written and captivating."

—Jillian Cantor, author of *Margot* and *The Hours Count*

"Amy Gottlieb's characters pray that they 'will find a way to live between the dual cracks of uncertainty and truth.' Readers will delight in Gottlieb's metaphors, which express the otherwise inexpressible. In *The Beautiful Possible*, Gottlieb's characters careen precariously from love to love, strength to strength, weakness to weakness. This is a lovely book, whose dual themes of faith and passion braid together powerfully like the wicks of a candle whose flame marks the transition between the ordinary and the holy, the sacred and the profane." —Nomi Eve, author of *The Family Orchard* and *Henna House*

"What makes *The Beautiful Possible* so astonishing is not simply its elegant prose and erudition or the compelling love story at its core with its moments of joy and heartbreak but the novel's deep sense of wisdom that comes from the mysterious between places of the heart and soul, a wisdom that in Gottlieb's hands is never insistent or boastful but a grand meditation on human and godly grace."

—Aryeh Lev Stollman, author of *The Far Euphrates* and *The Illuminated Soul*

"*The Beautiful Possible* is impossibly beautiful, also luminous, lyrical, and unforgettable. With this stunning first novel, Amy Gottlieb announces herself as a formidable literary talent and a bright star in the firmament of twenty-first-century Jewish writers."

—Letty Cottin Pogrebin, author of *Single Jewish Male Seeking Soul Mate*

"People always want to know what a book is about. That's a hard question to answer when it comes to *The Beautiful Possible*. I've never read anything quite like this lyrical and infinitely wise novel. There's a line in the book that reads, *Inside every story lies the hidden kernel of an infinite one.* That's what this book is about.

"If I had to say more, I would add that this novel is about a woman in love with two men, and the way that she sustains both relationships over a lifetime, not without signifiant cost. It's about faith and love and lust and mysticism and poetry and the eroticism of spices. It's about the things we give our children but prompts us to think about what we should give them, and what they, in turn, should give us.

"Mostly though, it's about how a book can be a wonder. If books could shimmer, this one would."

—Elizabeth Berg, author of *The Dream Lover*

"*The Beautfiul Possible* is a deeply felt and evocative novel that draws on history, memory, all the senses, and the author's own considerable conjuring skills. Alive with characters and unafraid to examine ambigous emotional complexities, this is a moving debut."

—Meg Wolitzer, author of *The Interestings*

"This enchanting novel is a 'braid' of romance, passion, and betrayal; of marriage, family, and loss; of three characters whose love is incomplete in the secrets each conceal; of the beauty that is possible and the wrong that makes it possible. It's also a delightful and brilliant commentary—a midrash on the Song of Songs and Tagore and Whitman, on Hasidic wisdom and Hindu wisdom, on the mundane and the sublime and how we live between them. Read it once for its story, again for its wisdom, and one more time for its poetry and truth."

—Rodger Kamenetz, author of *The Jew in the Lotus* and *The History of Last Night's Dream*

THE
BEAUTIFUL
POSSIBLE

a novel

AMY GOTTLIEB

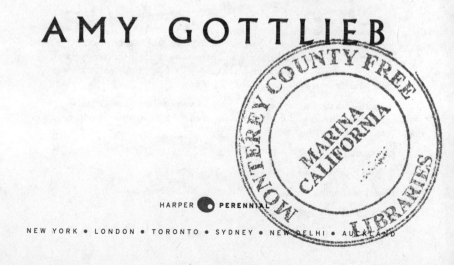

HARPER ● PERENNIAL

NEW YORK ● LONDON ● TORONTO ● SYDNEY ● NEW DELHI ● AUCKLAND

HARPER ● PERENNIAL

Grateful acknowledgment is made to the following for permission to reprint previously published material:

Robert Bly. The translation of "Dusk" by Rabindranath Tagore is from *The Soul Is Here for Its Own Joy* edited and translated by Robert Bly. Copyright © 1995 by Robert Bly. Reprinted by permission of Georges Borchardt, Inc., for Robert Bly.

Coleman Barks. The translation of "There Is a Light Seed Grain Inside" by Rumi is from *The Essential Rumi*. Copyright © 2004 by Coleman Barks. Reprinted by permission of Coleman Barks.

This novel is a work of fiction. Characters, places, dialogue, and events are the products of the author's imagination, and any references to real people, events, establishments, organizations, or locales are used fictitiously.

P.S.™ is a trademark of HarperCollins Publishers.

HarperCollins books may be purchased for educational, business, or sales promotional use. For information please e-mail the Special Markets Department at SPsales@harpercollins.com.

FIRST EDITION

Designed by Jamie Kerner

Library of Congress Cataloging-in-Publication Data has been applied for.

ISBN 978-0-06-238336-5 (pbk.)

16 17 18 19 20   OV/RRD   10 9 8 7 6 5 4 3 2 1

for my family

THE
BEAUTIFUL
POSSIBLE

When my mother and I would enter the paneled sanctuary on Shabbat mornings my father would peer down from his red velvet rabbi's chair and bite his lip. It was a wink of recognition, barely a gesture. I would fold my hand in hers and we would swing our arms in a proclamation of private joy. The congregants would turn toward the aisle, gaze at their sultry rebbetzin in her wide-brimmed hat, and behold her as if she were a queen.

My mother's body was a source of pleasure to me: the strawberry scent of her face cream, the delicate veins on the backs of her hands, the satiny texture of her summer Shabbat dresses. One dress was made of crisp white cotton, patterned with red bricks. The sleeves ended at her elbow, huge flower-shaped buttons ran down the front, a thick patent leather belt cinched her waist. I would sit next to her in the front row and lay my cheek against the bricks that covered her upper arm. My father would read from the Torah and deliver his sermon and I would twirl the buttons of my mother's dress as if they were radio dials and I controlled the frequency.

The synagogue stairwell was my first jungle gym; its parking lot my first hopscotch course. I was the congregants' flower child, their little pet. Come sit on my lap, Maya! Point out the words to me; have a lollipop; sing me a little song. As soon as I learned Hebrew, my father taught me how to move my fingers around a page of Talmud as if I were a blind person reading Braille. I once believed all the words of the Torah were true, just as I once assumed that my mother and father belonged to each other in the way of ordinary married people.

I was Sol and Rosalie Kerem's late-life consolation prize: accident, miracle, and redemption rolled into the form of a lanky girl whose bangs reached her nose. Whenever my mother invited me to make a birthday wish, I would close my eyes and imagine things already present in this world: a white flower, an arched doorway, a footpath crossing a river. I lip-synced my favorite songs in front of a mirror, and when no one was watching I would peek into the ancient books on my father's shelves, hungry for a phrase to swirl on my tongue and taste its meaning.

At night my parents would sit on the sofa in my father's study and listen to records. Fly me to the moon, sang Frank. Dance me to the end of love, sang Leonard. I say a little prayer, sang Dionne. I would spy them studying the liner notes as if the lyrics were sacred texts, yet something about their marriage always eluded me. Our house was a palace of stories—the ancient ones in the books, the love stories in the songs, the secrets my mother whispered into the phone late at night. At times, I would drift off to sleep and imagine how all the stories were part of one great book that hummed with sadness and longing.

I was once content with my flower, my doorway, my footpath. What I had was more than enough. I did not know that I was also written into this great book, and that my parents were entangled in a web of desire that began long before I was born.

PART ONE

All the streams flow into the sea—
the wisdom of a person comes from the heart.
Yet the sea is never full—but the heart can never be filled.

—ECCLESIASTES RABBAH 1:4

LIEDER

November 1938

Walter awakens to the smell of burning paper. With the bedroom shades drawn, the late afternoon street sounds are muffled. He untangles Sonia's hair from his hand, steps to the door and peeks. His father kneels before the fireplace, feeding the flames with rolled-up sheet music. Josef rips the pages from their bindings and shapes them into logs, the edges cinched tight. Walter winces at the sight of his father's fuel supply. Maybe the fire will release some kind of strange music, he thinks. A prompt, a sign, a directive. *Leave this place; embrace your future.* But a flute étude cackles like ordinary paper, heats the living room for a brief spell, and then flickers out.

Josef lights a cigar with the last embers and steps over to his typewriter. He taps a few keys slowly, then attacks the whole alphabet with ardor. Here he goes again, thinks Walter. Another afternoon of futility for the father; another afternoon of love for the son. He listens to the keys explode under Josef's fingers and knows his father is writing yet another letter to his former colleagues at the university that no longer employs him, claiming that Josef Westhaus educated a generation of Berliners to understand Plato and Aristotle and this defrocked professor is not like other Jews. For a while Josef mailed these but now he doesn't even address the envelopes.

Walter would give themselves another two weeks. Enough time to convince his father that he could teach philosophy and make music in Palestine, that he could survive the heat and possibly again know happiness. Two weeks would be enough time for Walter to arrange for their visas and pack up the whole traveling circus: Josef, Sonia, her parents in Leipzig, their embroidered tablecloths and Sabbath samovar, his father's flute, the unburnt sheet music—and himself, an eighteen-year-old student who needs no luggage of his own, a man who memorizes all the poems he loves. Walter imagines a caravan of loaded camels meandering through the streets of Berlin, Sonia riding in the lead, wearing a white veil, her long blond hair brushing the camel's skin.

"What's the plan?" asks Sonia, her voice thin and hoarse.

Walter returns to the bed and spoons behind her.

"My father's burning up his études," he whispers.

Sonia presses her nose to his hand and inhales the faint smell of vodka they drank sometime that morning, in between the lines of poetry, the languid sex, the hours he spent sketching her toes, her incessant question: *when*, schatzi, *when?*

He pulls at her long curtain of hair and sniffs the ends.

"Cardamom?"

"Cheap perfume."

"I could smell you forever."

"Palestine will be our forever."

Sonia winces, thinking of the flute études burning on the other side of the wall.

She once believed every piece of sheet music was holy, that the pages filled with Italian words—*con brio, andante, agitato, subito piano*—were her cues for how to shape time with her voice. Even if Sonia had memorized Brahms lieder she would hold the sheet music in her hand and fix her eyes on its elegant code. She misses the nights she sang in a café, and longs for the moments after the applause when a stranger would approach her with words of praise.

If Billie Holiday sang Brahms she would be you.

"I asked you about the plan, Walter."

"What?"

"Stop dreaming, schatzi. The currency of real life. Certificates and visas. We can't live in your childhood bedroom forever, waiting for your father to pack his bags. I can't breathe in here. His cigars, the burning—"

"Think of us standing on the deck of the boat," says Walter.

Sonia points to her wrist. "When?"

"Two weeks."

"Promise?"

He holds up two fingers and presses them against her lips.

"Yes."

"Thank God," says Sonia. "The minute we arrive, let's buy your father new music."

Walter tries to imagine his father crossing an arid desert in Palestine with a folio of études under his arm, but he can't picture him anywhere except this apartment, or laying flowers at his wife's grave, or delivering lectures at the university, speaking the only language he knows. No new verb forms lie ahead for Josef Westhaus; no tender pangs of a life marked by change.

"And if he won't come?" asks Walter. "I can't leave him behind."

Sonia springs up and sits on her heels. "We will convince him! There will be orchestras and cafés and Arabs selling rugs so we can buy him one that doesn't stink of old smoke. He will be happy again; he will remarry! And he will find new students, even if he has to stand before them wearing short sleeves for the first time in his life."

"And us? What will we do over there?"

"I'll sing lieder in the cafés."

Walter's friends talk about this haven called Palestine but he can only imagine the words from the Bible he learned in poetry classes. Sonia's café would be built from a pile of stones, a dish of gold, and a measure of barley.

"You won't be singing lieder over there."

"But everyone loves Brahms."

Walter maps her gaze. He can tell when her thoughts careen into a private fog, and he waits until she finds her way back.

"What are you remembering?"

"Nothing important." She shakes out her hair, piles it on top of her head and lets it down again.

"I'll sing a new kind of lieder then. I'll set the Song of Songs to music and we'll play it at our wedding."

"And me? What will I do?"

"You will sketch Mediterranean beauties and become a professor of world religions. It's your destiny! How many men your age see their work translated into English and then published in a journal?"

"A silly joke. I only wrote that paper to impress you."

"My seducer. *The words of the texts echo in the lives of the people who read them.* If I had told you I was in love with the Book of Lamentations and not the Song of Songs would you have written a paper on that?"

"I'm glad you didn't try me," says Walter.

"I wouldn't have. I'm not one for sorrow."

"Then you were born into the wrong time."

Sonia sits up and straddles her legs around his. "A few more weeks and life with you will be beautiful."

Walter runs his hands through her hair.

"I could swear it's cardamom." He inhales. "One day I will rub spices on your belly."

"And?"

"We will pluck dates from our own trees—"

"And—"

"Stand in a wadi—"

"And—"

"With our children—"

Sonia wraps her palm around Walter's wrist, shaping her hand into a bracelet. "We will make the beautiful possible." She closes her eyes and shudders.

"Are you okay?"

"Not really," she says. "Toss me a line, please."

"Tagore or Heine?"

"Oh, Tagore. And say it slowly."

"*The butterfly counts not months but moments, and has time enough.*"

"Now Whitman."

"*The scent of these arm-pits is aroma finer than prayer.*"

"You and your faithless American poet! How can you believe that?"

"Poetry is my god, Sonia. My one and only."

"When I read your paper on the Song of Songs, I honestly thought you were religious in some way."

"The Song is a poem. Nothing more. Are you disappointed?"

"You never disappoint."

"Two weeks. All of us. I promise," he says.

"One more line and maybe I can trust you."

"Tagore? Whitman?"

She smiles. "Ours. The Song."

"*His belly is an ivory tablet on a sapphire stone.*"

"Sounds like you. Only they didn't have *spritzkuchen* back then. You, schatzi, have an excuse for your untableted belly."

She rubs her cheek along Walter's chest, draws circles around his torso.

"Promise we'll go to Palestine?"

"Promise," he says.

The fire has gone out. The cackling from the living room has stopped, along with the thrum of the typewriter keys. Walter pulls the blanket over their shoulders, and Sonia closes her eyes, listening to Josef warm up with a minor scale, then an arpeggio, then the first movement of the Bach Flute Sonata, unaccompanied.

"Your father sounds good today. Softer. I feel as if I'm underwater."

Walter slithers to the edge of the bed. "Need anything from the kitchen?"

"We finished the crackers last night," she says. "Every crumb."

"I'll look."

"No, Walter. Let me. I'll go crazy if I spend another minute inside this love cave."

"Check for vodka too. There may be a drop left."

She reaches for a slip and laughs. "Will your father faint from the sight of me?"

"Possibly." Walter passes Sonia his sweater. She wraps it around her shoulders, twirls, and winks.

Her face will never age, he thinks. One day we will both be old and I will brush her long white hair and remember her standing before me like this, half-dressed, fully ripe, smelling like cardamom.

"Better, yes?"

"When you come back, stay just as you are so I can sketch you."

She winks again.

The bedroom door closes behind her and Walter reaches for his pad and charcoal. He gazes at a blank piece of paper and imagines Sonia in the center of it, his sweater wrapped around her breasts, a glass in her hand. This time he will sketch with focus, committing this moment with her to a kind of permanence. Everything is backwards, he thinks. His world is ending and he and Sonia stand on the edge of a new story to be lived in a new land. Sonia's love will keep him safe and when she gets lost in the tangle of her thoughts he will recite lines of poetry, surround her with words of comfort.

"*Scheiss!*" yells Josef.

Parading herself in a slip was a mistake, thinks Walter. *Forget the crackers! Come back!* Glass breaks, shatters, the front door pops, the music stops, Josef screams. From the bed, Walter smells gunmetal and grime, stench from another world. An icy shrill passes from Sonia's throat, then a shot rings out, then another, another. The flute crashes to the floor, two bodies fall. Walter reaches for a shirt—*save them!*—but then freezes and slips under the bed, lies facedown, his arms wrapped tightly around his head. *Save them, you coward! Save them—*

The bedroom door cracks open, *that stench!*

The profile of a man's boot is close enough for him to touch, gleaming, black. A bloody footprint. Another pair of boots casts a shadow at the door. Walter flinches.

"*Lass uns gehen!*"

Hands press on the bed above him; a man sniffs the sheets like a crazed dog.

"*Kardamom. Das fraülein—*"

The boot pivots.

"*Gehen!*"

A sharp inhale; a groan.

"*Gehen!*"

The men gallop down the back stairs, a door flails on its hinge, a woman shouts in the street. Breaking glass, a gunshot, more glass.

The living room is silent; his father's cigar is ash. The radiator hisses, stops, and hisses once more. Walter lies under his bed, facedown in his own vomit, shit oozing between his legs. He slithers on his belly, reaches for the bed frame, and stops himself. Sonia. His father. One more body left to fall. Too soon to get out of here alone; too late to save them. It should have been me, he thinks. *It was meant for me.* Walter pulls his arm close to his torso, his body a rolled-up rug.

He hears nothing, just the rasp of his breathing and the rodent sound of his teeth chewing off his thumbnail. *Come back to me, Sonia. Forget the crackers. Forget the vodka.* His tongue finds his lips and just before Walter fades out he tastes the last remains of cardamom, and there he finds her, climbing a mountain where spices grow, and she takes his hand and pulls him onto a slab of rock. *The words echo in our lives now, just like you wrote in your paper,* she says. And then Sonia lets go of his hand and runs onto the hills where hyssop grows alongside mint and she runs and runs and then she is gone.

SPICES

December 1938

The alabaster moon brightens the surface of the Mediterranean and Walter leans against the rail of the *Conte Rosso*, staring at the shimmering light. His jacket rests loosely on his shoulders and his body feels untethered, a feather in free fall. He could jump, he thinks; his body would float in the vastness like a swirl of seaweed and then descend. As a child, Walter loved swimming across Lake Wannsee, caressed by buoyancy. His father would wait at the shore and Walter would propel his arms and reach him in a few strokes. But now he has been washed into the ocean by sorrow, saved so he can live out his days in mourning. The passengers babble about the mysterious destination called Shanghai. *What a shithole! Illness and poverty await us all! But Shanghai is the promised land! Silks! Opium! Tea!* The sound of laughter wafts from the ship's bar and cackles like fireworks against the night sky.

Walter has not spoken to anyone on board and he wonders if he has gone mute. The lights of Brindisi flicker in the distance and he holds up his hands. The left is steadier than the right, even though he has chewed off his thumbnail and the raw skin throbs. Perhaps in Shanghai he will see a doctor.

Sorry, Sonia. No promise kept. This boat isn't sailing to Palestine. Only a month ago he had promised her they would live the words of the Song in the place where they were written.

Nard and saffron, fragrant reed and cinnamon, with all aromatic woods, myrrh and aloes—all the choice perfumes.

As if poetry would save them.

At night, the boisterous chatter of cocktail parties fills the decks. Every kiss is welcomed; every stranger's touch encouraged. Women paint their lips red and invite men to rest their palms at the small of their backs; older couples lie in each other's arms on narrow chairs and gaze up at the stars. To Walter it all seems like a display of relief or a vast delusion. When the Aga Khan and his wife board at Djibouti Walter peers at their elegant costumes as if he is standing on the other side of a painted screen. Life has two shades of color: muted grays that cover some kind of pain, and vivid primary hues that strain to defy death. Walter can intuit how each person on the *Conte Rosso* is either wounded or miraculously unscathed.

He tries to utter simple phrases to his fellow passengers—*pass the salt* or *where are you going?*—but he can only stammer. The effort to speak feels overwhelming. Walter shares his cabin with three other men, two of whom entertain women during the day. The third man has a mustache and wears a brown felt hat that he only removes at night. He sneaks glances at Walter and then snaps his head away, revealing a twitch in his left eye. Walter watches his every move and decides that he won't go to Shanghai after all; wherever this man disembarks, Walter will follow. After losing Sonia and his father and boarding the wrong ship, the code of his life will be random. Tagging along like a loyal mutt to a stranger is the perfect course for him, a roll of the dice that will determine his future.

When the ship docks in Bombay Walter is half-asleep in the cabin. His head swims with voices he can't reach: his father calls his name and Sonia sings lieder that fade into murmurs. Walter hears the whistle and commotion on the decks above, but his thumb throbs harder than ever, and just as he imagines a Shanghai doctor standing above him with a scalpel, he spots the man with the brown felt hat fold his coat under his arm and step out of the cabin. He turns toward Walter and winks.

"Follow me," he says. "You will be better off here."

Walter jumps to his feet, grabs his suitcase, and trails the man down the gangplank, striding in his shadow. No one asks for his ticket; no one asks his name. Walter could be invisible. He pauses to tie his shoelace and then looks around for the man he followed, but he only spots different hats worn by other strangers. Throughout his life, he will leave out the details but will say, I followed a man wearing a brown felt hat and ended up alone in Bombay.

He wanders the streets for hours, a single suitcase in hand. The thick air and unfamiliar sounds give Walter a migraine but he can't find a place to sit. Cows loiter on the roads and rickshaws speed past, shaking up dust that blinds his eyes. Just before sunset, Walter finds a brothel and arranges to rent an empty room.

He spends his first days in India lying on a thin cot, clutching a pillow to his chest. Every morning a prostitute named Kavita brings him soap and a towel and teaches him the English words she learned from her British clients. Walter asks her to stare at his hands and tell him if they still tremble. Her eyes glance from one to the other and every day she measures the level of tremors on a chart she has drawn. After many days the line is flat.

As Walter saunters through the city, he can hear Sonia's voice calling to him. *When are we going to Palestine, schatzi?* Beggars line the streets and pungent spices waft around him but Walter cannot discern them; he can't even smell his own sweat. When passersby veer away from lepers, Walter moves in close enough for the flies to circle his arms. The world holds no perfume and no stench; his nose is oblivious to its offerings.

Four months pass in a haze. Every afternoon Kavita shaves Walter's face and ties his hair into a ponytail. Walter asks her to bring him some charcoal and a sketchbook. At first he only writes numbers, the tally of days since it happened. The day after the gunshots. The day after that. The futile attempt to find Sonia's parents. The train to Trieste and the confusion at the port. The man who handed him a ticket and told him that the *Conte Rosso* was not sailing to Palestine, but he should board anyway. Another man who pointed to the ship and said, "Shanghai is good for the Jews." The haze of dialects. His aching thumb. The porter's question: Is *anyone traveling with you?* Not anymore.

Walter sleeps with the sketchbook nestled in the crook of

his arm. When Kavita comes into his room each morning she moves the book aside and lies beside him, waiting for a response, but Walter does not break away from sleep until the afternoon. After her last client leaves at midnight, Kavita poses for him and Walter uses the shape of her body to remember Sonia. Her neck is longer than Sonia's, her hips slimmer; Kavita's toes are stubby like a small girl's, while Sonia's toes were shaped like question marks. Instead of sketching Kavita, he sketches Sonia as if she were still alive. *This is a picture of my fiancée,* he tells Kavita. When he opens his eyes after long naps, Walter can hear Sonia asking him if he can rub spices on her belly and if they have packed their bags for the journey home. He can feel her lips on his earlobe, her hand resting on his chest. At times he speaks to her as if they are a long-married couple. *Taste this, schatzi. You like fluffy rice.*

One night he falls asleep with a fresh drawing resting beneath his cheek and wakes up to the chalky smell of charcoal. Walter asks Kavita to bring him a clean bedsheet and he envelops himself in its faint whiff of lemon, soap, and women's hands. He runs outside and the smells overwhelm him: the acrid cow shit, the lepers that reek of rotting skin, and the carnival of spices—arousing cumin, sweet tamarind, the dungy stench of *hing*—that fills his nostrils and saturates his brain.

Walter runs from market to market, plunging his hands into barrels of seeds and herbs. He inhales turmeric root and clutches thick chunks of it until his palms turn yellow. He rubs fenugreek seeds into his hair and chews on them until the bitter center pops open on his tongue. He hoards fistfuls of coriander seeds and sucks on them until he releases the soapy center that makes him feel giddy. He snaps apart black cardamom pods that carry the earthy smell of the Grunewald Forest he visited as a boy and he clutches the cracked pieces in his fingers and sways from side to side. In the street markets of Bombay, where the sight of the deranged and the lost is not unusual, Walter covers his head with a shawl, holds seeds and roots to his nose, and *shuckles* like a Jew in prayer. A merchant named Rohan teaches him the names of the spices and shows him how to use a *sil batta* so he can grind them in the traditional Hindu way. At night, Walter sprinkles Kavita's naked body with the spices he's hoarded.

With his senses awakened, Walter rises at dawn and arrives at the market when the merchants are setting up their stalls. He learns the names of every spice and in time Rohan hires him as an assistant. He lifts heavy seed sacks from a rickshaw and carries them to the stall. The muscles in his arms twitch from the effort but then grow tighter with each passing day. Walter summons Sonia a bit less and responds to Rohan's prompts to carry a sack of hyssop from one corner to another, grind turmeric root into powder, help an elderly woman load her bags.

"I haven't seen this one before," says Walter. Rohan has just finished arranging the stall and the first customers meander in. Walter sticks his head inside a sack filled with pods and inhales.

"*Kamal kakdi*," says Rohan. "Lotus seeds."

"A well-known aphrodisiac," someone says in German.

Walter leans deeper into the sack.

"Don't you remember your own language, Walter? A handful of those pods could seduce the world."

Walter pops his head out and glances at the man's sandals.

"Who are you?"

"Be careful whom you follow next time."

Walter looks up at a man with a mustache who is dressed for a cricket game. The man's left eye twitches.

"You were on the *Conte Rosso*."

"Until I got off, with you walking in my shadow."

"You told me to. And then I couldn't find you anywhere."

"See that? I'm not a stranger after all."

Walter feels lightheaded. He has chores to do, new spices to sample. This is no time to play rhetorical games with a cricket player. Back to work. Kamal kakdi. Lotus seeds.

"Look at me, Walter."

He glances up. The man's twitch seems absurd to him.

"How do you know my name? I didn't talk to you on the ship," says Walter. "I didn't talk to anyone."

"I know your work."

"What work? What have I ever done?"

The man laughs. "Join the club! All of human accomplishments are as illusive as dust. Every one of us is in the process of becoming, aren't we, my friend?"

Walter glares. "I have no idea what you're talking about."

"I apologize. Subtlety is not my strong point." He offers his hand. "Paul Richardson. I read your paper on religious desire in the Song of Songs."

"That was a lifetime ago," says Walter.

"Do you have any idea what you wrote? You pulled the words of the Song outside of their context; you opened all the windows.

If you apply your erudition to the entire Bible, future generations will read the words in a brand new way."

Walter grimaces. "Who are you to care?"

"I teach this stuff. An itinerant underpaid scholar or a professor of enlightenment—take your pick."

Walter shrugs, then lowers his head into the sack and sniffs.

"I heard about your father and your fiancée. I'm very sorry. Maybe I can help you in some way."

Walter pops his head out.

"Have we met? Before the *Conte Rosso*?"

Paul laughs. "In a karmic way, of course. But no, we were never introduced. I was a student at Oxford, had a fellowship in Berlin. And now I bounce around the American university system with frequent interludes in India."

"A guru without the robes."

"A small iota of scholarship and a whole lot of preaching to eager young students. At the end of the day, it's a livelihood. You might consider it—academia would suit you."

Walter shakes his head.

"You have no idea what you hit upon in that paper," says Paul

"I wrote it to impress my fiancée. She loved the Song."

"Your work had traces of brilliance."

"I wrote that paper as a romantic wink, an inside joke."

"That was some wink, Walter. A love letter like that can alter the field of religious studies."

"It's yours for the taking."

Paul grabs Walter's hands. "Study with me," he says.

"Thank you, but no."

"Look. I don't need another young man to turn misty-eyed over my stories about Hindu gods. My American students think scholarship is a slot machine for wisdom. Line up the cherries and out pop the aphorisms."

"What makes you think I can do any better?"

"I'd love to find out."

"You're looking for a protégé."

"As a matter of fact, yes."

Walter stares at Paul's face, looking for a sign, a hint of an idea. He boarded the wrong ship, followed a man wearing a hat, and wound up here. In Bombay. He has a friend named Kavita and a job in a spice market. Isn't that enough?

"I don't think so," says Walter.

"You are such a lost man."

"I have a job."

"You haul sacks and get high on spices. I'd call that a dalliance, a goddamn waste."

Walter shakes his head. *Go play cricket. Go off to your American students and teach them Tagore's line about the butterfly that counts moments and tell them how my Sonia was shot. Just go—*

"Please leave me," says Walter.

"Is that what you really want?"

"Yes, it is. I never should have followed you. There were other strangers on that ship. Beautiful women. I should have trailed someone else. Or stayed until Shanghai, where no one would have found me."

"I will leave you then. I'm sorry."

Paul leaves and wanders off, first slowly and then more quickly, winding his way through a maze of alleys.

That night, Walter asks Kavita if she knows Tagore's work.

"Of course," she says. "Even a Bengali whore knows her national poet." She closes her eyes and Walter listens to her sing in a scratchy high-pitched voice. When she finishes, she opens her eyes and takes his hand.

"*Gitanjali*," she says.

"What is the song about?"

Kavita pulls a sheet of paper from Walter's sketchbook and draws a footpath crossing a river. Then she sketches a primitive boat with a stick figure standing at the helm, playing a flute. Walter lies beside Kavita and closes his eyes. He has no boat, no river, no flute. Sonia and his father are dead. Kavita, Rohan, and Paul are the only people in the world he knows. One. Two. Three. No more.

The following morning Paul spies Walter in the market, inhaling peppercorns.

"Getting off on the ambrosia again?" asks Paul.

"I asked you to leave me alone."

Paul reaches out and grabs Walter's shoulders. "Staying here is a mistake."

Walter pushes away his hands.

"Suit yourself then. Disappear as if you had never been saved. One day your fingers will turn yellow from turmeric and your skin will harden into citrus peel."

Walter pulls a shawl over his head and begins to sway.

"You look like a crazy Jew, shuckling in prayer."

"I don't pray."

"You're not like the Jews I know," says Paul. "Not at all."

"How would you know what kind of Jew I am? I wrote a damn paper on the Song of Songs. And I'm not dead. So what am I?"

"Smart and lucky."

"Neither," whispers Walter.

"If you come to America with me I'll set you up for a brilliant career. Students will admire your erudition; you will enlighten the world about the burning heart of theology."

Walter adjusts his shawl and closes his eyes. *You will become a professor of world religions. It is your destiny,* Sonia had said. *But, Sonia, my love, what is destiny when the future has been rendered into ash? What now for us? What now?*

"First stop New York," says Paul. "The Jewish Theological Seminary of America."

"That's ridiculous. I'm not religious. And I'm not looking for the Bible."

"Beyond the Bible, Walter! You will study with rabbis. *Wissenschaft:* the science of plumbing ancient texts. Your fingers will touch the words you need to learn. You will weave yourself into the story, morph yourself into my Jewish protégé."

"Don't label me."

"Agreed. No labels for the young man with boundless potential."

Walter scans the market stalls and alleys that are beginning to feel like home. He doesn't have to give in. He has Kavita and

Rohan. He has spices. He has charcoal and a sketchbook. He has lost everything and now he has quite enough. *Dream on, Professor.*

"Look," says Paul. "I give up. If you change your mind, prepare yourself for a long train ride and find your way to Shantiniketan—Tagore's ashram. It's the only place where history won't intrude on you, a sanctuary of respite where you can heal, wipe yourself clean."

"How long do I have?"

"Forever, Walter! You can squander your life here or you can come to America and climb the steps of scholarly achievement. Write your own ticket."

"And you?"

"I come to India every year. I will find you."

Walter pulls the shawl from his head and drapes it around his shoulders. "Why me?" he asks. "Am I really of such benefit to you?"

"Just consider my offer."

"You haven't answered my question," says Walter.

Paul turns. As he ambles off, he reaches into his pocket, pulls out the brown felt hat, and places it on his head.

Walter reaches into the barrels of spice and picks up palmfuls of fenugreek and saffron. He replaces the shawl on his head and inhales, then looks up and scans the horizon for Sonia. The back of her dress appears before his eyes, the fallen hem, her strong calves wrapped around his. Walter stands and sways in the middle of the market, praying in no words and to no god, searching for the outlines of her face.

Walter will stand and sway during his years at Shantiniketan, where he will live until the war is over. He will study Eastern philosophy with dreamers and seekers in an adobe house where the words of the Koran mingle with the Upanishads and he will learn the verb forms and idioms of English and Sanskrit. He will meditate on the myth of the eternal return and wonder if Sonia will ever come back to him. He will study the Bengali words that Kavita sang for him, and he will translate them into English. *I don't know if I'll go back home tonight or not. I have the feeling I'm going to meet someone. And sure enough, where the footpath crosses the river, there is a boat. Floating in the boat is a person whom I've never seen, playing a flute.*

In the hot afternoons, Walter will venture out to the plain behind the adobe and cool himself in the shade of date palm trees. In the monsoon season, he will place a shawl over his head and stand out in the rain and cry for all he has lost. And when the rain stops Paul will arrive and tell him the war has ended and it is time for them to go to New York so he can begin learning with the rabbis—all because Walter once wrote a paper on the Song of Songs to impress the woman he loved.

BOOKS, SEEDS

November 1946

Rosalie Wachs pulls her father's books off the shelves and sorts them into piles: Mishnah here, Maimonides over there, Hasidic commentaries placed in a box for his students. Shakespeare, Freud, and William James on one side of the living room floor; journals and clippings from Yiddish papers in a carton. She places the torn prayer books in a shopping bag labeled SHAIMOS—FOR BURIAL for the man who will collect the defective volumes to be laid to eternal rest. One at a time, she blows the dust from the books that she is saving for Sol, her fiancé. Rosalie opens a volume of Talmud and pictures her father's hand resting on top of hers, coaxing her finger toward a word he wanted her to understand. *This way, Rosalie. Up in the corner.* Rachmones. *Compassion. A good word for you to know.*

Her mother leans against the doorway.

"Be careful," says Ida. "Your father's heart lived in these books."

"You don't need to tell me," says Rosalie. "I know everything about Tateh."

"You understand so little. Old enough to be a bride, far too young to be a rabbi's wife."

"What's that supposed to mean?"

"You have so much to learn."

"Like?"

"Like you won't always come first."

"So I'm selfish, Ma?"

Ida folds her arms over her chest. "You're still a child, that's all."

Rosalie shrugs.

"Your father used to describe you as a beautiful colt, ready to break out of its pen and gallop. Does this sound like a rebbetzin to you?"

"Sol understands me," says Rosalie.

"Thank God," says Ida. "A marriage needs at least one who keeps watch."

Rosalie returns to the books. Her father's Chekhov, Dostoyevsky, Pushkin. How could her mother pretend that her own marriage was fixed by tradition? It was anything but. She opens her father's prayer book and riffles through the pages. The Ashrei prayer he taught her to recite in a singsong melody. The Shema he taught her to recite slowly, because, he said, *you want each syllable to feel sad when it departs from your lips.* She was five when he taught her those prayers; it could have been yesterday.

Ida stands next to Rosalie and pulls a thin volume off the shelf, tucks it under her arm.

"Something I shouldn't see, Ma?"

"Every marriage has its secrets."

Rosalie knows the contents of her father's library by heart but she can't figure out which book her mother is hiding from her.

"The Spinoza, Ma?"

"Guess again."

"The *Mei HaShiloach*?"

"Of course not. I already put that one in the *shaimos* pile." Ida smiles. "Tateh's students won't understand the Ishbitzer's teachings, and it's not a suitable book for a young rabbi and his beautiful bride."

Rosalie remembers her father sharing his interpretation of the Ishbitzer Rebbe's work. *God is in all things, even in your doubts and desires. So let your heart be your master; let your life become a sacred story.* He insisted she tell no one that he was teaching her a nineteenth-century Hasidic book considered so heretical that Polish Jews would keep it hidden in an outhouse. *I can't teach this to my students. They will learn the language of transgression before they understand their own boundaries.*

Ida carries the book into the kitchen.

"You hid the Spinoza with the blue cover," shouts Rosalie. "Right?"

"Oh, that Spinoza. His writings nearly destroyed our marriage. These books aren't so innocent. None of them. I carried faith in my bones, from Lublin to Brooklyn, I never wavered. But he—"

"Tateh was a Hasid, Ma. His doubts only brought him closer to God."

"Whatever he was he was. We survived each other and it worked out."

Rosalie doesn't know whether to cry or laugh. She spent her childhood watching her parents' separate orbits grow distant and then even more remote until something realigned and they began to revolve around each other like the earth circles the sun. Rabbi Shmuel and Ida Wachs, spinning celestial objects. Rosalie would lie in bed at night and listen to her father talk to his students in the living room while her mother hummed in a singsong voice in the bedroom. It wasn't until after her father died that she found a tin filled with notes he wrote to her mother.

My head is in the books but every word reminds me of our kisses.

Buy a chicken and remember to ask the man for some livers on the side. And then pick out a pastry for us. One bite for you, one bite for me, my sweet butterfly.

While her mother seemed to uphold the wheel of tradition, blessing every morsel of food before she took a bite, Shmuel played with the edges of his beliefs, testing the parameters of his faith. When Rosalie was small, he experimented with keeping Shabbat on a Tuesday, just to see how it would feel. He wore his silk-lined coat, blessed wine and challah, sang zemirot, napped, and meditated. When the sun set he told Rosalie it was a failed experiment. *Tuesday cannot be Shabbat. Next time I'll try Wednesday.*

After her father read a book review that quoted Saint Augustine, he borrowed *The Confessions* from the Brooklyn Public Library. Then he perused the shelves. Pascal. Rousseau. He peered at the Koran, dabbled in Sufism, considered Buddhism and Zen, but always returned to his beloved Hasidic masters. He told Rosalie that these rabbis gathered sparks from all of human experience, packaged them up for their students so they could taste the essence of the entire world without needing to leave home.

A year before he died, Shmuel shocked his students by espousing the works of Spinoza alongside his Hasidic texts. He shaved his beard and tucked his *tzitzit* inside his pants pockets, keeping the fringes of his *tallit kattan* a secret from the outside world. *You are just like me*, he had said to Rosalie. *The boundaries of this life will not be wide enough to contain your longings.*

Ida's voice wafts from the kitchen. "It's your turn now. Grow yourself up."

"You mean grow up," says Rosalie. "Use proper English."

"Whatever. As long as you do it."

"Why hide the Spinoza, Ma? Tateh taught me everything; I'm not such an innocent."

"Of course you're not. And I didn't hide the Spinoza."

Ida emerges from the kitchen. Her mother looks like a sparrow whose gummy beige shoes keep her tethered to the earth. Rosalie kisses her cheek.

"I didn't mean to offend—"

"This apartment may seem small to you but your father and I lived a big life here. Faith, doubt—everything seeped into these walls."

"What did you ever doubt, Ma?"

"More than anyone will ever know, little rebbetzin."

Rosalie laughs. "And what book are you hiding from me?"

"That's none of your business. Just remember that as long as you look the part you can be a secret heretic. Be as daring as you want on the inside. And on the outside, you set a nice table on

Shabbat, keep the holidays, go to shul for Kol Nidre. And keep quiet. Your life will be hard enough; don't let anyone pin you down."

That's a comfort, thinks Rosalie.

"Do you understand what I'm saying?"

"Of course, Ma." Rosalie picks up her father's prayer book, closes her eyes, and recalls their last conversation.

Don't squander your wisdom. You may know much more than this man you found.

Sol is learned. He will be a good rabbi.

Rabbis come in different flavors, Rosalie. What flavor is your Sol?

Tateh?

Is he the God kind of rabbi or the law kind of rabbi? Which does he love more?

Both, I think.

And you. Are you in love?

I am.

There are many flavors of love too. Be free of him, be devoted to him, both at the same time. Keep your soul open; dream beyond your marriage.

"Finish up already," says Ida. "The shaimos man is on his way."

Rosalie closes the last book and places it on top of a pile. What she had with her father has ended. She had learned from him, yes. And now she will learn with her new rabbi. Sol will lead her fingers across the page and point out the words that will help her comprehend the mysteries of this life.

Two months before he died, Rosalie's father had insisted she attend a lecture by Abraham Joshua Heschel. *He knows how to*

*translate Hasidic wisdom into the words American Jews can under-
stand*, he had said. *Go listen and you'll see what I mean.* At a packed
YIVO Conference, Rosalie sat scrunched between an overweight
man who reeked of sauerkraut and a handsome rabbinical student whose arm brushed against hers. At first the student edged
away from her, but as Heschel spoke she leaned close enough to
inhale his aftershave. Rosalie's comprehension of Yiddish was
spotty but when Heschel said, "Books are no more than seeds; we
must be both the soil and the atmosphere in which they grow,"
the student turned to her and smiled. "Sol Kerem," he whispered.
"Rosalie Wachs," she whispered back. For the rest of the lecture,
she thought only of the man named Sol who sat beside her and
decided that he was her *bashert*, her soul mate.

Rosalie places Sol's books in a shopping bag and carries them
down to the subway. Her wedding is eight months away. She still
has time to find a white flapper dress, just like the one she saw
in a bridal magazine, and time to convince Sol that a traditional
gown would not suit her at all. She has eight more months of
sleeping alone in her childhood bed, plenty of time to consider
the ways she loves Sol (how he leans his ear close to her lips when
she speaks, how he shuckles in prayer and raises his arms as if
to touch God, how he gazes into her eyes whether they speak of
China patterns or theology). Even when they disagree over wedding plans, Rosalie feels a quiver behind her knees every time he
says her name.

She glances at the ring on her finger: a large diamond he
could barely afford. When he asked her to marry him, she said,

You will be the Humphrey Bogart of the rabbis. He laughed and said, *And you will be the Lauren Bacall of the rebbetzins. Together we'll build a pulpit fit for the silver screen.* She carries the bag of books tightly, ready to hand it off, father-in-law to son-in-law, rabbi to rabbi. She will find a way to live as a secret heretic, inventing new ways to spool out everything she was taught as a girl: the cycle of the six-day week that links one Shabbat to the next, the holidays with their distinct flavors and outfits—cheese-filled blintzes in the springtime, pungent etrogim for Sukkot, white clothes for Yom Kippur, and stained shirts on Tisha b'Av. Ritual is the clock with which Rosalie measures time; her bones ring with the reliable thrum of the holidays coursing through the seasons.

Paul Richardson and Walter Westhaus arrive at the Seminary during a late November snowfall. Walter wears his green kurta pajamas from Shantiniketan, with Paul's tweed jacket draped over his shoulders for warmth. His cloth shoes are caked with snow. As they enter the seminar room, a rabbi hands each man a black satin yarmulke. The rabbinical students slouch around a table, their arms crossed over their narrow ties. Paul talks about his research in India and how one spiritual tradition is porous to another. *We are all connected in the unending chain of belief and doubt. Together we can answer each other's questions.*

Sol wrinkles his nose and turns to his friend Morris. "Welcome to the Seminary Clown Show."

"Or a new class in practical rabbinics."

"Who's the sidekick?" asks Sol.

"A German Jew by way of India," says Morris. "Testing our tolerance for guilt. *Your final exam, gentlemen. In this corner we place a guru and in this corner a Jewish survivor. How will your teachings hold up now?*"

Sol stares at Walter. This man with high cheekbones has come dressed for a Purim party. He hopes someone will bury the yarmulke that covers his long brown stringy hair; surely he picked up microbes on the streets of Bombay. To Sol, Walter does not seem like a Jewish refugee at all, but like a character who stepped out of a storybook he read as a boy. Sol shuts his eyes and wonders if this man is a figment of his imagination, but when he opens them Walter smiles at him.

Morris turns to Sol. "The refugee likes you," he whispers.

Sol gazes down at the table as Paul explains the myth of the eternal return. "Everything cycles back to its cosmic origins," he says. "Even the Bible considers this, yet much is imperceptible to us. We misread so many cues. How about a line of poetry, Walter?"

"*We cross infinity with every step; we meet eternity in every second.*" Walter looks up and smiles. "Rabindranath Tagore."

Morris turns to Sol. "What the hell is that supposed to mean? And who is Rabbi Tagore?"

"I'm guessing Hasidic," says Sol.

The Seminary rabbis stand in the back of the room and cast awkward glances at one another. After he finishes his remarks Paul announces that Walter will be joining the rabbinical students for the remainder of the academic year. "Teach my student Hebrew and Bible. Show him how to wander through a text and uncover meaning. One day you will be proud to have known him."

Sol Kerem's father was a Warsaw-born yeshiva student who rose to American prominence as the owner of Kerem's Brooklyn Kosher Emporium. After he died of a sudden heart attack, his wife Lotte would say, *What Chaim could not provide in progeny, he made up for with flanken and braised beef.* On Shabbat the Kerem house swelled with visitors who could not afford to buy their own meat. Chaim would sit at the head of the table and pontificate about some minute aspect of Jewish law to the guests who had only come for the food. As a boy Sol stayed at the table for a short time, preferring to sit alone in the kitchen, immersed in an adventure book. On a Shabbat afternoon when he was seven, Sol warmed himself beside the stove while the guests crowded around the dining table, relishing the assortment of cold cuts, stuffed cabbage, and tongue. He was alone in the kitchen when the gas oven exploded and lifted him from his stove-side chair and threw him on the floor, momentarily unconscious, then awake and stunned, leaving him deaf in one ear for the rest of his life.

Soon after they met at the Heschel lecture, Sol told Rosalie about his deaf ear and she said, "Let me guess which one." She took in his chocolate eyes and artfully matched sideburns. His plump lips and elegant nose. A faint cleft in his chin. Her Sol was the Casanova of the study hall, the matinee idol of the *beit midrash.* When he stood before her she focused on his broad shoulders and when he turned she admired the elegance of his slender back. He was a catch, her Sol.

"You are perfect," she said to him. "Your deaf ear is your secret to the world."

"It's the left one," he said. "Don't tell anyone."

"My best secret," said Rosalie.

When they announced their engagement, Sol and Rosalie invited their widowed mothers to meet them at Ratner's Restaurant. The four of them broke an engagement plate in honor of the wedding that was scheduled to coincide with Sol's graduation from rabbinical school. Ida Wachs and Lotte Kerem wrapped their arms around the couple and wept.

Rosalie and Sol meet in Riverside Park, just hours after the gossip about the refugee and his guru-escort dissipated into vague cackles. Rosalie pushes the bag of books into Sol's arms, picks up a handful of snow, takes a lick, and offers it to him. Sol shakes his head and peers into the bag.

"I feel as if I'm carrying the foundation of our first home," he says.

"Careful with that metaphor, rabbi," says Rosalie. "*Books are no more than seeds*, remember? Your holy books will only take you so far."

Sol turns and kisses her cheek. "You will take me the rest of the way."

"Wherever you want to go, sweetheart."

"I can't wait for everything to start," he says. "Time to shake up a few lives."

"That's ambitious, Sol. People don't like to change."

"But that's the whole point! Inspire, teach, guide. And along the way, our lives will become so textured—like living doubly! The days will seem ordinary, but the sanctity will shine through."

"And what if life proves you wrong? One day you'll wake up and realize that when Moses received the tablets on Sinai a great myth was born."

"Every word of that myth is true."

"You have to be kidding."

"It's not literal truth; I'm not an idiot. But the suspension of disbelief permits me to park my faith in the Torah. It's a choice I make, again and again."

Rosalie rolls her eyes. At times Sol seems to be speaking a lofty, foreign language. She knows its vocabulary and idioms, but she prefers to talk about religion with the language she learned from her parents: recipes and rituals flavored with a good Hasidic story. Sol is nothing like her. *Find a man who complements you,* her mother once said, *and you will honor your differences.* When they kiss Rosalie loves to rest her fingers on the tips of Sol's ears and lightly circle the left ear that holds the world in silence. At times Sol reads passages aloud from Maimonides's *Guide for the Perplexed* and she closes her eyes and follows the timbre of his voice, listening to him articulate every syllable as if he is making love to the words.

Sol tells Rosalie about the men who visited that day: the pompous man who said that all of humanity was sewn from a single piece of spiritual cloth and the Jewish refugee who wore a green nightgown made of thin cotton.

"Oddballs," says Sol.

"Or opportunities, Rabbi Kerem. You have to start behaving like a holy man. Everything in your path has something to teach you."

Sol reaches down and scoops a palmful of snow. He shapes it into a tight ball and holds it in his ungloved hand. As the chill seeps in, he thinks about how Walter smiled at him. There were other students in that room; what was Walter trying to say? Rosalie would have an answer, of course; something vaguely mystical and very silly. He was Elijah the prophet. He was the Messiah. He was the hearing that Sol lost in one ear. And of course Rosalie would think that; his fiancée was the daughter of a Hasid.

"I wish your father had liked me," says Sol.

Rosalie laughs. "Oh, sweetness. My father knew my heart. You have nothing to worry about."

She pulls the snowball out of his hand, carries his fingers to her lips, and blows warm air on them.

"Soon," she says.

"Eight more months."

"No time at all."

Barely enough, yet just enough, thinks Sol. Time enough for the last shaping of the clay before he drives out to a pulpit and puts his hand on a lectern and imparts meaning to a sanctuary full of congregants. Time enough to complete the final revisions of his boyhood self, to grow into a proper groom for his bride. Enough time, barely enough. It would take him a lifetime to be ready.

"Did you choose yet?" asks Sol.

"I'm still deciding."

"A bride needs a dress."

"I'm holding out for a flapper."

"I can't make you do anything," says Sol.

"Then we understand each other perfectly."

Sol's hand wraps around Rosalie's and she laces her fingers between his. "*She'elah* and *teshuvah*," says Sol. "Question and answer. Want to play?"

"I'm always up for a round of Ask the rabbi," she says.

Rosalie remembers how one of her father's students would show up at the apartment, sit beside her father, and lean close. The student would whisper a *she'elah*—a personal question about faith or practice. After a few moments, her father would respond with a *teshuvah*—a ruling, an explanation, or a sideways answer that left the student hungry to ask something more.

"Remember: the answer lies between the lines," says Sol.

"Of course. My father taught me. So, rabbi, what's your she'elah?"

"How does a man know if he is intended to be a rabbi?"

"Teshuvah," says Rosalie. "If the man yearns to live in the place where the words of the texts brush up against real life, maybe it's meant to be."

"Good one!" says Sol.

"And how would you answer the question, rabbi?"

"Teshuvah," says Sol. "Do not ask if the man knows his way around a text. Better to ask if he burns with passion for his intended wife. As it is written, *the only calling is the calling of love.*"

Rosalie laughs. "You sound like some kind of romantic. Did those strange visitors sprinkle you with fairy dust?"

Sol takes her face in his hands and kisses her nose.

"I'm in love," he says. "With you."

In the Radish's intermediate Talmud class, the students are required to stumble through an entire Aramaic passage aloud, correct each mistake, read through the text again, then offer a translation. Sol sits in the front row. He is the only student who does not refer to Rabbi Radnitsky as the vegetable he most resembles, especially when a passage in the text—usually concerning bodily emissions—makes him blush.

Walter sits in the last row, leans back in his chair, and stares out the window.

"Read, Westhaus!" yells the Radish. "Take a turn with your brethren."

Walter slowly articulates the first three words, the easy ones that bear no message but announce the opening of a gate:

"*Rabban Gamliel omer.* Rabbi Gamliel says."

Walter looks up at the Radish. "That's all I know." He stands, closes his book, and exits the classroom.

Sol casts his eyes around the room, waiting for someone to follow Walter, but no one moves. The Radish continues with the class, and Sol stares at the page of Talmud, wondering where oddball Walter had vanished. He hears Rosalie's voice whispering in his good ear, *Opportunities, Rabbi Kerem. You have to start behaving like a holy man.*

After class, Sol finds Walter in the hallway. "Has anyone claimed you yet?"

"What are you talking about?"

"Everyone needs a study partner. A *chavrusa.* You'd be good for me."

"I'm only visiting here."

"I want to learn with you," says Sol. "The others are ambitious and smart but you have the gall of someone who doesn't care." He thinks of what Rosalie said in the park. "Maybe you can teach me something."

"Your school is a temporary shelter for me," says Walter. "I am not one of you."

"That's exactly why I'm asking," says Sol.

Rosalie spreads a blanket over a snow-laced boulder in Central Park. She has brought plates from her mother's house and places a pastrami sandwich on each one.

"Leave it to you to propose a winter picnic," says Sol.

"It's not officially winter and a sandwich is not quite a picnic. Did you bring the wine?"

"It's not the Sabbath," says Sol. "I prefer to save my blessings."

"You are the master of saving everything for another time. Picnics for spring, wine for the Sabbath, sex for marriage." Rosalie sighs. "Does it ever stop?"

Sol wraps his arms around her. "Be patient with me."

She rests her head on his shoulder and spies a man and woman kissing on a nearby bench. The man's hand reaches inside the woman's skirt.

"I just wish," says Rosalie.

"Wish what?"

"Oh, don't pretend to be naïve. The other students don't follow these rules. It's the Seminary, Sol. The Conservative movement, not some crazy Orthodox yeshiva where men and women are forbidden to touch before marriage—"

"I'm not like other men."

"Clearly."

"What's that supposed to mean? Do you think this is easy for me? I touch myself at night and think of you."

"Really?"

"I'm counting the days."

"Look at those two. We could be enjoying ourselves right now. No leap of time, no waiting. We decide the course of our lives, free of prescriptives."

"But—"

"The law doesn't have to be a fence," says Rosalie. "It wasn't for my father."

"I'm not like your father."

Be free of him; be devoted to him. Rosalie closes her eyes. Give yourself over to your rabbi, see where it goes, she thinks. Rosalie Wachs soon to be Rosalie Kerem. Kerem means vineyard. Rosalie Vineyard. Where grapes are saturated with light and grow into their fullness in time. Rosalie rests her hand in Sol's palm.

"We have this," he says. "What is suggested is more arousing than its fulfillment."

"Sometimes I feel it's all too challenging and lofty and—"

"And?"

Rosalie closes her eyes. The woman on the bench knows the man she kisses; she studies him through his touch. Necessary information. But Rosalie knows so little about Sol; he is filled with words that Rosalie cannot translate. And yet he is her bashert; she knows this. Intended, perfect, inevitable as rain.

She'elah: What can the body teach the mind?

Teshuvah: The body delivers its truth without words.

Sol and Walter sit side by side at a table in the beit midrash, a tower of books stacked before them. Walter reaches into his pocket, pulls out a bag of yellow spice and inhales.

"Want some?"

"Don't get your powder on the books! If they get ruined, we'll have to bury them."

Walter laughs. "These books were written under the influence of all kinds of spices, Sol. Just imagine your beloved ancient rabbis picking at the roots of plants and sniffing with abandon. They craved all kinds of knowledge, just like you do."

Sol opens tractate Berakhot and scans the pages. He begins to sway.

"Oh, look," he says, his voice falling into the cadence of Talmudic singsong. "Rabbi Meir says that to love God with all of your soul means that you should love God with your good inclinations and your evil ones too. And Ben Azzai says, *with all of your soul* means you should give your soul to the commandments."

"That's ridiculous," says Walter.

"But there's more to the story," says Sol. "Ben Azzai was engaged to Rabbi Akiva's daughter. He broke it off because he wanted to devote his life to studying Torah."

"Idiot," says Walter. "What a waste."

"Not necessarily," says Sol. "Yearning can be that deep."

"For a woman. Not for the words of a book."

"And God?"

"What does God have to do with this? I'm not a believer, Sol. You're wasting your time with me." Walter stands and gathers his books.

Sol pulls at Walter's sleeve. "Please stay," he says.

"Ben Azzai was scared," says Walter. "Just like you."

Sol stares at the page of Talmud and bites his lip. "Let's move on," he says. "Your turn to crack the Jastrow."

Walter perches on the table and flips through the pages of the Talmudic dictionary. "I hate looking up words," he says. "I'm a miserable foil for a promising rabbinical student. You cursed yourself by choosing me."

Sol pulls the dictionary from Walter's hands. "I'll look up the words. Then we'll be free to learn."

By the end of the week, Sol and Walter no longer study the text in any prescribed order. They open volumes of Talmud at random, choose sentences out of context, and conjure their meanings.

"Look at this one," says Sol. "A *slave belongs to its master forever.*"

"How long is forever? How long does it last?"

"The rabbis suggest that forever lasts until the Jubilee. That's fifty years."

"But does forever refer to a unit of time or a condition of the heart?" asks Walter.

They spend hours like this, throwing snippets of text between them like the finest baseball players, pitching and catching with playful perfection. Sol offers Walter a translation—any string of words will do—and Walter sets off on a tangent. When they learn the laws pertaining to lost objects in Bava Metzia,

Walter talks about lost thoughts and how an isolated human idea can survive for generations. When they peruse the dictionary, Sol remarks how the Hebrew word *zeman* means time and invite and opportunity, their connotations perfectly linked like a string of pearls. They riff on how people's lives are written into the Hebrew language, and how the ancient words are never static.

One afternoon Sol writes out the words of the Shema and asks Walter to ponder their meaning.

"It's a haiku," says Walter. "Three lines. Five syllables, then seven, then five. *She-ma yis-ra-el*. Five. *A-do-noi El-o-hei-nu*. Seven. *A-do-noi Ech-ad*. Five. It works out perfectly."

"Nu?"

"A haiku asks us to reenvision the object it describes. A simple frog becomes more green, more moist, more embodied; a white butterfly becomes an acrobat, a ballet dancer, a celestial being."

"And the words of the Shema transform how we understand God at any given moment," says Sol.

"As you wish. But God is not a noun."

"Is God a verb?" asks Sol.

"God is a parenthetical thought, rabbi. A commentary you add to your days; something to justify the karma of your actions."

"I wish I could ride on your caravan of brilliance. My mind would be so open."

"Your mind is beautiful just the way it is," says Walter. "You wear your learning well. It doesn't constrict you."

Sol smiles at him. In just a few weeks, Walter has morphed from a dirty-haired stranger to an intriguing friend. He still dresses in his green kurta, but his hair is clean and when he remembers to wear a yarmulke, it no longer sits awkwardly on his head.

"You could be one of us if you wanted," says Sol. "You would be a good rabbi."

"Don't kid yourself."

To Sol, the refugee's lack of faith challenges him to sharpen his own. After they learn together, Sol sits alone in the beit midrash and thinks of ways he can counter Walter's arguments, prove to him that God is really a noun. He wishes he could see Walter as Morris does: a lost soul, an illiterate Jew who wears the wrong clothes and sniffs yellow powder. But Sol loves what Walter teaches him; together they release interpretations as if they are breaking open pistachio nuts and savoring the sweet green meats. With Walter as his chavrusa, Sol believes he will never stray as a rabbi; he will always know how to unlock kernels of passion and meaning.

"She'elah: If a man claims a chavrusa in his youth, are they destined to learn together in the future?" asks Sol.

"Teshuvah: Everything is explained in the World to Come," says Walter.

Sol thinks of Rosalie and Walter as milk and meat, requiring separate dishes and a designated lapse of time that must pass between eating one or the other. Rosalie is his bashert, his soulmate, who insists on wearing a flapper dress to their wedding. At night before sleep he imagines their first time together. Like he did as a boy Sol practices kissing the back of his hand, only now he imagines how he will kiss her *down there*, as the Radish explained during an impromptu counseling session. Sol has no idea what to expect but he believes Rosalie will guide him well. She is that kind of woman.

Wife here. Chavrusa there. Another set of dishes. His father had once said to him, I *left behind my chavrusa in Poland and he was the love of my life. God only knows what happened to him. If you have a chavrusa keep him close and he will sustain you as a husband sustains a wife.* Day after day Sol and Walter envelop themselves in the words that carry them to ancient study halls, steamy bathhouses of men and Hebrew letters dancing together in an eternal tango. Whatever sex may be, thinks Sol, nothing beats the frolic of two men's minds, this holy fire, thought merging with thought in perfect knowing and boundless joy.

IN THE GENIZA

December 1946

A December blizzard blankets the city with three feet of snow. Classes are cancelled and Sol invites Rosalie to the Seminary for afternoon tea. She arrives early and steps out to the courtyard, a silent field of white. Rosalie digs her boots into the knee-deep snow, steps forward into the middle of the yard, opens her arms, and spins. This is happiness, she thinks. This cushion of snow, this gray shawl of a sky, and Sol, the man who will escort her into the future. She is ready to cast aside any lingering doubts and buy a wedding dress. Rosalie picks up a twig and writes:

SOL

ROSALIE + SOL

ROSALIE

She spins again, opening her mouth to catch the falling flakes, and spies Sol standing at a window. He runs out to the courtyard, pulls her by the waist, and leads her to the arcade where they kiss in the shadows. Rosalie opens her eyes and notices a man without a jacket standing beside Sol.

The man shivers and Rosalie turns to him.

"You must be freezing!"

She pulls on Sol's lapels. "Give this man your coat!"

"This is not any man," says Sol, smiling. "Rosalie, meet Walter Westhaus, my beloved chavrusa."

Sol drapes his coat over Walter's shoulders and clears his throat. "You sneaked up on us. Walter. Meet Rosalie, my fiancée."

"At last!" says Rosalie. "I have been waiting for this. Sol adores you! I hope you'll tell me about India and the ashram and how you got here—Sol is so secretive."

Walter glances from Rosalie to Sol and then back to Rosalie. "You make a beautiful couple," he says.

"Thank you," says Rosalie. "Don't you have any boots?"

When the arrangements were made for Walter to study at the Seminary, he was assigned a dorm room that was infested with mice. Walter would be awakened by a mouse nibbling on his arm and another one slinking up the sleeve of his tunic. Rather than ask the other students how they tolerate the infestation he scouts out other places to sleep. He samples every closet and crawl space in the building, choosing a different place to lay his head each night. No place in the building is rodent-free, but he never returns to his room.

On cold nights Walter sleeps in a basement boiler room, huddled in the warmest corner. When he wants to study he camps out in attic rooms crowded with Hebrew books, some torn and used, others stored in their original boxes. He opens volumes at random, forcing himself to decipher the meaning of the words. On nights when he can't sleep, Walter finds an empty classroom and takes a seat. He imagines a rabbi who would not teach law and textual criticism as the real rabbis do. Walter's rabbi would pull away a curtain and reveal Sonia to him. Sonia would not appear as she was in this life—blond hair cascading down her back, her voice poised for Brahms—this Sonia would step out from the curtain and escort him on his American journey, explaining the meaning of things. Then the rabbi would vanish and Sonia would become the rabbi. Instead of lieder she would sing wordless songs and answer all his questions.

She'elah: *Why do these men wear leather straps that tear into their arms?*

Teshuvah: The straps are a ladder to the infinite. They spiral on the arm and twist around the middle finger because one day the body will lie in the ground but the spiral goes on forever.

She'elah: Why won't I wear those straps, no matter how many times the rabbis insist?

Teshuvah: You can't cross your own boundaries, schatzi. The scent of these arm-pits is aroma finer than prayer. But you will help them understand their strange tribal ways.

She'elah: Why did you die and I am here?

Teshuvah: I left the bedroom to look for crackers. I was shot instead of you. And now you are alone in this building where Paul Richardson dropped you off like a parcel of laundry.

As he sits in the empty classroom Walter feels certain that Rabbi Sonia has touched his shoulder but when he looks up he remembers that he is alone. This building where men learn about God and Torah is the only home he has.

On Friday nights the rabbinical students dress up in bow ties and serve dinner to one another in the dining hall. Sol is an eager waiter. He escorts Rosalie to an empty table and pours her a glass of water. She spots Walter standing in a corner, perfectly still.

"Walter!" she calls.

He nods and smiles at her. He looks so thin, she thinks. So very lost. She walks over and offers her arm.

"Open spaces in this building make me wary," he says. "I can't always make my way across the wide foyers."

"But you live here. Didn't they give you a room?"

"Overrun by mice. I find other places to sleep."

"Sol didn't mention—"

"Your Sol doesn't know me as well as he thinks."

Rosalie escorts Walter to her table, now occupied by Morris and two other students. Walter's leg trembles under the tablecloth and Rosalie places her hand on his knee to keep it steady. Morris glances at them and nods.

"Gentlemen and Rosalie," he says. "I have a burning question, an inquiry that will affect the course of Jewish life in America. Maybe our refugee friend can answer."

Walter turns to Morris. "Go ahead, rabbi."

"On Shabbat is one allowed to dip a tea bag in a cup of hot water? Or—and here is the clincher—should the hot water be poured over the tea bag?"

"Is this religion?" asks Walter.

"Every detail," says Rosalie. "Art lives in the minutiae."

"Then religious practice is an art form," adds Walter.

"You remind me of Professor Heschel," says Morris.

"I hear he's teaching here now," says Rosalie. "He was my matchmaker! Any of you in his class?"

"I am," says Morris. "But he's too mystical for me. I can't figure him out."

Rosalie closes her eyes for a moment and remembers Heschel's lecture, and how Sol smiled at her for the first time. She glances at Walter and then turns to Morris.

"Isn't that your job from now on? To understand people?"

Morris laughs. "When I graduate I become a rabbi. Here I am still a boy, a fountain pen, an ingénue in the ways of God."

Walter turns to Rosalie and whispers in her ear. "That's the problem," he says. "No enlightenment. Rabbis like Morris with their picayune questions. How can a tea bag open a door to transcendence?"

"Ah," says Rosalie. She pulls a bag of Swee-Touch-Nee from her pocketbook and immerses it in her water glass. First a blush, then a darkening stain, then saturation.

Rosalie smiles. "Transcendence in a glass."

"But you haven't answered my question," says Morris. "The pouring of the water is what matters, not your little home economics demonstration."

"Jewish life is home ec," says Rosalie. "Who is going to make Shabbat for you when you graduate, Morris?"

"That's enough, Rosalie." He moves to another table and the other students follow.

Walter and Rosalie are alone.

"She'elah," says Walter. "If a woman learns with men will they be seduced by her presence in the beit midrash?"

"Teshuvah," says Rosalie. "The woman will be permitted to learn with the men if she agrees not to speak. After all, her voice may arouse and distract them from their holy Torah."

"Why don't you sit next to me in the Radish's class? I could use a companion."

"No women allowed," says Rosalie.

"I can ask. Your fiancé would be proud to have you as his audience. The Radish calls him an *ilui*, a Talmudic prodigy."

"My handsome genius."

"Your Sol is a man of deep faith," says Walter.

"One of us has to be," says Rosalie.

After he finishes serving, Sol sits beside Walter, grabs a fork, and helps himself to the leftover chicken on Walter's plate.

"How about we find a coveted place for Rosalie in the Radish's class?" asks Walter.

"That," says Sol, "will never be permitted."

Rosalie turns to him. "You're the one who is refusing me."

"Of course not," he says. "I'd love for you to be in my class. You would be so proud of me."

"We will test it out," says Walter. "If you don't ask the Radish, I will. I'm the treasured guest—he won't say no to me."

"Okay with you, Sol?" asks Rosalie.

He reaches over and kisses her cheek.

"If that's what you want."

———————

The Seminary attic is cluttered with books and papers waiting for burial—faded prayer books with missing pages, a volume of Talmud munched on by bugs, discarded source sheets, solicitation letters inscribed with biblical verses that were never mailed. Prayer shawls are strewn about, some with holes, some never worn. Just like in the dorm rooms, mice scurry everywhere. In a corner, a Torah scroll lies on a low table, properly covered with a suit jacket that Walter borrows when one of the rabbis scolds him for improper dress.

The attic has become Walter's sleeping loft. He has named it the geniza, a holding place for cast-off sacred books, which he has begun to sort and shelve into an organized library. After class he invites Sol for a tour. "It's the place," says Walter, "where the dead visit on Mondays and Thursdays to read Torah, enlighten me, and then return to the World to Come."

The floor is littered with books and Sol is reluctant to step over them.

"I can't walk on a prayer book," he says. "I'll look from here."

Walter takes Sol's hand. "Trust me," he says. "I won't let you tread all over your holy words. I'll keep my rabbi fit for his profession."

Walter points out the books he shelved. "Look at my feat of organization. Rashi here, mysticism over there, Talmudic *responsa* in this corner."

"Did you bring me up here to show off how you've progressed in your learning?"

Walter sits against a wall, opens a file drawer, and pulls out a bottle of whiskey. Sol sidles up beside him.

"Yours?"

"Someone shares it with me. Every time I check, it's down a bit. One of your rabbis."

"And yours."

"Ha!" says Walter. "This is your world, not mine."

"Why don't you talk about what happened?" asks Sol. "All the students are trying to figure out how you escaped from Berlin, traveled to India, and wound up here, with us."

Walter offers the bottle to Sol who takes a swig and passes it back.

"What are you looking for, Sol? A tale of suffering so you can try out your pastoral skills before you graduate?"

"It's not that—"

"What's motivating your great curiosity? A tad of voyeurism, perhaps? Or maybe I can give you a way to test-drive your compassion—extra sweet because you get the full package in one story. So here it is, my friend. When she was shot, her wetness was still fresh on my hands. Both of us so tender. Had she not been killed with my father we all would have probably been gassed by now. I am your living symbol—"

"Stop," says Sol.

"No. Take it all. Take my life. Take it so you can seem learned, wiser, so you can pretend to be a real rabbi who has seen something outside the four cubits of your small American life. No one will dare call you a thief if you use my material for your sermons."

"I'm sorry. I'm only trying—"

"You have no idea that you mock me. You actually believe you can offer me consolation. I find that incomprehensible."

"I want to help," says Sol.

"What do you see when you look at me? A lost man wearing a cotton tunic in the middle of winter? An emblem of tragedy you can use to test out some kind of theology? Even now, you are thinking of a way to offer some comfort, show off your rabbinic talents."

"I'm not vulgar," says Sol.

"And I'm not one of your teachers, preparing you to lead a deluded flock. I'm a guest here. And I couldn't care less about your profession."

"But I care," says Sol. "Deeply."

"That's obvious," says Walter. "So go ahead. Practice your craft. Offer me your best words."

"I can't."

"Of course you can. Go ahead."

"Your fiancée who was shot," says Sol. "You will chase her all your days. She calls to you from the World to Come."

"Oh! That's a good one. Home run on your first time out, rabbi."

"I'm not insincere," says Sol.

"I can see that."

Sol inches closer to Walter. "You could be one of us too."

"I hold nothing of your wisdom."

"I was cruel," says Sol. "I'm sorry."

"You will be a good rabbi," says Walter. "And I understand. Honestly, I do."

They pass the whiskey bottle in silence. I went too far, thinks Sol. I will lose him if I'm not careful. *Keep your chavrusa close to you always*, his father had said. *Do not let the flame of your learning burn out with time or misunderstanding. Let it be a marriage for you. Never be mean, always be loving—*

Sol takes the last swig and lets the bottle roll on the floor. Walter turns to Sol and takes his face in his hands, bringing their noses to touch. The gesture is one of apology. Walter is just about to let go when Sol grabs his cheeks and kisses him.

Sol's lips tremble against Walter's and he closes his eyes. Walter lays his hands on top of Sol's, removes them from his cheeks, and holds them together.

"This, my rabbi," says Walter. "This is not meant for you."

Sol pulls away and covers his face with his hands.

"Of course not," says Sol. "I lost myself."

He brushes himself off and steps toward the door.

"I was mistaken. I'm sorry—"

"It's all right," says Walter. "I understand."

Sol closes the door behind him and sits at the top of the staircase, resting his head in his palms. Of course Walter understands. The refugee knows me too well, he thinks. Sol imagines Walter leading him by the hand through an intricate palace made of Hebrew words. *You don't need language to find your way through these rooms,* he says. *You can leave your conjugations behind; no need to know Aramaic, no need for your Jastrow dictionary.*

Sol listens to the traffic of students milling about in the hallway and shifts his body to the side of the stair so he won't cast a shadow.

She'elah: Can the body ask one question and the mind another?

Teshuvah: As God is one, the mind and the body are one.

———

Alone in the attic that night, Walter lies on the floor and gazes at the ceiling as he once gazed at the night stars in the fields of Shantiniketan. No one had intruded on him at the ashram; no one had tried to claim him as a fellow Jew. He could learn philosophy without the spitfire of Talmudic debate; he could digest the language of the spirit without a chavrusa leaning in for a kiss. And yet when Sol's lips pressed against his, Walter knew that this kiss was not a whiskey-hazed indiscretion, but a declaration of love. Sol's yearnings may have been misplaced, but Walter feels touched by his audacity.

He listens to the mice scurrying beneath the floorboards. Earned time, he thinks. The afterlife, the footnote. The students' faces are question marks, asking everything of him. *Be one of us, deliver the goods, enlighten us, or confess! Who are you, Walter? What kind of Jew are you? Speak when you are ready; open the gate: Rabbi Walter omer.* He does not belong in this building, his way station to some vague future. *Soothe me with the words of the Song,* Sonia had said. *Walter, please. Promise me we will go home.* Walter lays his ear to the floorboards and listens to the laughter of the students in the hallway beneath the attic, their voices erupting with a joy he will never understand.

The next day, Sol rushes along Riverside Drive, muttering Talmudic phrases to himself. Rosalie trails behind, then sprints and grabs his hand.

"Slow down, sweetheart."

"I need to get back and study."

"Talk to me, Sol. I can't marry a man who has his thoughts parked elsewhere."

He slows down. "I'm sorry. Of course you can't."

"Why don't you tell me," she says.

"What?"

"Everything. All the details. What you are learning, how one becomes a rabbi, something. Anything. I need to prepare for your Talmud class."

"So much doesn't translate."

"You make it sound like a secret society."

"It's not a cabal," he says.

"But it is! Hebrew and Aramaic are your secret keys to the treasures that you twist around to make an argument. You use your implied wisdom to manipulate people into believing what cannot be proven."

"You sound crass."

"Look, you knew my father. One can be skeptical and still embrace a daring life of faith. And I don't say this without love."

"I have found a wise woman. Your price is above rubies."

"Don't toss me your rabbi lines. You haven't even earned the title yet."

"Rosalie, what—"

She puts a finger to his lips. "If you see me as a threat we won't get very far. I'm on your side, sweetheart; I'm marrying you."

Sol kisses her finger and takes her hand. He remembers how their arms touched at the Heschel lecture and how he literally felt a spark binding them together. Their courtship began so simply: a tinge of desire that felt inevitable. And his desire for Walter started off simply too—the lifelong bond of a true chavrusa— and then he corrupted it with a thoughtless gesture, a mistaken kiss, a mistranslation. He had been listening with his deaf ear and misunderstood what was said. But no more.

"Thank God," says Sol.

Rosalie smiles. "My handsome ilui. It's going to be fun, driving off to the suburbs in a new car, starting a shul—"

"I was thinking about a Dodge. Morris has a friend who owns a dealership."

"A Dodge is fine," says Rosalie. "As long as you're honest with me."

"Then let me become the rabbi I am meant to be. The next few months are demanding."

"So we will only speak of china patterns and the make of our car?"

"And the number of children you want. I still say three will be enough."

"And I always wanted four," says Rosalie. "Happy and layered and crowded with laughter, tables laden with food, the clanging of dishes, small hands wiping against my skirt. That's what I want."

"You," says Sol, "are all I want."

Rosalie and Walter sit together in the back row. The Radish has warned his students never to tell anyone that he invited a woman to his Talmud class, and he asked each man to seal his promise in the Talmudic way, holding one end of a handkerchief while the Radish held the other.

Sol sits up front. He is the Radish's pet student, the first to volunteer to read, the one who understands the precise meaning of the most obscure Aramaic phrases. At first Sol turns back and winks at Rosalie, but he doesn't want to make eye contact with Walter, so he stares straight ahead at the Radish, allowing his mind to tether to his teacher's words.

Walter and Rosalie pass notes: he draws a sketch of the Radish, passes it to Rosalie, who adds eyeglasses, styles a beard, earrings, a hat. In each class they draw more variations of the Radish until they fill an entire notepad with drawings of the Radish as a woman, the Radish fully naked, the Radish as a goat, the Radish as two goats having sex, the Radish as a radish. When he passes notes to her, Rosalie admires Walter's long fingers. One afternoon she writes him a note that has nothing to do with the Radish, folds it slowly into quarters, and passes it to him under the desk.

With fingers like that you could be a pianist.

Walter writes back.

I am a sketcher, a dreamer, a lost man.

Rosalie takes the note, crosses out *lost* and replaces it with *found.*

Walter writes back, I *believe Sol has a meeting with the placement commission today. Meet me at the top of the stairs after class. I want to show you something.*

Walter is waiting for her, his head balanced in his hands, his elbows resting on his knees. She sits beside him and can smell the spices on his breath. After a few moments, he takes her hand, opens the door to the attic, and begins his tour. She pauses at the section of Hasidic books and pulls out a volume.

"Ah! The Ishbitzer," she says. "The *Mei HaShiloach*. My father taught me this." She reads: "*When a man yearns for something, he should see that the object of his desire is the will of God.*"

"What if the man has no God?"

"Let desire be your God," says Rosalie.

"That works for me," says Walter.

Rosalie points out the letters crowding the page. "This is easier than learning Talmud."

Walter takes the book from her hands and turns it upside down. When he shakes the pages, a single sprig of faded freesia drops onto the floor. He picks it up, sniffs, and carefully tucks it behind her ear.

She runs her fingers along the spines of the books and Walter's long fingers follow hers.

"I can teach you how to understand these books," she says.

"My Hebrew is miserable. I can play games with the text but I make up the meanings."

Rosalie laughs. "That's half of it. These rabbis were playing games too. They were creating a new art form."

She pulls out a random book and points to a word. "Look. Here's the *shoresh*, the root. And then you have a starting place. The seed of the concept."

"You should be a rabbi," says Walter.

"Ha! The daughter of a rabbi marries a rabbi. That's how it goes. A link in a chain."

"You can be my rabbi," says Walter. He opens a file drawer and pulls out a fresh bottle of whiskey.

"Is this where you and Sol come to study?"

"Yes," he says. "Now you know."

"The secrets of men."

"I come here when I want to be alone. I sleep here most nights."

"I'll buy you better bedding," she says. "This is America! No need to sleep under a dirty, frayed blanket—"

"Don't tell Sol I brought you here."

"Why would I do that?"

Rosalie brushes her lips against Walter's and waits for him to respond. The first kiss is soft, nothing declarative. A dip in the waters. Walter's kiss bears no reminder of Sol; his thumbs rest lightly on her neck and welcome her to a new country.

He pulls away. "We can't—"

"Of course not," she says.

Walter stands, extends his hand, and pulls Rosalie to her feet. They kiss again.

"That's enough," he says.

"More than enough." She rests her head on his shoulder.

"Sol," she says.

"Sol," he echoes.

"This never happened."

Walter rests his fingers in Rosalie's hair and smiles.

"I will leave first," he says. "Wait several moments and close the door behind you."

She starts to say something but then stops and waits for Walter to walk out the door.

That night Rosalie lies awake in her childhood bed and counts the days until she will say goodbye to the only mattress she has ever known. She imagines all her girlhood fantasies lodged within the bed's casing: Her longings to shrink herself into a girl tiny enough to jump onto the pages of her father's books, swim through the words, wrap her legs around the letters. Her yearning to know Hebrew as fluently as her father did, and Aramaic, and a few words of Ancient Greek. Her wish, when she was eight, for a Shetland pony that she could ride from one end of Brooklyn to the other. Her desire for a first kiss, practiced on the back of her hand for so many years. That desire vanished when Sol kissed her the first time and she closed her eyes and tasted him and believed he was meant for her. Her dreams of marriage and children, how she would crowd a table with more laughter than her own parents did: four children at least, how she would kiss their heads and hold their small fingers as they drifted off to sleep. And then there were the dreams within the dreams: the pony's name (Spangle), the Hebrew letter she would wrap her legs around (lamed), how she would stand on a bench on upper Fifth Avenue and recite Hebrew poetry with perfect fluency. Rosalie wraps her arms around herself and then reaches under her nightgown, feeling Walter's fingers resting on hers and then departing, as they travel across her belly and thighs, circling until they arrive. She knows her body well and holds out until she imagines Walter inside of her and then she bursts into tears.

The next morning Rosalie takes the subway to the Seminary, marches up to the attic, and bangs on the heavy door. She has rehearsed the scenario in her head. Walter will answer, she will look down at the floor instead of into his eyes, tell him that she cannot see him again, that she will not return to the Radish's class and certainly not back to this geniza. She will say to him, *It was a regrettable mistake*, and then she thinks, *no, it was a beautiful mistake*, and then she decides she will tell him, *that was beautiful and not a mistake at all.* She opens the door and lets herself in.

Walter stands beside the file cabinet and holds a plastic bag filled with brown seeds. He picks up his sil batta from India and methodically crushes the seeds into powder. Rosalie stands at a distance, watching the twitch of his arm muscles.

He looks up.

"I—"

"Shh," he whispers. He takes her hand and they stand in front of the table where the Torah lies covered with a suit jacket. One kiss lasts for a long time, long enough for Rosalie to allow herself to say yes and long enough for Walter to move his hand up her skirt and explore her slowly and with care. Nothing is awkward between them; everything is permitted. Walter teaches Rosalie what she was waiting to learn about her body and Rosalie teaches Walter that it is possible, once again, to know pleasure.

Hours later, Rosalie skips down the attic stairs alone. She sprints outside the building, crosses Broadway, and runs into Riverside Park, where she collapses on the chilly grass, and reviews what just happened. Walter's hands and tongue. The inside of her thighs, the unfolded map of her longing. The spice he held to her nose and rubbed on her leg. What she did not know. What she knows now. *Something so beautiful cannot ever be a mistake.*

Rosalie presses her feet into the earth and stares at the clouds. She had left her shoes behind in the attic and when she returns to the Seminary an hour later Sol greets her in the lobby and asks why she is barefoot. She raises her hand to her mouth, pretending to be surprised.

No one can promenade around a text with Sol Kerem's alacrity. While his fellow students stumble through the guttural Aramaic, Sol pirouettes with brisk confidence. He thinks of every text as a field that welcomes him to linger and listen to the rustling of the trees. The letters are alive to him; the words of the Talmud make Sol ache with longing for more words, more pages, more paths toward knowing his God.

Sol is in his final months of learning. He has completed his first round of interviews and the wedding invitations have been mailed. He has no use for Walter now. Why did he let his chavrusa slow down his learning? All those hours wasted while they pillaged the text for fun. Had he had a real chavrusa, someone like Morris with actual skills, Sol would have had a proper partner to challenge his thinking. He never should have crossed the threshold of Walter's geniza. Something was calling out to him during those winter months—*more moments, more life, more love*—but what he craved was not another man but the words of the texts themselves. A sea of words. Law and lore. Storehouses of stories. Scripture in its skin. The tellings told anew. A rabbi without a Talmud is a heretic and Sol Kerem is anything but a heretic.

In the hallways he brushes past Walter and does not speak to him; in class he no longer turns to look at the back row. There is no more time for goodwill toward refugees who wear cloth shoes and Indian outfits—Sol needs to shape himself into the next great American rabbi. Now, late at night, when Sol touches himself before sleep, he thinks of Rosalie, imagines their first time after the wedding, soon, so soon. Sol will ask his wife to undress slowly; he will elongate the seduction, making it last after all these months of waiting. He feels himself touching Rosalie's thighs, her breasts, the skin he has not yet seen. When he is just about to come he can taste Walter's kiss, at first like fruit and then like ashes.

Walter and Rosalie return once more to the back row of the Radish's class. They stare straight ahead and pretend to listen to the Radish lecture about ancient laws of taxation. They do not pass notes. Rosalie senses Walter's every gesture: his hand moving across a page, the turn of his head when he brushes his hair out of his eyes. When she has the urge to pull him close, she focuses on how the lining of her skirt presses tightly against her hips. She considers the silk of the fabric, conjures the person who wove the silk with his fingers, the silkworm that spun the cocoon from its body. She reaches for a sheet of paper and writes:

She'elah: If the finest silk is woven into a fabric used for impure purposes, is the silkworm unholy in its spinning?

She passes her note to Walter. He pauses for a moment, then writes:

Teshuvah: The silkworm is always holy. True love is never impure.

MILK OR MEAT

February 1947

While Sol attends his afternoon seminars on practical rabbinics—
how to conduct funerals, unveil gravestones, bless converts, write
marriage contracts—Walter and Rosalie spread a blanket in the
darkest corners of the attic and explore the possibilities of their
bodies in the shadows of the eaves where bats have left their droppings. They call the attic the upper geniza and Rosalie keeps the
Ishbitzer's *Mei HaShiloach* right beside them.

"This book serves as our witness," she says.

"Of what?"

"That we are a vessel for God's desires."

"Even now?"

"Especially now. Don't you think so?"

"Your fiancé is the expert on theology, not me."

Walter leads Rosalie downstairs to the Seminary basement and
guides her through an endless warren of corridors. He opens

doors to rooms that lead to other rooms littered with office furniture, cartons of unmailed letters, and boxes of torn books, labeled SHAIMOS—FOR BURIAL. They name this labyrinth the lower geniza. When Rosalie learns her way around the maze of rooms, Walter picks up an abandoned prayer shawl and uses it to make a blindfold for her eyes.

"Now," he says. "Look for me."

"It's too confusing," she says. "I'll get lost."

"Look, darling. I will hold an open jar of coriander in my hand. The wisdom of your nose will help you."

Rosalie finds Walter hiding in a broom closet and they call this home base, the place to which they always return. At night when the students retreat to their dorm rooms, Walter and Rosalie play the spice game in the basement until they either find each other, or abandon the game and rendezvous in the closet. In the upper geniza they seduce each other with words: her quotes from the Ishbitzer and his quotes from Tagore. The upper geniza is where they talk about Rosalie's past—lessons from her father, her desire to embrace all of life—and Walter's future as a historian of religions, just as Paul Richardson has scripted for him. In the upper geniza Walter repeats the story of how he followed a man wearing a brown felt hat and wound up in Bombay, and how he didn't know that man was Paul Richardson. Rosalie listens to Walter's words and follows the music of his accent, but she does not pry for details.

In the lower geniza Walter and Rosalie speak little. They forget that time is measured in minutes and hours and that the sun sets at dusk. They look for hints of each other's bodies in empty broom closets and play hiding games that arouse them both. They touch each other with daring and mark each other's skin with turmeric. In the lower geniza they sniff the strongest spices, the ones that make them forget that Sol and his classmates inhabit the floors above, learning their final lessons in how to name and how to marry and how to bury; how to consecrate, how to nullify, and how to explain things that defy comprehension.

Rosalie and Sol sit across from each other at a Friday night dinner in the dining hall.

"Did you find a dress yet?" he asks.

"I'm working on it."

"Get the flapper. Get whatever you want."

"Yes," says Rosalie. "I plan to. Get what I want, I mean."

"Your choice."

Morris sits down next to Sol. "May I interrupt?"

"Of course!" Sol turns to Rosalie. "Morris and I are learning together now. He's a much better chavrusa for me than Walter."

"No more refugees clouding the thoughts of our ilui!" says Morris. He laughs and turns toward Rosalie. "What did Sol ever see in that man?"

"I don't know, Morris."

"Now, I can see how women would adore him. The mysterious stranger who wears a tunic the color of pea soup. He's a real lady-killer."

Rosalie looks down at the table.

"Really," says Morris. "Can you imagine anyone considering him an object of desire?"

"Walter is a good man," says Sol. "Sad and confused and decent."

Morris laughs. "Sounds just like you. Just think, Rosalie. All over this building you have your choice of sad, confused, and decent men."

"And I chose this one, Morris. This beautiful man is my fiancé." Rosalie smiles at Sol.

Morris winks. "I expect an invitation to the wedding."

Sol and Rosalie leave before dessert is served. It is always as it was, she thinks. I love him no less. Walter is a dream, a figment, a palace gate that will soon be closed. I will be a mother and a grandmother and the secret of these weeks will resound in my bones as private music that only I will be able to hear.

The following Monday Rosalie tells Sol she plans to spend the day in Brooklyn with her mother, buying a dress at Kleinfeld's and celebrating over lunch. But instead she takes the subway alone to the Birth Control Clinical Research Bureau on West 16th Street. She sits in the reception area, waiting for her name to be called. Rosalie fidgets in her seat and her eyes dart toward the other women in the room. What do they know that she doesn't? She is new at this, not much older than a child. Rosalie wants to ask someone for advice but what question would she ask first? *Sol or Walter? Milk or meat? The lockstep of generations or the seduction of spices?* She closes her eyes and imagines herself standing inside a circle of women who dance around her. Rosalie wears a traditional wedding dress; an opaque veil covers her face. The women gaze at her with admiration, except for her mother, who wears a black gown and glares. *You're too young to be a mother*, she says. She hands Rosalie a small round box and says, *No babies until you find your heart*. Rosalie opens the lid and holds a rubber diaphragm in her trembling hand.

Sol stares at his reflection and winks. He has grown a mustache to appear older for the second round of interviews. Rosalie will be pleased, he thinks. He hasn't seen her in two weeks. "So much to do, Sol," she had said to him over the phone. "My mother, your mother, all the lists! Just be glad you are not involved in this wedding insanity." All for the best, thinks Sol. In a few months they will drive off in their Dodge and leave everything behind: the Radish, Morris, Walter. He would stay in touch with his teacher and with Morris, but Walter would not travel with him beyond these walls. Yes, his one-time chavrusa offered him a diversion. They had some moments on the page, some memorable flights through the Talmud. But Walter knows so little; he is a pawn in Paul's academic scheme. And that regrettable moment! Best to erase the memory before it festers and Sol becomes like the Talmudic figure Reish Lakish who saw Rabbi Yochanan bathing in a river and thought he was a beautiful woman. What did the Talmud leave out? Did the two men kiss and part, or did one always long for the other? What misperception was fastened to the text, recorded into history? Sol's indiscretion, at least, would not be recorded anywhere; it was a moment of youthful abandon, an episode he would discard with the library books he would return on his last day of rabbinical school.

———————

The dogwood tree in the Seminary courtyard blossoms in March. Ivory petals float on the lawn, but interview season has begun and the students barely notice. While they prepare for their first pulpits and are quizzed on their knowledge of Jewish law—how to build a mikvah and how to *kasher* a metal pot—the fiancée and the refugee explore each other's bodies in the upper geniza and in the lower geniza: the upper where they speak in words and the lower where they find each other in silence and surprise.

One afternoon in the lower geniza, Walter pulls a bag of black seeds from his pocket. "Close your eyes, Rosalie. Sniff. Now, give the smell a name. Make one up."

"Teacup."

"Black cardamom."

"Winded spice."

"Fenugreek. Good for digestion."

"Apple dust. Coriander. Good for awakening the spirit."

"Thighbone. Lotus seed."

"Serenity check. Borage flower."

"Camel skin. Turmeric root."

"Latke festival. Mustard seed."

There is no end to the variety of spices he puts before Rosalie's nose; the associations she conjures fly from her mouth like birds. Sometimes Walter grinds a mix of seeds against her skin, sniffs, and licks it off until her body smells like a spice garden, just like in the Song of Songs.

Walter and Rosalie have fallen asleep in the broom closet and she wakes up with tears in her eyes.

"How will Sol know me as you do?"

"You will educate him," says Walter. "In time he will learn how to please you."

"But this can't be translated."

"You will teach him as I was once taught before you came along. Every man learns from the first woman."

"Adam learned from Eve."

"Yes, my chavrusa. And Jacob and his two wives. Leah was given to him first so she could teach him how to satisfy Rachel."

"You make it sound like a daisy chain of lovemaking."

Walter laughs. "The infinite, single story of a man and a woman."

"How on earth," she asks, "will I ever let you go?"

Ida Wachs carries three dresses under her arm and follows Rosalie into a dressing room. Ida tells her the first dress is too revealing; a sleeveless flapper is unfit for a rebbetzin. The second dress doesn't flatter Rosalie's tiny waist, she adds. "A bride should be modest, yet give a hint of what lies ahead." When Rosalie tries on a traditional wedding gown, her mother rubs her palms together and beams. "You look like the kind of bride I was, only more elegant, more American, a regular movie star! You have made me so happy."

Rosalie thinks of her father's question: *Are you in love?*

"What about Tateh?" asks Rosalie. "Do you think he would have approved of this wedding?"

"Don't question what we both wanted for you."

Rosalie convulses in tears and Ida kisses her hair.

"A typical bride," says Ida. "I was the same."

As her mother walks out with the gown, Rosalie imagines the filmstrip of her unfolding life: making love with Sol in the light of the Shabbat candles, the welcoming of the babies, the fresh leather of the childrens' holiday shoes, her hands rubbing fresh thyme on the brisket, the rolling of the rugelach dough just as her mother taught—roll once, twice, three times for the flakiest pastry. More rolling, more specialness, more holiness. A sequence of kitchen sanctity spun out by rebbetzin Kerem, soon-to-be household goddess and patron saint of whatever synagogue would offer her husband his first job.

She'elah: What does one do with the unsolvable question?

Teshuvah: The bride will live her question, mold it under her hands, just like rolling out pastry dough on a table.

Rosalie returns to the spot in the grass where she laid her body after she and Walter made love in the upper geniza for the first time. The grass is slightly wet but she doesn't care about ruining her dress. She lies down and thinks of this patch of earth as her holy spot, a place on this planet that holds something of her heart. *Something so beautiful cannot be a mistake.* She flips onto her belly and rests her face on her forearms. It is possible, she thinks. Possible to tell Sol she cannot marry him. Possible to say *I'm sorry but.* At first he would doubt his hearing and touch his bad ear and then he would realize that he'd heard her correctly. *I cannot.* Sol's face would contort and he would let out a whimper. She would look at him and turn away because it would be unbearable to watch. And then she would run to the attic and find Walter. *I told him,* she would say. And she would contort her face as Sol had contorted his and Walter would shake his head slowly. *No. No. This is not my way. How could you have misunderstood me?* Rosalie would burst into tears because she would have shredded her future for that gesture, that question, that definitive refusal.

Her lover is a homeless man, caught between worlds. He wears the wrong clothes in the wrong seasons. She wants to live in a house, a real house with two tables: one in the kitchen and one in the dining room. One table adorned with a crystal vase of long roses, the other table offering a wooden bowl of fresh peaches. She wants bedrooms filled with children, their toys and books scattered about the floor, evidence of their joy. She wants to build a family, create a link in the chain of generations. And she wants to do this with Sol, who is learned and sincere and who will teach her Talmud early in the morning before the children wake up. And late at night she will lie beside him and teach him how she wants to be touched. What she learned with Walter. She will translate what is possible. It would not be everything — translation is an imperfect art and Sol would balk at the spices— but she will find a way to live with her husband's touch. His small hands. His one deaf ear. His big heart. It will take a lifetime to teach him what she wants but she, Rosalie Wachs, soon to be Rosalie Kerem, will find a way.

Walter lies on the floor of the upper geniza and listens to the faint laughter of the students gathering for their graduation party. Rosalie has told him about the progression of their remaining weeks here. Sol will be told where to report for his first pulpit.

The wedding will take place at the end of the month but Rosalie will not disclose the exact date or location, even though she knows Walter will not show up. Sol and Rosalie will marry and drive away in their new car. The rest of the rabbinical students will pack their bags and Walter will remain. Someone on the faculty will notice him lingering in a room and ask what he learned during his stay, and it will become obvious that Paul Richardson's arrangement was a sham. The rabbis housed him for a while; they lent shelter to a refugee whose sole contribution to the Seminary was offered in the upper geniza and the lower geniza, those holding places for discarded books and source sheets, unmailed letters and spoken words that would never be recorded into history.

"Where are you now, Sonia?" Walter asks aloud. "Where are you going, Rosalie?"

Rosalie wears her white satin wedding shoes to Sol's graduation party so she can break them in. She totters on the spiked heels and leans on Sol's arm for balance. Her face is smeared with a paste of makeup, and she holds her neck high. This is who I will be, she thinks. A first lady. A queen. A rebbetzin who is foolish beyond words. She enters the Seminary party room, her arm linked with Sol's.

The students and faculty erupt into the traditional wedding song: "*Od yishoma be'arei yehuda, uvechutzot yerushalayim: kol sasson v'kol simcha kol chatan v'kol kallah.* Still will be heard in the cities of Judea and in the courtyards of Jerusalem: the voice of laughter and the voice of joy, the voice of a groom, and the voice of a bride."

Walter crosses the courtyard, following the sound of raucous singing. When he first met Rosalie, he was afraid to walk across this open space alone and would linger in the shadows of the arcade. But he no longer worries that he will be murdered by a Nazi, or exposed for being less than an authentic Jew. Rosalie's love had made him feel safe; her affection felt like a canopy over his head. Let the rabbis wrap themselves in prayer shawls; if Walter were to ever become a man of prayer, Rosalie would be his tallit.

He stands at the doorway of the party room and peeks. With her upswept hair and veneer of makeup, he can barely recognize her. They look perfect together, he thinks. They will have beautiful babies. Walter pictures Sol and Rosalie's mothers sitting together at the wedding, admiring their grown children cascading across the dance floor, perfectly matched in each other's arms.

Walter turns and Rosalie calls to him.

"Wait—"

"It's a lovely party," he says. "You and Sol are a perfect fit."

"Don't—"

"Go back to your fiancé, darling."

Her voice quivers. "Find me when this is over. I'm so confused—"

He takes her face in his hands and kisses her tears.

"Better now," he says.

"Not better at all," she whimpers.

"Go to him, Rosalie. Sol is waiting for you."

After the party Sol is invited to the Radish's apartment for drinks and final words of congratulations. Rosalie and Walter sit side by side in the upper geniza, and stare straight ahead at the unread Torah scroll resting under the suit jacket. Rosalie kicks off her party shoes.

"I want to go back in time," she says. "Our first kiss."

Walter shrugs.

"Don't you?" asks Rosalie.

"My relationship to the past is very different from yours," says Walter. "I've lived through many chapters before this one." He reaches over and rubs her feet. "You have fresh blisters."

Rosalie closes her eyes. Remember how he touches you, she thinks. You will need every moment to be a repository for when this is over.

"Those shoes are finished," she says. "I'll be wearing flats to my wedding."

"You will look elegant in flats. Very stylish."

"I don't know how to end this," she says.

"I followed a man off a boat and wound up in Bombay," says Walter. "A man wearing a hat. I was on my way to Palestine and then to Shanghai and I never arrived."

Rosalie wipes her eyes with the back of her hand. "I don't want to go to Shanghai or Bombay or anywhere that doesn't include you. I don't want to go to my own wedding."

Rosalie brings her palm to her mouth so Walter won't see her lips quiver.

"You belong to each other," he says.

"I don't hold back from you."

"And you won't hold back from Sol."

"You spoiled me completely."

"Sol will spoil you."

Rosalie shakes her head. "Would he understand this?"

"Do you expect him to?"

"Of course not," says Rosalie.

"Sol is a true Talmudic scholar. He knows how to parse obscurities, plumb the meaning of things. So maybe he'll figure it out. Or he won't."

"And me? Will he figure out the meaning of me?"

Walter stops rubbing Rosalie's feet and rests his head in her lap.

"I believe in the two of you, Rabbi and Mrs. Kerem. You will grow to love your life, you'll see."

"But I—"

Walter reaches up and puts his finger to her lips.

"What was I thinking? I followed my body and now I can't bear to lose you. I don't want to spend my life longing for you."

"You are immense, Rosalie. You can carry the challenge."

"I want to carry your children," she says.

"I'm not looking for a family."

Of course not. She tries to imagine Walter cradling a baby in his arms, standing at the head of a Shabbat table reciting kiddush over a goblet of wine, laying his hands above a child's head, offering a blessing. But all she can see is Walter lying naked in her arms, their bodies sprawled on a blanket that covers a dirty floor.

Walter closes his eyes and Rosalie stares straight ahead. Neither of them speak for a long time.

"I will leave first," says Rosalie. "And I will close the door behind me."

"Yes," says Walter. "For now."

She'elah: How does one prepare to depart?

Teshuvah: Every ending is a beginning. Every departure carries the seeds of homecoming.

THE BRIDE

Rosalie has bathed, scraped off her nail polish, and gently whirled a Q-tip inside her ears and navel. Her pearl earrings and engagement ring rest in a small dish next to the sink. She pushes a button on the wall and waits. The mikvah attendant has young eyes, but her stiff wig and housedress make her look old enough to be Rosalie's mother.

"Come, my bride." The attendant loosens the robe from Rosalie's shoulders and lets it drop to the floor.

"Such a figure you have." She runs a finger down the length of Rosalie's spine and pauses to remove a loose hair. "Show me your hands."

Rosalie holds them out, palms up, then palms down.

"What's this yellow here?"

"I was cooking with spices."

"It's on your hip too," says the attendant. "And your belly. You cook naked?"

Rosalie lets a tear fall.

"Your husband will think he's getting a painted lady. *Vey iz mir*."

"I just—"

"Don't be like those Sephardic girls with their crazy spices. A little white pepper and salt will season a soup just fine."

Rosalie begins to sob.

"Another crying bride. Hasn't your mother taught you anything?" She offers Rosalie a tissue.

"Mothers never prepare their daughters. After you get used to it, sex is a pleasure. You have nothing to worry about."

Rosalie laughs.

"I heated the mikvah for you, made it extra special. The water carries blessings for your marriage. You will immerse three times. After each one I will call out 'Kosher!' The first time you go down, I want you to think about all your childhood dreams and longings floating away like seaweed in the water. The second time I want you to think about your husband and how much you love him and the children you will have. It will be a beautiful life. And the third time I want you to plunge as deep as you can, open your eyes wide and let everything you desire enter your body in a single holy moment."

Rosalie steps down into the mikvah and runs her arms through the water. She stands in the deepest part, hesitates, then immerses. She thinks of her mother and how she hid a book from her the day she sorted through her father's library. Was it the Spinoza? She pictures her father pulling the *Mei HaShiloach* off the shelf, and then she sees Walter's hands shake open the same book in the geniza, freeing a sprig of faded freesia that he places behind her ear. She kisses him, runs barefoot down Broadway and then Walter catches her, enters her from behind.

"Kosher!"

Rosalie mumbles the Hebrew blessing her mother taught her. She immerses again and summons Sol, who smiles at her and leans close. She can see his wedding suit, the fresh creases in the pants, the narrow lapels, and the silver cuff links that brush against her face when they kiss. *He will spoil you,* Walter said. *You will educate him.* Rosalie can see the braid of the three of them crossing over throughout their lives, knotted in places, tangled and impossible, her head resting on a wall of stone, ribbons and challah dough under her fingers, a single thread of fine hair streaming down a child's back—

"Kosher!"

Rosalie dives deep this time, opens her eyes. She sees her hands tremble in the water, the dank green tiles at the bottom, her feet shimmering like fish. She followed a scent in a geniza and wound up in an illicit forest that has no trail, no borders, no end. Rosalie plunges deeper, allowing her knees to fan out. She exhales bubbles, circles her arms wide, feels the water open her up as she empties her lungs and finds the last still place until it is too late and then she pushes down another inch and springs up.

"Kosher!"

Sol has asked the Radish to officiate at their wedding. When he meets with Rosalie before the ceremony, the Radish instructs her to circle Sol seven times under the wedding canopy. Her mother will follow closely behind and carry her train. "It's a meaningful ritual," says the Radish. Rosalie remembers how her father explained that seven circles represent the completion of the world, but the Radish has another explanation.

"You will be like seven wives to your husband," he says.

"And how many husbands will my one husband be to me?" asks Rosalie.

She'elah: If a bride thinks of another man when she stands under the wedding canopy, will the marriage be rendered impure?

Teshuvah: Three stand under the wedding canopy: the groom, the bride, and the presence of the holy one.

Walter knocks on the door of the Radish's office and hands him a package to mail to Sol and Rosalie.

"You should have been at their wedding," says the Radish. "You and Sol had something special. You lit him up. He should have kept you as a chavrusa, instead of starting up with Morris."

"I was a corrupting influence on your prized student."

"He had a spark when he was learning with you. I could see it."

"It was all too much for him," says Walter.

"I just hope—"

"Hope what?"

"That he can handle his wife," says the Radish. "She's a handful."

"How did she seem?" asks Walter. "How did she look?"

The Radish blushes. "She was radiant. Reminded me of Lauren Bacall."

"Lauren Bacall?"

"Hollywood."

Walter shakes his head. He can't imagine Rosalie as an actress on a silver screen.

"You should have seen them dance together."

Walter pictures Sol and Rosalie sweeping across a dance floor and wonders if she ended up wearing flats to her wedding and if the turmeric powder ever faded from her hip, her belly, and the places that only he knew how to find.

On their wedding night, Sol and Rosalie check into a hotel in Queens, close enough to the airport to hear the roar of the planes. Sol lies on his back on the cheap brocade bedspread, waiting for Rosalie to emerge from the bathroom. He closes his eyes and tries to picture his wife's body: the naked thighs he has imagined beneath her pencil skirts but never touched, the nipples he has seen outlined beneath her blouses but never kissed. This night is not what he anticipated. No seduction, no tantalizing first kiss as husband and wife. Rosalie drank too much at the wedding and wobbled into the taxi that brought them here. As soon as they checked in, she ran into the bathroom, vomited, and then closed the door behind her.

When she finally emerges, Rosalie is still wearing her wedding dress. She lies beside her husband and wraps her arms around herself.

"Can you take this off?" he whispers.

"Go ahead," she says, turning her back toward him.

Sol begins to unzip her dress but the lace gets caught and he can't untangle it.

"What's taking so long?"

"I didn't realize I would need my reading glasses."

"Never mind." She rolls onto her back and lifts up her gown.

"You're not wearing underwear," he says.

"Of course not." She opens her legs and gently pushes his head down. Sol flinches.

Know what I want, she thinks. *Do what Walter would do.*

Sol rubs his hands around her buttocks for a moment and then surfaces to lie beside her.

"I love you, Rosalie."

"Love you too," she says.

"Can we just start now?"

"I am showing you how we begin," she says.

"I'm sorry. I am new at this."

"Of course you are."

Sol closes his eyes and remembers sitting beside Walter in the Seminary attic. *When she was shot*, Walter had said, *her wetness was still fresh on my hands.* Walter knew how to make love to a woman; he knew so much about everything. Sol thinks of their kiss and shudders.

"No one taught us anything, Rosalie."

A plane careens outside, rattling the windows. Rosalie jolts up and covers herself with the bedspread. *Save me, Walter. Find me, touch me, never let go—* She begins to sob.

"It's late," says Sol. "Let's get some sleep. We have the rest of our lives."

Sol and Rosalie live in a hotel room on the side of a highway in rural Pennsylvania, waiting to find out when they can visit the synagogue under renovation and inspect their new house. Sol spends the days pacing; Rosalie suggests they play rummy to pass the time. Each morning she lies under the covers and watches

Sol wind his tefillin around his arm, wrap himself in his tallit, and daven at the foot of the bed, his body swaying as he sings the words of the Shema. She takes in his body, his face. This is the man I married. This stranger is now my husband. My prayers are on his lips; he is to become my home, my kingdom.

Since their wedding night, they have avoided touching. At first Sol asked and Rosalie refused, feigning nausea or a headache. After a few weeks, Sol stopped trying. Every night, they fall asleep on opposite ends of the bed, quenching any hope of desire. When Sol raises the possibility of making love, Rosalie explains that the time isn't right, that they are both too nervous about his impending pulpit, too worried about the state of the house they are not welcome to visit. "Not right," she says. "I want this to be perfect." Then Rosalie tells Sol she misplaced her diaphragm and she is too young to be a mother.

"There are other means," says Sol.

"You're not allowed to spill your seed into a bag of rubber," says Rosalie. "Your rebbetzin knows the law."

"I thought you didn't care about that," says Sol. "And anyway, the law is fluid."

She kisses him on the cheek. "Soon. I promise."

Days turn into weeks and for a month they live in a hotel room, waiting for a home. They play rummy and drink Scotch in the late afternoons, and every night Rosalie turns away from Sol and wraps her arms around herself.

Why, wonders Sol. There is a reason for everything. Every action derives from an intention; every teshuvah is borne from a she'elah. So much of life is rational, sequenced, then this, then this, and, inevitably, this. Some nights he falls asleep clutching a pillow between his legs for warmth, Rosalie on the far side of the bed. He is ignorant about her body, about how she wants to be touched. He knows so much about the intricacies of the letters that crowd a page of Talmud, but nothing about the strange flower that lies between his wife's legs.

But maybe it's something else, Sol wonders. Maybe Rosalie heard about the time he kissed Walter, and maybe she thinks he is less than a man. After all, Rosalie and Walter spent time together; perhaps Walter felt betrayed by him and told Rosalie about the kiss. *Sol kissed me*, he would have said. *Sol desired me.* And if Walter had said something to her, where would the truth lie? Was the kiss a momentary lapse of judgment, or the opening of a gate?

Dear Paul,

I'm ready to move on. I have slept in every room of this building. I can find my way around a sacred text. I don't know how to build a mikvah or how to kasher a pot, but I learned how to design a meaningful source sheet, which may be the most useful skill of all. My time here has not been a waste.

Please arrange for my studies in Chicago. I am lost in this country, and without a university to shelter me I will never find my way. There is so much I miss but I cannot name what or whom I am longing for the most.

With gratitude,

Walter

Sol and Rosalie are told that the job promised to Sol no longer exists; the synagogue building never passed inspection, and a congregant's father moved to town and agreed to lead services for free at a local rotary club. "But it's good news," Sol says to Rosalie. "We've been offered a shul in Westchester. With a brand new house." They drive to New York, find the sign that says TEMPLE BRIAR WOOD ENTER HERE, and career into a parking lot with a small circus tent in its center. They walk across the lot to their new split-level house. Rosalie steps inside the kitchen and brushes her hands on the granite countertop, while Sol runs upstairs and counts the rooms. Three bedrooms for their children and a master suite for the rabbi and rebbetzin. Even if Rosalie doesn't desire him, he thinks, she will behold the emptiness of these carpeted rooms that wait for their babies and she will take the hint, God willing, and soon.

The holidays are a month away. Sol spends his time writing sermons and organizing the services that will take place in the tent. Rosalie samples paint chips for the empty rooms, but she loses interest in Plymouth Green and Burma Jade, and can't imagine how this big house will ever fill with the voices of children. She enrolls in a driving school and passes her road test. For her first solo drive in the Dodge, she cruises down to Manhattan and parks outside the Seminary. As if she never left, she marches up to the upper geniza and looks for traces of Walter. New file cabinets line the walls and the Torah scroll has been removed. She searches the bookshelf and file drawers for leftover hints—his powdered spices, bottles of whiskey—but finds nothing. She scans the books on the shelf but the *Mei HaShiloach* is gone. No more words of the Ishbitzer, no more sprigs of faded freesia left to fall.

Rosalie saunters downstairs to the lower geniza and passes a custodian who asks if she is lost. She shakes her head and runs to the broom closet, hoping to find something he left behind, but the room smells of disinfectant. Rosalie bursts into tears and lies down on the cold floor, her face close to the wet mops. She inhales the sickening stench of ammonia and tries to pretend she is smelling turmeric or coriander, but her imagination fails her and she covers her mouth to muffle her sobs. When her crying softens into a whimper, she rises, straightens her skirt, and exits the Seminary for good. As she drives home under a darkening sky, she decides to tell Sol that she is ready. She will be patient with him and she will teach him how to be patient with her. She will touch him and she will allow herself to be touched. She will map his body and she will allow him to map hers.

She is ready for her marriage to begin.

The Kol Nidre service marks the annulment of all vows, the annual window of time when all past promises are broken, creating space for new prayers. Every synagogue in the world is saturated with expectation, crowded with men and women who have waited all year to listen to the swell of the Kol Nidre melody—the notes in a minor key that descend a staircase, lower and lower, and then rise up with hope. Every folding chair in the Temple Briar Wood tent is filled, except for Rosalie's because she has a headache and doesn't want to leave the house.

The tent stands fifty yards from their backyard, close enough to hear the prayer from the open porch. As Rosalie stands alone under the darkening sky the spell of the Aramaic wraps around her like a celestial dress. The low notes of Kol Nidre take her down to the cellar of her deepest longing and the high notes pull her into the night air, along with everything she wants to leave behind: every dashed possibility, every regret, every moment of sadness.

The prayer is recited the first time in a whisper, the second time to be heard, and the third time to be as declarative as a trumpet. Who needs a synagogue to receive this? Rosalie has a porch. She can be alone and take stock of her life. This, now. This husband, this house, this tent that will be Sol's lifeblood, these congregants that he will draw out of their homes and welcome to a place of sanctity.

Rosalie makes a pact with herself and decides that she will always stay home on Kol Nidre, close enough to hear the words, yet distant enough to let the prayer resonate in her bones. If every Jew is standing to face a Torah scroll on the first hour of the Yom Kippur fast, Rosalie will face a yard, a tree, a night sky. Closer to Walter. Closer to remembering how she felt when they climbed the stairs from the lower geniza, how her skin was a fibrous membrane that could hold memory and music, and if she listened well enough, the symphony of her own body would teach her everything she would need to know.

PART TWO

The small truth has words that are clear;
the great truth has great silence.

—RABINDRANATH TAGORE

VINEYARD

March 1952

On a rainy Sunday in March, Sol digs a hole in a patch of earth in central Westchester, the very spot that will mark the foundation of their synagogue. Rosalie watches her husband bite his lip as the shovel hits the dirt and splatters mud on his new suit. He pauses for a moment, lifts the shovel above his head and shouts, *"Shehecheyanu! We have a shul!"*

Rosalie's hair is done up in a beehive for the ceremony and she wears a tweed dress and heels. Nathan and Missy Samuels are named the first board members of the *real* Temple Briar Wood—Nathan will be president and Missy will represent the Sisterhood—and the four of them hold hands and dance the hora around the hole, raising their arms in unison.

The die is cast, thinks Rosalie. Our lives will be etched on this patch of land. This man who calls out my name in his sleep is the rabbi whose words will inspire these first families, when they lie down and when they wake up, when they love and when they work, when the women gossip about who is pregnant and whose baby has colic. The words that Sol delivers from the lectern every Shabbat morning will be the words the men recall when they stand behind their folded newspapers on the train platform each weekday morning. The words of his Rosh Hashanah sermons will echo in their brains when they feel an occasional vague thirst at the back of their throats, wondering if the quiet streets of Briar Wood are bold enough to sustain the yearnings that once seemed so vast.

Nathan and Missy and the other first families of Temple Briar Wood call themselves the charter members, the foundation-stoners, or the niners because all together they are nine couples, plus their small children who lay their hands in a corner of wet concrete they name the Children's Square. Some of the foundation-stoners refer to Briar Wood as the shul; some call it the temple, or the building-that-is-no-longer-the-tent. When they dedicate the synagogue, Sol says, "From now on, we will call Temple Briar Wood *The Shul*, as if this is the only shul in the world."

Rosalie asks how they can ever sustain a congregation with only nine families, and Sol says the math is simple. "We need ten men for a minyan, a prayer quorum. At first, three men will show up: an elderly man who recites the Mourner's Kaddish, another man who comes on Shabbat morning out of habit, and his friend who comes out of curiosity, then out of devotion. You start with those. And then you add. Only the men count, of course. You add the widowed father who has moved in with his son. The son will accompany his father to shul even though he does not remember the prayers he learned as a child. Then the son's own son will grow and he will need bar mitzvah lessons.

"Others you will find by pacing the nearby streets when you are desperate for a minyan at nine o'clock on a Saturday morning. You will spot a mezuzah on the doorpost and knock. Here you will find them: the man you rouse from morning sex, the man who repairs his car in the first light of day, the man who flips pancakes for his children. *Rabbi! We were just sitting down to breakfast. Honey—the rabbi needs a tenth man. Tell him to take his strange tribal customs elsewhere. Sshh— he can hear you! Put on your pants. I'll finish the pancakes.*"

"And you, Sol? Is this what you want?"

He kisses Rosalie. Everything he needs is here. The walls of his synagogue will contain multitudes. He will convert his beloved texts into words of meaning for those who enter. What more could he want?

"I hope so," he says.

In Chicago Walter buys a pair of lined boots but they don't warm his feet. A single wool scarf is useless on the coldest winter days so he wraps two of them tightly around his neck and then yanks them off because they constrict his movement. He can't get warm in the winter and he can't cool off in the summer. He yearns to return to the time before he arrived in New York, back to the long afternoons he spent reading under a tree in Shantiniketan. Walter would trade the life he has now for a single hour in the dusty Indian heat, fresh dates sweetening his tongue while he memorizes poems by Rumi and Tagore.

He is a doctoral candidate at the Divinity School and Paul oversees his work. Walter teaches an occasional class. He touches upon what he learned in Shantiniketan but the lecture halls and seminar tables are weak settings for the Brihadaranyaka Upanishad's honey of all beings. His mind hooks on certain lines: *As a man acts, as he behaves, so does he become. Whoso does good, becomes good: whoso does evil, becomes evil. . . . Whatever deeds he does on earth, their rewards he reaps.* Walter weaves himself into the ancient words: *as I act, as I love, as I become. Whoso fucks his chavrusa's fiancée just months before her wedding becomes the man who loves a woman who will never belong to him.*

Most evenings Walter eats dinner alone in a Hyde Park coffee shop. Every morsel of food tastes bland and he sprinkles his own garam masala mix onto the mashed potatoes and chicken pot pie. Had he stayed in India, Walter could have returned to Bombay and married Kavita. He would be a father by now, he thinks. He would be the father of an Indian-German-Jewish child they would have named for Sonia. Sanjiv for a boy, Satya for a girl. *No promises kept, Sonia. Your Walter is a refugee who won't tether himself to any post in this strange country.*

Women alight on Walter's body like butterflies in a garden. He has hesitant, brief affairs: a single night with a teaching assistant, a furtive hour with an English major in a library stack. Trish is a ballet student, Ellen is an anthropologist, and Deidre works at the coffee shop. He sleeps with each of them in turn and repeats this in a weekly cycle. When Walter makes love to Ellen he calls out Trish's name, but when he falls asleep in Deidre's arms he dreams of Rosalie and is surprised when he wakes up next to a

Jamaican waitress who chants his name in a singsong dialect that makes him swoon. He closes his eyes and reaches back to find Rosalie in the path of his dream but she is gone.

Ida Wachs and Lotte Kerem join Rosalie and Sol for Shabbat dinner at their new dining table. The formal chairs have wide seats, plush with green velvet, and Ida's feet don't touch the floor.

"Why such enormous chairs?" she asks Rosalie. "Are you expecting your children to be giants?"

Lotte beams with pride, as if she was born to sit at the throne of her son's new Ethan Allen set. She turns to Rosalie.

"What a dignified table for your family, rebbetzin! So rabbinic."

Sol stands, goblet in hand, ready to recite kiddush.

"Do you want to tell them, sweetheart?" He winks at Rosalie.

What is she supposed to say? That she hates this ornate table and only agreed to buy it as a concession to Sol's taste? That the man in the Ethan Allen store stared at her Capri pants and sneakers, then whispered to Sol that his wife should dress like a real rebbetzin? That when the table was delivered and set up, Sol proposed they make love, right there, in the place where the challah and roasted chicken will sit every Friday night of their lives? That his proposition was—so far—Sol's most brazen suggestion and a good one? Should she tell them that?

"Rosalie?"

"I'm pregnant," she says. "A little bit." She holds up three fingers.

"B'sha'ah tova!" says Lotte. "Not so little!"

"May you have a girl," says Ida. "You are meant to have a girl."

"No limits!" says Lotte. "May God bless you with a healthy baby!"

Lying in bed that night, Rosalie runs her hands over the faint rise of her belly. A girl, she thinks. How lovely. A baby girl to wipe away the past, claim their territory as a new family: Sol, Rosalie, and the baby. An elemental threesome, their own Garden of Eden.

Rosalie miscarries later that week. As she weeps in bed, she thinks of a seed being flushed away, a seed that held her intended first child. She is certain this baby would have been a girl. News in the small synagogue travels fast; Missy Samuels and her new Sisterhood friends Bev and Serena deliver casseroles and pastries to their rebbetzin's door. Each woman hugs Rosalie and says, "Soon, rebbetzin, soon." And Missy whispers in Rosalie's ear, "First we will make a shul and then we will welcome your children."

Sol becomes Temple Briar Wood's tradesman of holiness and Rosalie his helpmate. In time the men come in numbers slightly greater than the required ten and then the women follow the men to shul, wearing doilies or hats on top of their teased beehives, pulling their children along, girls in patent leather shoes, boys in their first dress slacks. On the High Holidays that Sol calls The Big Show he peers down from his red velvet seat on the bima and notes how many chairs are empty and how many full. When he speaks he pounds his fist on the lectern and shakes his forefinger for emphasis, a sermonic gesture he learned from Morris just before they graduated.

Rosalie counts on frizzy-haired Bev to decorate the sukkah with popcorn balls, paper chains, and cardboard Stars of David dangling low enough for the smallest children to touch. Sol relies on Nathan's father to chant the Torah portion and serve as a cantor. In time the layers of involvement become thick and textured until the shul has a board, with Nathan at the helm. When the congregants exit the sanctuary, Sol greets each one and says, "Have a good week, and give my regards to your mother." And then he whispers to Rosalie, "I think I got it wrong. I can't remember if the regards should be for the father instead of the mother and how do I keep track of all these names and lives in my care?"

When delivering his sermons, Sol's voice rises with each sentence; he caresses each word and enunciates the final syllables emphatically. *The details teach us how to live! Our forefathers teach us that the furnishings in the Tabernacle were placed from the inside outward, from the most sacred to the least. This teaches us many important lessons! We should live our lives from the Sabbath outward. What do I mean by this? Think of Sunday as the day closest to the holy Sabbath. How many of you come to morning services on Sunday? You should carry over the Sabbath for at least one day, help us make a minyan and then stay for coffee and cake.*

Rosalie sits in the front row, listening to the people behind her rustle through their prayer books, counting how many pages remain until the service is finished. What would wake them up? Certainly not Sol's empty words or his pounding fist. Rosalie believes the congregants deserve a love story: the Song of Songs rendered as a modern love affair. She would deliver it, of course. She would speak of her love for Walter, but she would tell it slant and disguise all the facts. Rosalie would set the story in prewar Poland and portray Walter, Sol, and herself as Hasidim who craved to hear the voice of God. Sol would sit in the first row and would frown at her, but Walter, if Walter ever set foot in a synagogue, would be proud. Everyone would be wide-awake. Missy Samuels would listen with rapture and she would grab Nathan's hand; Nathan would fantasize that if Rosalie were the rabbi the shul would be teeming with congregants, aroused by her words. How lovers touch—now that would prompt people to wake early on a Saturday morning, dress in their best clothes, and take up their seats in this paneled room.

When Rosalie can't sleep at night, she stands in front of Sol's bookcase and brushes her hand over the spines of the Mishnah, the volumes of Talmud, and Maimonides's *Guide for the Perplexed*. She lets her fingers trace the letters burnished onto the brown leatherette, and then lingers on an English translation of the Song of Songs that Walter sent them as a wedding present. Rosalie caresses the inked inscription on the opening page, follows the line of his handwriting:

> *Rosalie and Sol,*
>> *Blessings on your house.*
>>> *Herzlich,*
>>> *Walter*

This is a dangerous act for her, this simple brushing of her fingers against his handwriting, bringing something dead to life. Walter had written their two names as if it were one name, *Rosalieand Sol*, in his precise painterly script. The W in his name takes up half the page, his winged spirit etched in the book. When Rosalie follows the curve of Walter's hand shaping the cursive W she can feel his hand on her neck, his fingers brushing her jaw, pausing at her bottom lip. She brings the book to her nose and tries to summon the memory of cardamom or turmeric, but the pages hold no scent.

Walter came to the Seminary; they had a few precious months, no time at all. Long enough to open an envelope, read a message, and tuck it back inside.

Paul has found an adjunct position for Walter in Berkeley, teaching South Asian religions with an occasional foray into Jewish studies. He teaches a class in creation myths, and compares the lonely Lord Brahma who split himself into man and woman to the lonely Jewish God who created Adam and Eve. He talks about how the lotus flower that sprouted from Lord Vishnu's navel gave birth to Lord Brahma, the mother of creation, and how this flower image relates to the Jewish concept of the Shekhinah, the feminine aspect of God.

You are on your way, Paul tells him. *The refugee I found in Bombay has become my true protégé.* Together they edit a book on the religious themes in Tagore's poetry and Paul composes Walter's bio for the flap: *Walter Westhaus was a prized student of Tagore in the Shantiniketan ashram*—even though Walter didn't study with

Tagore and spent most of his time in Shantiniketan longing for a home and waiting for Paul to take him to America.

When the synagogue building is complete, Sol commissions a sign to be posted on the lawn: TEMPLE BRIAR WOOD, COME FOR A VISIT & STAY FOR A LIFETIME. Just as Missy Samuels had predicted, Rosalie grows round with a healthy baby, the first to be delivered by Stu Katz, Briar Wood's unofficial obstetrician, the self-declared master of the epidural who promises pain-free deliveries. In her ninth month Rosalie falls asleep with a pillow sandwiched between her legs, her immense body moored to the bed.

When her breath grows shallow in the final weeks of pregnancy, Rosalie makes a decision. She will banish Walter from her thoughts, along with the narrow-waisted dresses that she will never wear again. He was a young woman's fantasy, a dreamscape from another phase of her life. She is no longer too young to be a mother. She is too old to pine for the upper geniza and the lower geniza, for every touch and every word and every rub of powdered spice. She cannot live an impossibility. She prepares the house for Passover, purging it of chametz, those leftover crumbs that must be swept away from every kitchen crevice and every coat pocket. As she tapes shelf paper to the cabinet shelves, she reviews the litany of everything she and Walter did. With the mere thought of every kiss, every game, every word he spoke, Rosalie pulls off the ache of her longing. With every rip of tape, she unpeels Walter's skin from hers. She summons the sound of his voice and then she lets it echo into the distance. She imagines Walter getting smaller and smaller until he is a bit of chametz she sweeps to the back of the cabinet.

As Stu Katz promised, the epidural works like magic; childbirth is not quite painless, but somehow empty of high drama. Rosalie senses the contractions as they surge through her body and she receives them with indifference. Stu announces the birth of their baby boy and hands Rosalie her swaddled infant, along with a pill that prevents her breasts from leaking milk. Eight days later she wears a brand new dress to the baby's bris. Charlie is named for Chaim, Sol's father; the middle name Samuel is for Shmuel, Rosalie's father. The baby clings to Rosalie and is slow to walk, but once he takes his first steps Charlie runs around the shul with abandon and in time leads the other children in jaunts around the building. Charlie teaches them where to hide from their parents and shows them the cot where the custodian sleeps, his toupee loose on the pillow. At night, Rosalie reads him stories of K'tonton who was as big as a thumb and fell into the folds of his father's tallit. She calls Charlie *my happiness, my honeydew, my boychik sunshine.*

Two years later Rosalie gives birth to another son. She has the same epidural nurse, the same Stu Katz, the same sensation of surge, the same pill to dry up her milk, and another new dress for the bris. Sol wants to name this son Pinchas in memory of the Radish who singled out Sol as his protégé before he died. *No Pinky in this family*, says Rosalie, and they name him Philip. As soon as he can walk Philip becomes Charlie's next in command. At shul he sticks out his tongue at the congregants and at home he plasters wet peas into his hair. Philip pulls at the ends of Sol's mustache, and at night he can only fall asleep if Rosalie lies beside him.

Once a week Sol and Rosalie hire a babysitter and go to concerts in Manhattan. Sol reveres Leonard Bernstein, and he listens to recordings of the Mahler symphonies with rapture. He explains to Rosalie how a single large gesture—the sweep of Bernstein's hands at the perfect moment, his own arms raised to offer a blessing at the end of services—can blaze a hole through the sky and change the direction of a life. Nathan Samuels gives his rabbi and rebbetzin orchestra seats to *West Side Story*. After the final standing ovation Rosalie tells Sol she is pregnant again.

"If we are blessed with another boy," says Sol, "let's name him Leonard. Aryeh. A lion. In honor of our great conductor."

"It's bad luck to name for the living," says Rosalie, but Sol says that the superstition only applies to a member of one's immediate family.

In 1961 Stu Katz has grown sideburns, and his office teems with women wearing batik muumuus and iridescent lipsticks. This time the surge that roars beneath the blanketing silence of the epidural fills Rosalie with curiosity and she wonders what she is missing, what is this pain that other women bear in childbirth, while she watches television and waits for Stu to tell her to push. When she holds her third son in her arms Rosalie tells Stu she might like to try breastfeeding—*what do you think?*—and he says, why bother when your other babies grew so strong on formula, and you, rebbetzin—*such a role model!*—should leave that to the hippies.

Sol speaks from the pulpit of how their three boys mark the ideal American Jewish family: one child for each parent and a third child to represent one who was lost in the Holocaust. He rests the baby on his shoulder while delivering his sermons. Rosalie watches Lenny's face staring out from his paternal perch, and she sees herself in him, eyes scoping the room, mouth shaped into a half smile. After she reads to him at night, Rosalie rests her fingers on the curls that drape his forehead, letting them linger as he drifts toward sleep.

Day after day the three boys pull at the hem of Rosalie's skirts. She feels as if her life is tossing her around on its wild sea and she will land on a shore far away from the cove made of turmeric rocks that she once thought of as her true home.

She says to herself, no one ever tells you that the incessant demands of small children will colonize your brain and make you forget the woman you once believed yourself to be.

She says to herself, no one tells you that you will fall in love with the journey, no matter how unexpected it seems.

She says to herself, no one calls to you and says, I *am waiting, darling. I will wait. However long it takes.*

And how would she answer? *My children wait for me too. They need me to trim the edges of their cheese sandwiches, pour them apple juice, cut their nails, and hem their pants before Shabbat so they won't shame their father whose eyes shine with love.*

One year follows another. Charlie's snowsuit is passed down to Philip and the same snowsuit is passed down to Lenny and they call it the Three Brothers' Snowsuit. Each year is held aloft with the poles of holidays that intercept the flow of time. The warp is the calendar; the weave is made of the boys who grow taller and the husband whom Rosalie has learned to desire. Some nights after the boys are asleep Sol goes into his study, puts a Frank Sinatra record on the turntable, and waits for her. Rosalie tiptoes in, stands behind his chair, and kisses the back of his neck. Sol rises, wraps his hands around her waist, and they dance far into the night.

One summer morning Rosalie wakes up to the faint scent of turmeric on her fingers. She sniffs her palms but the source of the smell eludes her. No, she thinks, I haven't forgotten him at all. Walter lives here on my hands; Sol lies beside me in our marriage bed. Milk and meat. Two classifications of food, each distinct. Separate dishes, different utensils. Rosalie uses cornflower-blue dishtowels for dairy, red-checked towels for meat. And then there is the waiting time. Some people count six hours between eating milk and meat, some three, Sol says, according to the custom of their tribe.

Walter is named assistant professor of religion at UC Berkeley. He rents a single-room house in the hills that he calls his studio. A pair of black-framed windows face the Bay; the morning fog obliterates the view but at night the Bay Bridge lights up like a string of pearls. Walter's life radiates from this single large room cornered by a kitchen barely wider than his arms and a bathroom the size of a small closet. In his Introduction to Religion class, some students ask if he is a Jew, if he survived the Holocaust, and Walter says, "Yes and yes, end of conversation. Now turn to your source sheets and look up the Sanskrit definition of *samskara*. For this week's essay, select a family story from Genesis, reflect on the text's unconscious imprints, and then write about the hidden traces—*samskara*—in your own lives."

Walter teaches one class, then five more; at night he sits on the floor of his studio and grades papers. He places an ad in the local weekly for an artist's model and in time he has three young women in rotation, each of whom becomes an eager lover. After he sketches the contours of each one's body, he rubs spices onto her skin as he once did with Rosalie but none of his lovers summon her and no one can take him back to the past. In the parade of women who have passed through his life, Sonia feels to him like a distant relic that has changed shape through erosion, while Rosalie is perched at the edge of every thought.

One afternoon Walter tears a sheet of paper from his sketch-book and writes.

Dear Rosalie, I long for—

Dear Rosalie, I long for the upper geniza where we first kissed—

Dear Rosalie, I hope you are well and that Sol treats you as—

Nothing works. He rips out another page and another, and then writes a few words that spill onto the page like tears. He phones a rabbinical organization and asks for the address of Rabbi and Mrs. Kerem, *old friends of mine*, he says.

On Kol Nidre night the boys gleam in their holiday outfits: navy blue suits for Charlie and Philip, pale blue Fauntleroy for Lenny who stands sandwiched between his brothers. Picture-perfect. Rosalie tousles the hair of her three sons and tells them to pray for her.

"How about just this once?" asks Sol. "Everyone notices the rebbetzin stays home for Kol Nidre. Missy Samuels asked me if you're pregnant again."

"Tell her I'm on the pill. Tell her I keep the little blue box in our medicine cabinet, behind the aspirin. Tell her to ask Stu Katz about my reproductive life. He knows everything, just like a pulpit rabbi should."

"For God's sake, Rosalie. It's Kol Nidre. *This matters.*"

"And it matters to me. Very much. I can hear every word from the porch."

"Once, when we had the tent, yes. Now it's not so easy."

"How would you know what I hear or how I pray? This is enough for me. It's perfect."

"I can't build this shul without you," says Sol.

"And your shul includes this porch. I'm the outer edge of your boundary."

"Clearly."

"Meaning?"

"Meaning nothing," says Sol. "I just wish—"

"Wish what? That I would be a different kind of rebbetzin? More earnest, more devout?" She lays her hands on Sol's shoulders and kisses his cheek. "Look at me. I'm yours. And while you lead your flock in Kol Nidre I will be here. In our sacred little home. Ours."

Alone in the house, Rosalie challenges herself to find a glimpse of holiness, something she can think about before she begins her twenty-five-hour fast. She sits at her husband's desk and sorts through his file of readings. A source sheet with obscure Talmudic references makes her feel sad; a newspaper clipping with popular Jewish jokes makes her feel even worse. If he only quoted a Hasidic master like the Ishbitzer, maybe Sol would be a different rabbi, a different man. Yet she is not disappointed. Her husband has learned to satisfy her and while she misses the daring she enjoyed with Walter, Rosalie has grown to love the way Sol removes his tallit kattan before they have sex, how he is slow and passionate, how he sometimes bursts into tears and thanks her for being his companion on this journey.

Underneath a pile of bills, Rosalie finds Walter's handwriting. Unmistakable. The winged W that takes up the entire page.

June 10, 1966

Dear Sol and Rosalie,

I tracked down your address through a rabbinic organization. I trust you are taking care of each other on the holy path you chose. My address is below. I hope you will stay in touch.

Herzlich,
Walter Westhaus
23 Rose Terrace
Berkeley, California

Over the years Rosalie has imagined Walter in all his homes. First in Chicago, a city Rosalie has never seen. At times she imagined him holding onto a railing during the famous winds, crouching close to the sidewalk to keep himself tethered to the earth. Then Berkeley. When she watched the students protesting the war on the news she tried to picture Walter holding up a placard but her imagination failed her.

She tried to forget him, worked to banish him from every thought. When she shampooed the boys' hair and sang, *Gonna wash that man right out of my hair*, her children laughed but for Rosalie the song was all about Walter. She tried to forget him when she pulled out spice jars and sniffed coriander and cumin, simply to remember the feel of the spices on her skin, and then she would challenge herself to let go of her longing.

But then she would wake up with a start in the middle of the night and realize she had lost him. She had forgotten to think of him when Charlie had the flu and the chimney needed repair, when Philip refused to go to school in second grade, when the car was in the shop and Sol was away at a conference—one ordinary encumbered day after another—but then when Rosalie felt calm again, there he was, waiting, asking for nothing.

And now. His cursive W rests in her hands. She copies his address on a scrap of paper and tucks it into her pocket. As the opening strains of Kol Nidre drift into the house, Rosalie runs to the porch. The first notes of the prayer run down her spine. Another year of life, unbound, new, open to possibility. With Walter's address in her pocket she is connected to all that she loves: the boys and Sol, the shul that has become an extension of their home, and on the other side of the country, Walter, found.

She stands alone on the porch and listens to the chant wafting from the shul, the words encircling her body like a gown. As Kol Nidre is repeated in its third and loudest iteration, Rosalie laughs. What she feels is not happiness, but something pulling at the edge of her skin that wakes her up. Nothing is enough. One life is not enough. The prayer that invites her to open her heart to God is her own call to Walter.

THE LITTLE
ASTONISHMENTS

November 1967

After teaching his Monday night class on Maimonides, Sol shuts
off the synagogue's master switch and lingers in his office. With
his desk lamp as the only source of light in the building, he
feels as if he is illuminating a path in a dark wood. The rabbinate was supposed to be like this, at least most of the time. Years
back the Radish had counseled Sol to expect some challenges
but assured him that he would grow to love his work. *Torah sells
itself*, his teacher had said. *As long as you express its meaning, your
suburban Jews will lap up its words like the sweetest milk.* But that
hasn't happened. No one praises his sermons; no one asks him
for advice. After he conducts a funeral, Sol gently touches the
mourners' shoulders, hands out business cards, and says, *Call
me anytime*, but no one does. He blames this on Briar Wood.
The Jews who moved here came for the top-rated schools, rea-
sonable taxes, forty-seven-minute commute to Grand Central,

and the gleaming Cosmos Diner with plastic menus as tall as Talmud volumes.

No one comes to a town like Briar Wood for the rabbi.

At first Sol thought he was reaching the students in his weekly Ask the Rabbi Anything class with four pre–bar mitzvah boys. The group was free-spirited; Mike, James, Mitch, and Ron loved to debate the Thirteen Principles of Faith and whether or not cheese rennet was kosher. Sol taught them the she'elah-teshuvah game, and was impressed with the boys' associative leaps. But after a handful of classes, the foursome stopped showing up. When Sol stumbled upon them getting high behind the parking lot, they averted their gaze.

"Why?" shouted Sol.

James looked up. "Our parents bribed us to come to your class. And it worked, rabbi. We raised enough money to buy a stash."

"That's educational," said Sol.

"You were building community," said James. "That's what you get paid for, right?"

When he called the boys' homes to report them, Mitch's mother said, "I'm sure you'd prefer they hang out behind the shul than near the train tracks. And if you care to listen to my real troubles, I can tell you about the restraining order I placed on Mitch's father, but because he always shows up for morning services, you wouldn't believe me. If you see us in shul on Shabbat— all dressed up and mouthing the prayers—you assume our lives are picture-perfect. If you want to know what's going on with us—any of us—just show up at the church AA meeting. Or come to the Cosmos Diner one night. You can overhear the lurid accounts of our lives, and when you find the details unbearable, turn on the jukebox to block out our voices. We are spilling our guts all over this town, rabbi. And you're missing all the interesting parts."

Sol never phoned a congregant again. He had no right to intrude on their private miseries and even if he did, what would he offer? A she'elah and teshuvah? A ruling about cheese rennet? A psalm? A slice of cake?

Pastoral disappointment tells one kind of story, but communal hope dictates another. After the Six-Day War the synagogue swells with members. Hebrew classes become popular, and congregants crowd into the social hall to perfect their Yemenite, Cherkessia, and Debka steps at Israeli folk dance parties. Sol remembers the oversized map of Jerusalem that was tacked on the wall of his boyhood Hebrew school classroom. He would imagine his body lying across the hand-drawn diagram of the Old City, his head resting on the Damascus Gate and his feet on the Zion Gate. Now he visualizes his hands touching the stones and monuments, the heels of Rosalie's shoes clacking like castanets as she approaches the Western Wall.

The synagogue grants Sol a one-month sabbatical to Jerusalem. Rosalie packs up the boys' belongings in a single shared suitcase and packs two bags for herself: one for her clothing, and one for her hats and shoes. Charlie, Philip, and Lenny are quickly absorbed into the hive of children who play in the streets of the German Colony; they are invited to other boys' homes for lunch and dinner, leaving Sol and Rosalie alone in their subletted flat. Every evening they sit together on the balcony, gaze out beyond the minarets and honey-colored rooftops, and hold hands in silence. Come morning, Sol strolls over to the yeshiva where he fills himself with new interpretations, new ways of looking at the Bible. *The light is different here,* he says to Rosalie. *The Bible comes to life with new music.*

Rosalie finds her way to the women's side of the Western Wall, wraps her head in a scarf, pulls up a folding chair, and leans her forehead on the cool stones. She has not written to Walter, but she carries his address folded inside her wallet, and often touches the scrap of paper like a talisman. *Write to him, already,* she thinks. *Just four words: I wish you well.* The sound of her sobs bounces off the stones. *I can't and I won't but I need to and enough with the craziness, rebbetzin, you have three beautiful sons and no business—* She imagines her longings seeping into the Wall, where they will be absorbed and carried elsewhere, freeing her from this impossible desire.

She returns the next day, hoping that another session of resting her head on the stones will offer some form of transcendent relief, but she only feels sodden and achy from sitting on a folding chair. She watches young women sway in prayer, and wonders how they are so good at piety, while she is such a bullshit artist with her headscarf, her scrap of paper, her confusion.

You don't have to believe, her father once said to her, *but you should live with some measure of faith.* Rosalie hands an elderly woman some shekels in exchange for a small book of psalms. She runs back to the Wall, rips out the last page, and around the margins of the 150th psalm she writes WALTER & ROSALIE. She folds the page into a tiny square, stands precariously on a chair, and pushes it through a crevice, higher than anyone could possibly reach.

"You'll hurt yourself standing like that," says a nearby woman with a British accent. "Those chairs are flimsy."

"Done," snaps Rosalie. "All tucked in."

A leggy woman with cropped hair and cat-eye glasses offers Rosalie her hand, helps her down. "No one reads these notes, pussycat. They fall to the ground, eventually. Picked up by beggars or swept into a sewer. Believe me, your words won't find their way into a geniza and God isn't reading them either. Are you religious?"

"I'm not religious but I'm not *not* religious," says Rosalie. "I'm a rebbetzin."

"Oh dear. An intrinsic contradiction. Proximity to the rabbi does not make anyone religious; it often inspires the desire to rebel."

"You've found me out."

"I share your fate, sweet pea! Madeline Rosenblum. Reform rebbetzin, visiting from London. The usual trappings of a rabbi's wife, plus I'm a hobby publisher. My little enterprise is as ambitious as knitting sweaters, but it makes the congregants proud. As you can see, I've got a big religion problem. You?"

"Not enough of one. My whole life is a riddle."

Madeline and Rosalie saunter arm and arm through the Old City, their strides perfectly in sync. Madeline confesses her struggles with infertility despite her excellent sex life, her flirtations with women, and the irony of spending her life as the rebbetzin of a London synagogue, when she would rather be working in a bank, where the terms of the transactions are obvious and clean.

"I like talking to you," says Madeline. "I hope we stay in touch."

Rosalie smiles. The women of Briar Wood flatter her and offer generous morsels of gossip, but they will always be congregants, not friends. Rosalie tugs on Madeline's arm and blurts, "His name is Walter and I have his address. I can't contact him and I can't not contact him and I can't—"

"Oh dear," says Madeline. "It sounds like you have a situation."

"You could call it that."

"You're on the pill, I hope."

"Now I am, yes. Thank God for the little blue box. Three boys are enough for the rabbi and his wife, don't you think?"

"I only wish I had such an overload," says Madeline.

"I'm sorry," says Rosalie.

"Every life has its parameters."

"I'm not good at understanding that."

"That's obvious," says Madeline. "This must be terrible for you. Fenced in by impossible love."

"Not very freeing, is it?"

Madeline leads Rosalie by the waist. "Let's give you some relief, pussycat. This is Jerusalem! You can either be burdened by ancient history or become transformed by something visionary. So tell me, rebbetzin, what do you wish to hold in your cup?"

"I'm sure you know the answer already."

"Have you been introduced to Madame Sylvie?"

"Who?"

"The French kabbalist in Old Katamon. Her courtyard is just down the street from where I'm staying. Everyone goes to see her—the new Jerusalem ritual, as popular these days as slipping a note into the Western Wall."

"I don't need a fortune teller."

"You just need to tuck notes between deaf stones."

Rosalie smiles. "At least I met you."

Madeline takes Rosalie's arm and leads her through a maze of streets. They approach a blue door framed with bougainvillea and enter a crowded courtyard ringed with chairs. Madeline kisses a white-haired woman on both cheeks, and whispers to Rosalie, "All these people have come to receive one of Madame's astonishments—a powerful visualization or a dollop of bullshit, depending on your attitude."

"Who are they?"

"American rabbis, mostly. Sprinkle in a few housewives, backpackers, academics, an occasional shrink."

Madame Sylvie announces that she will open the dam that has been closed within each of their bodies. No one volunteers to receive the first astonishment. Madame Sylvie looks around the circle and rests her eyes on Madeline. "Close your eyes, *ma chère*. A small bird rests in your hand. Pick it up and hold it close to your heart. Allow the bird to sniff and nibble at your skin, then nuzzle instead. Watch this procedure with bemusement; do not be afraid. Now allow the bird to separate your heart from its connective tissue. This is painless and quick. The bird carries your old heart in its beak and flies off. Your chest is now open. A new heart rests within, waiting to receive goodness and mercy. You are free. Now open your eyes."

Madame Sylvie parcels out little astonishments like a short-order cook. Imaginary birds fly off with hearts made of stone. A camel walks off into the desert sands carrying a mute throat in its load, leaving a blocked opera singer free to sing. Doors open and close and open again, garden gates fall off their hinges, tumors melt, the lame can walk. Two men in the circle burst into tears. One woman storms off, furious at what she calls shameful manipulation.

Madame Sylvie scans the circle of faces. "Our session is over," she says.

Rosalie raises her hand. "You forgot about me."

"Not yet, *ma chère*. For you I need more time. Please come back later in the week. What you need will be clearer to me then."

The next afternoon Sol's class ends early and he strolls the streets of Old Katamon, looking for a place to buy a volume of commentary. Studying with other rabbis in Jerusalem reminds him of what he's missed since he left the Seminary; once again he yearns to crawl between the Hebrew letters and immerse himself in the conversations that stretched over centuries, a she'elah in one era, answered by a teshuvah in another. With the right chavrusa, the words will close the gates of this world and reveal an infinite vineyard. *It is a torment to love religion as much as you do,* Walter once said to him. *The distance between your life and the one you crave will only make you suffer.*

Sol steps past an open blue door and hears the sounds of laughter. He lingers at the entrance to a courtyard rimmed with chairs, then takes a seat. Madame Sylvie smiles and instructs him to close his eyes.

"You are standing close to a mighty sea that rages with words. You want to jump in and swim, grasp the letters as if they are fish that will carry you out and return you safely. But the words are illusions that vanish in the water and dart away. The words you love are carried out to the sea. Now open your eyes."

When Sol looks up, Walter stands before him, beaming. In a button-down shirt, linen pants, and sunglasses, Sol barely recognizes him.

"My God! Is that really you? You look so different!" Sol reaches for Walter's hands.

"I never thought I'd see you in a place like this," says Walter. "You've morphed into a higher version of yourself."

"I am the same man you knew at the Seminary, only now I am a pitiful suburban rabbi."

"You could have written."

"It felt impossible—"

"Do you really think you're so pitiful?"

"Only half the time," says Sol. "The rest of the time I think I'm close to God. Both views seem like a dance of mirrors and I end up totally confused."

Walter laughs. "That sounds about right. Gurus, rabbis, imams, priests. The same messy brew of imposed grace."

"Imposed, yes. I'm not sure about the grace."

"You're not alone, Sol. I do research on this. A person who gets paid to make meaning for others wonders if he lives in a house of cards. It starts off quite innocently. First he is flattered when people ask him burning questions about God. Then he falls in love with the sound of his own answers, the phrases that float in his mouth like elegant water lilies. He gets hooked on the adulation of his flock, yet begins to wonder why he answered their questions with such certainty. After all, he eats cereal from a chipped bowl just like they do; he ponders ultimate truth just like they do. Who gave him the right to be so confident? An education? A teacher? A brilliant insight? But then it's too late. The flock won't let him be less than a clergyman, and he has no choice but to reach for more beautiful phrases, more meaning, more words to frame the essential mystery. He becomes stuck between the seduction of his words and the futility of his work."

Sol nods.

"He can deal with this conflict by finding a way to live with doubt, or he can deny everything and cloak himself with arrogance. This is the subject of my new book."

"I look forward to reading it." He places his hand on Walter's shoulder and leads him out to the street.

"Do you have time to walk with me?"

Walter glances at his watch. "I have a few minutes."

"I never imagined you would wear a watch."

"Life moves on, rabbi."

"I've missed you terribly," says Sol.

"Me too," says Walter. "How is Rosalie?"

"We have three boys now."

"Congratulations."

"And a synagogue, the centerpiece of our lives."

"Your wife. Is she happy?"

"Our lives are very full. And we have fallen in love with the symphony. Your chavrusa is smitten with Mahler. Have you heard Bernstein's recordings?"

"You haven't answered my question, Sol."

"What question?"

"Is Rosalie happy?"

"I believe she is. We have created something worthwhile."

"You have a family," says Walter.

"And a shul!"

"So you got what you wanted."

"I miss what we had," says Sol. "Our learning together."

"I am no longer the study partner you once took me for."

Sol squints at Walter. This man is the only person in the world who remembers what he is capable of. His flights of mind. His way of navigating a text, mining the ancient words for the brightest jewels, the most elegant nuances of meaning. Walter knows the part of Sol that lives inside the words. The part of him that leaps through the text with the elegance of a ballet dancer. The part of him that once believed he could teach people, that he could prosper in the holiness trade.

"Neither am I," says Sol. "Two men who fell from grace."

"I never had your grace. I was the strange refugee who blew in by way of India."

So strange and so beautiful, thinks Sol. He tries to remember the first time he saw Walter in the Seminary, how his hair was filthy and how he quoted some Indian poet whose name he can't recall.

"You've come quite far, it seems," says Sol.

"Most of the time I just figure it out as I go, like learning a new language."

"Do you have time to get a drink?"

"I wish," says Walter, "but I have to return to my conference. I'm only here for another two days."

He perches his sunglasses atop his head and for a moment Sol stares into Walter's eyes. Is this all he has? Five minutes in Madame Sylvie's courtyard and a brief stroll? A few minutes that will fade away like a dream?

"How about dinner?" asks Sol.

"The three of us?"

"Why not? I'm sure Rosalie would love to see you."

"I don't think that's a good idea," says Walter. "I'm rather busy." He strides off and Sol rushes to keep up.

"We can at least try!" calls Sol. "Where are you staying?"

Walter stops walking, hesitates, then turns to face Sol.

"The American Colony Hotel. I leave in two days."

The Jerusalem streets remind Walter of Bombay, though with fewer beggars and less crowds. Dry powdery dust sticks to his shoes and the pungent smell of *za'atar* itches his nostrils just like the Indian spices once did. He has become a man who delivers academic papers at conferences on religious thought, an American who wears short-sleeved shirts, linen pants, sunglasses, and a wristwatch. No one would suspect he is still lost, looking for the one place he can call home, longing for the only woman he desires. Why hadn't Rosalie written? Surely Sol shared the note with her. Walter feels dizzy. He looks around, half expecting to hear Paul calling his name, but when he turns he sees Sol, standing under an archway and crying into the crook of his arm. Walter stops and considers approaching his old friend, but he knows why Sol cries and he has no words or gestures to offer.

Back at the apartment that evening, Sol arranges a plate of sliced mangoes, olives, feta, and warm pita. He scowls at the haphazard jumble he created. If Rosalie were arranging this, he thinks, the mango would be evenly sliced and the warm pita would be placed in a separate basket. Where are the baskets in this apartment anyway? Sol opens and shuts the kitchen cabinets and then plops the pita on top of the food.

I'm not made for this, he thinks. Not for arranging plates, not for stumbling upon a former chavrusa who babbles on about the sad lives of clergymen, not for receiving astonishments from a strange French woman who surrounds herself with lost souls in a Jerusalem courtyard. Dinner with Walter and Rosalie would be so sweet; sharing a meal with the two of them would make him feel like an ilui again. Walter would ask him if he remembered their daring flights through the text and Rosalie would behold him with pride. Sol would feel less like a scam artist in the impossible holiness trade and more like an actual rabbi. Rosalie would never agree to it, of course. They were here for such a short time; the boys were occupied with new friends and were rarely at the apartment. His wife was free here. She could spend her time buying embroidered tablecloths and ornate silver candlesticks. She could explore the Old City and place a note at the Western Wall. It wouldn't have to be an actual prayer; a few jottings would do. The names of the boys. A prayer for peace. A she'elah that begs an answer, a line from a psalm, an acrostic on her name. He would suggest this to her; he was her rabbi, after all.

He brings the food out to the balcony and sits beside her.

"What's with the sudden gesture of hospitality? Are you suffering from Jerusalem syndrome?"

"No hallucinations yet. How about you?"

"So far, no," says Rosalie. "And I love your little spread. I'm famished."

"I went for a walk today."

"Of course you did, Sol. I strolled all over this city too. Ancient stones and Arabs and Hebrew slang and dusty confusion. All holy and perplexing and beautiful."

"He's here, Rosalie."

"Who?"

"Walter! He's here for a conference. I ran into him."

"When?"

"I stepped through a garden gate and found myself in a class taught by a crazy French kabbalist. She's all the rage."

"You were at Madame Sylvie's?"

"That's where I found him."

Rosalie smirks. "Did Madame astonish you with a river, or did she gift you with a bird?"

"Rivers, birds, camels, maybe a snake or two. I can't remember the details. You would like her."

"I've already been."

"Of course," says Sol. "You would have found her on your own."

Rosalie picks up a slice of mango and takes a bite.

"He's staying at the American Colony for two more days."

"Who?"

"I just told you! Walter! I thought the three of us could have dinner together before he leaves."

Rosalie brushes her skirt and stares at her hands.

"The three of us."

"Yes! When I saw him, everything came back to me. The Radish's class, the cloth shoes, the way he and I learned together."

"You lost interest in him, Sol. Don't you remember?"

"That was a mistake. He was so much smarter than the others."

Yes, he was a genius, thinks Rosalie. A seductive genius.

Rosalie gazes into her husband's eyes, not comprehending why this invitation comes from him. For Sol, seeing Walter would be a reunion of their student days, before they became parents, rabbi and rebbetzin, the holy chef and his devoted line cook. Walter is a few miles away, under the same dusky Jerusalem sky. And what kind of astonishment had Madame Sylvie dispensed to her husband? Did she astonish him with the image of the three of them gathering in a circle like deer in a forest, or sitting in the lobby of the American Colony Hotel and toasting their good fortunes to be meeting again? Did she open their hearts to receive a banquet set for three that Rosalie could not possibly survive?

"I'm sure it all came back to you," she says. "You were quite the ilui."

"I was so confident back then. Did I ever tell you that the Radish called me *a swimmer in the waters of faith*?"

"Yes," says Rosalie. "That suited you."

Sol smiles.

"How did he seem?" asks Rosalie.

"Who?"

"Walter! How did he look?"

"The same and different. He's gained some weight, cut his hair. Kind of resembles George Balanchine instead of a skinny Indian hippie. He's a beautiful man."

My beautiful man, thinks Rosalie. Mine. She gazes at the rooftops and balconies radiating out over Jerusalem. How can she find her way to the airport? Is there a car service that can take her back to Lod? Rosalie wouldn't have to go home to New York; she could hide out in the region, take a side trip to Cyprus or Turkey. Surely Madeline would be up for an adventure. Anything but being alone in this strange city, its unrelenting calls for prayer, the strands of Arabic and Hebrew that weave their ancient music into her brain and spin her around until she can't find her way. The alleys fall off at odd corners and the bougainvillea that grows on garden walls blocks the house numbers. In some parts of town Rosalie is accosted by beggars; in others elderly women smile at her and smooth her hair. She averts her gaze in the neighborhoods where bearded men patrol the streets with their hands clutched behind their backs as their eyes measure the length of her sleeves.

He is staying at the American Colony Hotel. Sol is merely the messenger and now Walter waits for her response. The world is wide open, thinks Rosalie, and I am a frozen woman sitting on a Jerusalem balcony in the setting sun, thinking of nothing but how my fingers have aged, how my waist has spread, how the memory of his touch lulled me to sleep at night all these years.

"So how about dinner?" asks Sol.

"I don't know. I made a new friend and was hoping she and I could visit some museums tomorrow. There won't be time for dinner."

The next morning Rosalie puts on a flowing skirt she bought from an Old City vendor and sets out for Walter's hotel. She carries a map but can't find her way around the streets of East Jerusalem. When she asks an Arab woman for directions, Rosalie doesn't understand the answer and when the woman responds in pidgin Hebrew, she is even more confused. Rosalie walks in circles until she recognizes the street where Madame Sylvie lives and where Madeline is staying and she knocks on Madeline's door.

"Walter is at the American Colony Hotel and I can't—"

"Give me a few minutes to change into a skirt and I'll make sure you find your way to him. Will you introduce me or will you slink off to his room like a thirsty paramour?"

"I can't do this."

Rosalie searches Madeline's eyes, waits for an answer.

"Do you want me to tell you to forget him? I can't do that for you."

Rosalie breathes deeply. She has Madeline now, the friend who will open the gate and allow her to step inside.

The lobby swirls with Arabs and sultans, a cacophony of languages and costumes. Rosalie hesitates at the entrance, tugs at Madeline's arm like a child.

"Let's go. I changed my mind."

"No, pussycat. Walter has to be here. Point him out."

Rosalie looks around. "The table off to the side. He is with a woman, see? He has someone now. A girlfriend. This is all wrong—"

"You didn't tell me that he looked like George Balanchine. He's lovely."

Rosalie pivots. "You can have him, Madeline. I'm turning back. He's all yours."

"I didn't bring you here," says Madeline. "You brought *me*. And I'm too curious to leave. And look—"

Walter glides toward them. Rosalie notices his cloth shoes, just like the ones that were caked with snow when they first met. He knew I would show up here, she thinks. He drew a circle and waited for me to step into its center.

"This is a mistake," says Rosalie. "I have to get back. The children—"

"You have time for me." Walter brushes his eyes with the back of his hand and smiles at Madeline.

"My new friend. Madeline made sure I didn't turn back," says Rosalie.

"Thank you for bringing her," he says.

Walter leads them to his table and pulls out chairs. "Everyone shows up in Jerusalem! This is Clara, a fellow passenger from the *Conte Rosso*."

A pale woman wearing a turban turns to Rosalie. "Your boyfriend was speechless on the ship. We called him the mute man," she says.

"He's not my—"

"Of course not," says Clara. "Another chameleon that survived the ship of chameleons! We were a horrid bunch, drinking and fucking each other into oblivion! And no one could understand why a certain silent man disembarked before we reached Shanghai. Did you know Helmut Newton was on our ship? I won't go into the salacious details. We were so young and so hungry."

"I followed a man off the boat," says Walter. "A man wearing a hat. Bombay."

"Whomever you followed off the ship led you to the promised land, Walter. America has been good to you," says Clara.

"I found my words," says Walter.

"We all did, eventually."

Walter wraps his arm around Rosalie. "This woman freed me."

"Your girlfriend is lovely," says Clara.

Madeline and Clara exchange glances and excuse themselves from the table. Rosalie glances down at her hands, her rings. The boys will be home soon. Sol will return from the market with another parcel of snacks to set out on the balcony. Her life is complete just as it is.

"I have to go," says Rosalie.

"You didn't find your way here to meet my old shipmate."

She follows Walter up a staircase and down a long hallway to his room. Rosalie sits on the side of his bed and Walter kneels at her feet and removes her sandals.

"The blisters from your wedding shoes have healed."

"Time will do that."

They make love silently, and then again with more languor and surprise, and then again, with all the daring of the lower geniza.

"You have become a mute man again," says Rosalie. "Just like on the ship."

Walter pauses. "I told you we would not be apart."

Rosalie begins to cry. "I wish I could despise you."

"It would be much simpler that way."

"Everything we did then seeped into my skin, a permanent stain."

"I can smell your life on your body. Your real life."

"Oh, that," says Rosalie.

"No. Not in the way of spices. Something else. I could smell it on your skin, the stretch marks on your belly, the way your breasts carry knowledge of the babies you nursed. You will always carry that smell—it marks you with found pleasure."

He doesn't know me at all, thinks Rosalie, picturing the rubber nipples floating in a pot of boiling water, night after night,

Charlie, Philip, Lenny, three little babies, thousands of floating nipples.

"Translation is so imperfect," she says. "My children—"

"You never have to tell me anything," says Walter. "No explanations."

They find each other again and stay in Walter's room until the sun begins to set over the city.

Walter tells Rosalie about his studio in the Berkeley hills, framed with bougainvillea, shrouded in fog. He invites her to visit, insists she find a way, use Madeline as an excuse—anything. Rosalie listens to the words flow from his mouth, his accent now softer, more American. But she can't tell Walter the details of her life. The children cannot be funneled into this hotel room; the synagogue is a distant dream. After all these years, she thinks. Walter is a child with his books, his models, his one-room studio. She is a mother. The past is a closed book on a shelf. An abandoned geniza.

"Sol told me he met you at Madame Sylvie's," says Rosalie.

"Yes," says Walter. "Your husband has become an adventurer of the spirit."

"I went with Madeline. When it was my turn, Madame Sylvie was speechless."

Walter laughs. "We'll go together and she will find a perfect astonishment for you. Madame Sylvie won't disappoint a friend of mine."

When they wander into her courtyard that evening, Madame Sylvie tells Walter that he cannot see her so often. "You keep coming back for more," she says. "This is not a candy shop."

"What you gave me wasn't enough," says Walter. "I want another."

"You're an exception," she says. "Now close your eyes and picture a path that winds through a forest, tangled with vines. A girl walks ahead of you. She begins to run and you cannot keep up. Watch her become smaller before your eyes, until she is no bigger than your thumb, then the tip of your finger, then a pinprick. She becomes a point of light. Open your mouth. A little pucker is all you need. Now let out a breath. This girl you left behind in this imagined forest has blown away."

Walter rests his palm over his eyes, holds Rosalie's hand with the other. He gathers his breath and whispers, "She is not you."

Madame Sylvie fixes her gaze on Rosalie. She tightens her lips and smiles.

"Ahh," she says. "I'm glad you returned. *Maintenant, c'est possible.*"

Rosalie closes her eyes softly enough to feel the light touching her eyelids.

"You see a braid, as long as a rope that pulls a ship into a harbor. Some strands of the braid are bright with colored ribbons and fresh flowers. Other strands are made from thorns and live wires—all tangled together. A woman walks in front of you and this braid runs down her back. You follow her, eyeing her braid, stepping with care. Keep going. Now open your eyes."

Rosalie stands and shouts, "Is that all you can give me? A braid? Where is my door, my astonishment, my open gate?"

"I cannot free you, ma chère," says Sylvie. "I dispense visualizations, small suggestive shocks that help you wake up, see something in a new way. I am not a fortune teller and I am not a psychoanalyst. You could recite psalms at the Western Wall or you could visit me. Some do both; keep the door flying open on both sides. Whatever you wish."

Rosalie grabs Walter by the hand and pulls him outside. Madame Sylvie turns to the next visitor who is asked to close her eyes and visualize a great river, light on one side and dark on the other.

FAITH IS THE BIRD

Rosalie lies awake and imagines Walter's room in the American Colony Hotel. She conjures the sultans and sheiks who have since slept in the bed that marked their reunion, how the traces of their bodies were washed away with the traffic of other lovers. She listens to Sol snore beside her and thinks about the woven braid that Madame Sylvie described to her. Some nights the braid is made of ribbon, wool, and wires; on other nights fish swim between the strands of hair and she has to shoo them out of her ears. A nasty conundrum, a riddle with no solution. Good sex in Jerusalem in exchange for a useless vision from the renowned kabbalist. Perhaps it was a ploy: had she not arrived at Madame Sylvie's with Walter she would have received an astonishment that would mean something to her now. But she waltzed into the courtyard holding hands with the very emblem of her betrayal and there was no fooling Madame Sylvie. Best now to obliterate the memory of that single episode, instead of wondering when they will meet again, and how does he see her when his eyes are closed and he explores her body like a blind man who can read with his hands?

The flow of holidays marks the seasons and Rosalie is carried along with the calendar's demands. Depending on the month, she shapes floured dough into a kreplach, a hamentashen, or a Passover noodle made from potato starch. The house pulses with the antics of her three boys who shred bedsheets to make flags of surrender for their raucous games. On Shabbat afternoons they wrestle each other in the yard until one of them—usually Philip—gets pummeled into the grass. At night Lenny calls to her and asks for another story, always another story. Rosalie sets her tales in Madame Sylvie's courtyard. In some, children climb the garden wall like cats and morph themselves into cheetahs that run wild around Jerusalem and uncover artifacts. In others, a boy and girl lie together under a flowering tree and press their ears to the ground, listening to the voices of the ancient past bubble up into their ears. Lenny falls asleep before Rosalie finishes and she sits on the edge of his bed and basks in the silence. Month follows month: stuffed knapsacks and leather mitts pile up in the foyer, dirty clothes are washed and clean clothes folded, meat marinates for weeknight dinners and chicken is roasted for Shabbat, and when it arrives, Rosalie and Sol lay their hands on their sons' heads, blessing them with long lives.

After Sol and the children are asleep, Rosalie sits on a stool at the kitchen counter and dials Walter's number. The time difference gives them hours to themselves. She speaks softly into the handset and winds the black phone cord around her arm as if it is a strap of tefillin. Her ordinary kitchen at night seems like an immense ocean and Rosalie is a ship afloat on its surface, drifting from one shore to another.

One night she tells Walter that she wishes he would get married.

"Make it possible for me to turn away from you," she says.

He laughs. "You don't mean that."

"I do and I don't. You deserve so much more—"

"Don't question what we have, Rosalie. We are creating something bigger than we are."

"Of course you'd think that," she says. "Talking about karma is your livelihood. You can justify anything."

"And you have religion, Rosalie. The karma game is all I have, and it is enough for me."

Rosalie never asks Walter about the woman in Madame Sylvie's astonishment. She doesn't pry into his past, and can sum up his known biography in two sentences: *He followed a man off the ship and that man was Paul Richardson. He went to Bombay and Shantiniketan and then to New York, where they found each other.* He is her personal Torah, written for her alone, a small necessary story that rings in her bones. The two of them can only live in the present tense. They are a word, a hyphen. Turmeric rubbed on a hip. Something faint and then lasting and then vapor. From the pulpit Sol speaks about the flow of Jewish history. *The stories course through our bloodstream,* he says. *Jacob's headrest made of rock is the foundation of our homeland; Joseph's dreams are linked to our eternal longing for image and interpretation.* Rosalie wonders if her love for Walter is an echo of an ancient story she hasn't yet learned.

A new housing development and good public schools have brought more Jews to Briar Wood, and new members to the shul. Sol offers Ask the Rabbi Anything to a fresh crop of pre–bar mitzvah students, and they also find their way to the wooded area behind the parking lot to get high. The only two girls in the Hebrew school skip class and teach each other how to French kiss in the girls' bathroom. The elderly Hebrew school teacher sits in the stairwell and weeps, not because the students mock her, but because the money she earns doesn't cover the cost of the trains and taxis that bring her to the suburbs twice a week. The shul is everyone's laboratory, the testing ground for what life holds on the outside.

On a winter Shabbat morning, Rosalie stands in the back of the sanctuary and watches the congregants shift in their folding chairs as they listen to the words of Sol's sermon. He explains how Jewish survival relies on core beliefs that stand the test of time but history judges a peoples' survival with fickle eyes. She has no idea what her husband is talking about, and neither do his congregants.

Sol is failing them, she thinks. New congregants, same old rabbi. His sermons are impersonal, his words obscure. How could anyone be moved? Why would anyone care? Yet still they arrive in this paneled room. Rosalie watches Bev who stands behind her father's wheelchair, smoothes the tallit over his sloping shoulders, and turns the pages of his prayer book. She watches Serena whose eyes dart nervously around the room. She finds Marv, who Rosalie knows is having an affair with his son's fifth-grade teacher, and Nadine who carries on with a local politician. She looks at Delia, who has breast cancer, and Missy Samuels, who swears by Weight Watchers and nibbles on carrot sticks during kiddush. Rosalie loses herself in watching them. She searches for the fragile broken center in each congregant, tries to name the one thing that makes anyone want to show up in this synagogue when the world offers so many other choices, so many better places to go.

Rosalie measures the distance between the yearnings of these people and her husband's words. She views this as a geometry problem. What is the length of the line between Nadine's love for the politician and Sol's words about the double meaning of the name Yisrael? The distance between high-strung Serena and Sol's sermon about the minor fast days? Between the hunched shoulders of Bev's father and Sol's hands that thump on the lectern like a heartbeat? Where does anyone's desire meet the pastoral response? She sees the sanctuary as a room full of gaping hearts that cannot be healed or touched by Sol's words. And yet, still they come, week after week: Bev and Serena and Nadine and Marv and Delia and Missy Samuels with her bag of carrot sticks. Missy winks at Nathan who stands in the back of the sanctuary. He fingers the fringes of his tallit and ponders his own geometry problem: the popularity of the rabbi and the duration of his contract.

On Sol's day off, Nathan asks Sol and Rosalie to meet him at the duck pond at the center of town. Rosalie carries a bag of leftover challah and tosses chunks into the water.

"Let me get to the point," says Nathan. "We—the board and I—want you to take a leave of absence."

"I don't need a vacation."

"Just a little break. Go back to Jerusalem and study for awhile. Every rabbi needs to hone his skills, fill in his gaps."

"I'm in my prime," says Sol. "So many new members. I just ordered new prayer books—"

"Real estate," says Nathan. "Housing prices. Public schools. The Cosmos Diner."

Rosalie stops walking and tosses the entire bag of challah into the pond. She glances at Sol and wishes he wasn't brushing tears from his eyes in front of Nathan Samuels.

"I'm good. You got one of the best."

"I know, Rabbi Kerem."

"So give me a chance."

Nathan turns to Rosalie. "Maybe you can help him out. Lend some inspiration."

"I'm the rabbi," says Sol. "You hired *me*."

"Yes, we did. We believed in you then, and Missy and I believe in you now. Just find better words; be less remote. Make us care."

"How long do I have?"

"Get back in the game and there's no limit."

As they drive home from the duck pond, Sol asks Rosalie what Nathan meant by *be less remote*. "Am I supposed to change into golf clothes and preach at the Cosmos? I thought they hired me to teach Torah, unravel meaning, make their lives better in some way. Now I utter a phrase and then cringe inside, wanting to take back what I said, but I can't hear myself clearly and my ideas gush in all the wrong directions."

"At least you're sincere."

"I stand up there on the bima, all alone, as if I'm supposed to be a symbol of something. But of what? My beloved texts are meaningless to them and they don't have the skills to understand the patterns behind the words."

"Then summarize. Reduce. Leave out the boring details. Serve them cake and aphorisms."

"I can't compromise my integrity."

"Figure it out, sweetheart."

"I sometimes feel as if I'm working an assembly line that doesn't stay still."

"You're a rabbi, for God's sake. And people are fluid. You need to dance with them, get playful."

"Walter called it a messy brew of imposed grace."

"That sounds about right."

"What am I supposed to do?" asks Sol.

"Let me try it," says Rosalie.

"What?"

"Being you. Next Shabbat. I'll give the sermon. Just a few remarks. I'll put myself in your shoes."

"That's impossible."

"Shh. I'm not replacing you. I'll just give my own talk, a little teaching from the rebbetzin. Hannah's tears, Miriam's tambourine—I'll wing it. And no one would ever compare me to you."

Rosalie phones Walter that night and asks what she should talk about.

"Think about what your father taught you. Mine your own life for material."

"Got it," says Rosalie.

Sol walks into the kitchen as Rosalie hangs up the phone.

"Who are you talking to?"

"No one. I'm just casting about for ideas."

"The phone won't help you but an open volume of Talmud could lead you somewhere."

Rosalie smiles.

"I have what I need now," she says.

Sol introduces Rosalie as his first lady who has some words she would like to share. She approaches the bima in a skirt she crocheted herself, a matching silk blouse, and a new hat. At first she speaks about her children, how Philip sometimes asks if they can keep Shabbat on Wednesday and if God knows the days of the week, and then Rosalie stops herself because she thinks of the congregants who don't have children and maybe she shouldn't speak as a mother, parading her private bounty.

"When I was young my father shared a teaching from the Ishbitzer Rebbe that has stayed with me all these years," she says. "The human experience—the story of your life—is a prism of God's desire. Think about how your eyes adjust to daylight when you first wake up; this is an entry in God's personal diary. The way you hand the dry cleaner your ticket and thank him for your pressed suit—also an entry in God's diary. And how you deny or respond to the dreams that tug at you until you find a way to make them come true—this, above all, is written in God's diary. Our lives are fodder for the great sacred story. Every moment."

She suddenly stops speaking. Nathan and Missy lean forward in their seats. Bev wraps her arm around her father's shoulders and looks up. Charlie and Philip sit in the back row with their friends, barely containing their laughter. Rosalie peers down at the congregants and feels as if she and the Ishbitzer have been standing on a distant planet, trying to emit a signal that will penetrate the silent darkness between the bima and the folding chairs. Mars to Earth. Jupiter to Saturn. Rosalie to everyone. She tugs on her skirt, adjusts her hat.

"Thank you for listening," she says. "We will now return to your regularly scheduled program."

Sol proceeds with services and after the final line of Adon Olam Bev tells Rosalie that her speech was just beautiful. Missy tells Rosalie that she cried. And Sol whispers in her ear, "Thank you. Maybe some of them will come back next week."

Rosalie spends her days behind the wheel of the Dodge, looping the circumference of Westchester County: soccer practices, dentist appointments, visits to the mall, and Lenny's trumpet lessons, an hour's drive each way. If these miles were spread out over an actual highway, she thinks, I would be on the other side of the country by now. I *would have actually traveled somewhere.* The force field of motherhood is unyielding; some weeks Rosalie cannot sit down long enough to read a magazine or write a letter. After dinner, if she stops washing dishes and daydreams out the kitchen window, Lenny stands close to her and takes her face in his small hands. *Earth to mom*, he says. *Come back to us.* Philip once drew a portrait of his family that showed Sol and the boys sitting at the table and Rosalie standing at a sink, washing a dish. She was of them and outside of them, their center and their distant star.

Rosalie believes Sol is showing improvement on the bima. Since she gave her speech, he asks her for insights on the Torah portion and uses her ideas. The congregants seem more attentive, less distracted. But she has no idea that Sol visits the wrong hospitals and drives to the wrong cemeteries, looking for a funeral he is scheduled to conduct at some other grave.

Sol's undoing is subtle at first. At an unveiling service in the rain, the pages of his Rabbi's Manual tumble into a muddy puddle. On the way out of the cemetery, he tosses the soggy remnants of the book into an open grave to fulfill the mitzvah of shaimos. But he never replaces the Manual, believing he has memorized all the prayers. Most of the congregants don't know Hebrew well enough to realize that Sol recites joyful psalms at burial services, and sings psalms of mourning at weddings.

Alone in his office one night, Sol turns out the lights, closes his eyes and lies on the floor. Maybe, he thinks, a lost rabbi is a question seeking an answer, a she'elah waiting for a teshuvah. His mind alights on a psalm and he tries to imagine Walter lying beside him, reciting the same words, but he can't find Walter's voice and even if he could, Walter would say, *This is not my way, rabbi. Keep your psalms to yourself.* I am becoming a master of forgetting, he thinks. A rabbi without memory, a teacher without channels, a man without a chavrusa, lying on a cold floor, waiting for a voice that doesn't arrive.

The following week Nathan tells Sol that the board wants to break the terms of his contract.

"You have one more year to win us over," says Nathan. "I tried to negotiate for more time, but it didn't go well. I'm sorry."

Sol lowers his eyes. *Be less remote* had traveled so far in the other direction that he could have been preaching from Bora Bora.

"Ask Rosalie to help you. Missy still talks about her speech. Maybe she can lend you a hand."

Sol thinks of Rosalie standing on the bima, how at first he cringed when she spoke of keeping Shabbat on a Wednesday. But then she said something about God's diary and the sanctuary seemed to come alive with silent rapture.

"Yes," says Sol. "Perhaps there is a way."

Every Saturday Walter stuffs his unopened mail and papers into a book bag, drives to Big Sur, and takes a table closest to the cliff's edge at Nepenthe Restaurant. It is not lost on him that while Rosalie and Sol are keeping their Sabbath on the other side of the country, he is enveloped in the Pacific fog.

He has not heard from Rosalie in months. He helped her find ideas for her speech, and then assumed she would keep calling him at night, after Sol and the boys were asleep. Walter phoned the house once, expecting Rosalie to answer, but Sol picked up. "What a surprise, Walter! I wish you would call me more often." Then Sol asked him to explain the phrase from Mishnah Peah, *the things in this world that have no measure,* and Walter snapped and replied, "If you stop measuring the cubits of your house and the liters of water in your kashering pot, maybe you would tell another story." To which Sol said, "Then I would be another kind of rabbi." And Walter said, "Yes, that's my point."

Walter wonders how much Sol knows. How much of Rosalie is permitted to him by Sol? Walter was never good at math and this arrangement seems to have something of a Venn diagram in it, with overlapping areas. Sol and Walter here, Walter and Rosalie here, Rosalie and Sol here. She is the perfect mate for him: The wife of his first American friend. The wife of a man who kissed him in the upper geniza, a man who looked at him and cried on a Jerusalem street, a man who considers his life through the lens of a text just like a groom gazes at his bride through a veil.

Quite a destiny, eh, Sonia?

He sorts through the pile of mail, opening each envelope with a butter knife. Paul is starting an ashram in southern California. *My own Shantiniketan. I'm naming it Eden Ranch.* A student has mailed him a final paper two weeks late: a comparison of Tagore and Heschel. Weakly argued, but not without merit. "Faith is the bird that feeds the light and sings when the dawn is still dark," wrote Tagore. And Heschel: "Faith is not the clinging to a shrine but an endless pilgrimage of the heart." Walter finds the shared threads intriguing and gives the student an A for the concept and a B for lateness.

He returns to the mail pile: three academic journals, the *Partisan Review,* a book on the Hindu prophetic tradition he has promised to endorse, and a letter marked with the return address of Temple Briar Wood.

June 8, 1969

Dear Walter,

When we spoke on the phone about the things in this world that have no measure you didn't give me a chance to explain myself. You assumed that I would bore you with an explanation about cubits and liters—and maybe once I would have. I didn't expect you to call me, but when I heard your voice I reached for a text that might suggest the depths of my despair, and that line popped out. When a musician loses his intonation, he can no longer play in tune; the same applies to a rabbi. I fear I've lost my ability to hear the music—if I ever had it at all.

When I saw you in Jerusalem I remembered what we created together—I'm not talking about the geniza, but I miss learning with you. Did all these years of academic life detract from the wisdom you once had, or did they endow you with an extra portion? I think of your words often— the messy brew of imposed grace—and understand that you were peering into my quite broken heart. The demands of my job have rendered the texts I love into an unforgiving clutter of words I no longer understand. I don't know where my faith lies. God? Law? I miss the certainty I once had, and I miss you.

In friendship,
Sol

If Sol begins writing in July he can stockpile twelve good sermons before the holidays touch down in September. But he doesn't go to his office all summer; every afternoon Sol draws the shades in the den and watches *Bewitched*, *Gilligan's Island*, and *As the World Turns*. The boys arrive home from their respective day camps and summer jobs, and barely notice that their father has grown a beard and lolls around in T-shirts, shorts, and slippers. He stops washing his hair before Shabbat and rehashes material from outdated sermons.

One evening in mid-August, Sol abruptly leaves the dinner table and runs upstairs to their bedroom. Rosalie follows.

"Let them fire me now," he says. "It's over."

"An inevitable crisis of faith," she says. "You'll get through it."

"I thought—"

"That you would be immune?"

"I wish it were simple," says Sol. "What once seemed so true to me has become as flat as the K'tonton stories you once read to the boys. What am I doing this for? And for whom? I stand on the bima, stare at those hungry faces, and no longer believe the words that fall from my lips."

"No one is asking you to believe, Sol. No one even cares. You just need to demonstrate faith that everything matters. This Torah, these words, every moment of their day—"

"I can barely summon meaning for myself; I have nothing in my pockets to give them. And why do they look at me with such longing? I can't stand it."

"They are in shul. Who else are they going to look at?"

"I once bought it all."

"A long time ago, Sol. When you were a boy."

"No. After."

"Didn't anyone warn you about this in rabbinical school?"

"Of course not."

"Didn't you and Walter wrangle with this?"

"We were so young, Rosalie."

"That we were."

"I'm an immoral scam."

"We all are."

"Not Bev," says Sol.

Rosalie smiles. "Everyone except Bev. The exception. One righteous person per shul; a common statistic, I'm sure." Rosalie imagines frizzy-haired Bev witnessing their conversation. *You inspire all of us, rabbi,* she would say. *Your teachings help me understand my life.* Thinking about Bev's sincerity makes Rosalie feel like crying.

"I'm simply empty," says Sol. "I need your help."

"I'm not giving another speech."

"You were very good, Rosalie. Better than I could ever be. I wish I could channel some of your words, make them come out of my mouth. Your words and—"

Rosalie sits beside Sol, lays her head on his shoulder, and reaches for his hand. Her husband chose an unbearable profession. People all over the world blindly follow faith healers, gurus, and missionaries, while a suburban rabbi is asked to inspire without daring anyone to change, to dig deep, to claim some pearl of meaning that could alter the course of their lives. How can anyone be good at this? It's impossible. Her father knew this, and Sol is finally catching on.

"Who were you talking to on the phone that night, Rosalie?"

"What night? When?"

"The night before you gave your speech. Who did you call? Honest to God, Rosalie, you weren't dialing your father in the World to Come."

She turns away, glances at her watch.

"I have a lot to do," she says. "We can talk about this tomorrow."

"I'm asking you a question," says Sol.

"Do you really want the answer?"

"Yes."

Rosalie sighs. "Walter called you that night and I picked up the phone. I asked him what he thought I should talk about."

"That's it? Why didn't you tell me he called? I ache to hear—"

"Ache?"

"Walter brought out the best in me, unraveled insights I didn't know I was capable of. He took me places—"

Rosalie gazes down at her hands. *Something we both share, my beloved husband. Our first bond, before the synagogue, before the children.* She closes her eyes and summons the smell of turmeric in the lower geniza, the yellow stains on her fingers and his, then on her hip, her lower back.

"Maybe Walter could save my pulpit," says Sol. "He could find the words that elude me."

"So call him."

"Walter doesn't know my audience. He wouldn't get the right tone for my Jews."

"You could help him with that."

"Or you, Rosalie."

"Me?"

"Why not?"

"Are you asking me to fly out to Berkeley?"

"Yes, I am. Walter knew me when I was strong. He will channel what I once was, give you the right words."

"Why don't you go? If that's what you want, why send me?"

Sol stares at her.

"Nu?" asks Rosalie.

He runs his fingers through his hair and pinches the skin on the backs of his hands. "How could I possibly get away, Rosalie? I have a board meeting and a class to teach, and things are so precarious now—"

"And I have boys to look after."

"I can't go!" he shouts. "Don't ask me to explain—"

"Calm down. Let me get this right. It's almost Rosh Hashanah and you're asking Walter and me to write your sermons for you? Who do you think I am, Moses?"

"You will be doing all of us a great service —the boys, me, the shul. You get this, Rosalie. Think of it as a business trip. I'll make a hotel reservation for you—"

"Sol—"

"I need ten of them! Make it twelve, enough to last through Sukkot. As many as you can write together. I'll call Walter and explain the details."

"Are you serious?"

Sol grabs her fingers and brings them to his lips.

"I need this from you," he says.

Rosalie closes her eyes, allows herself to think of Walter's hands, his face. Another reunion, this one granted with permission. She touches the folds of her dress to make sure she is not dreaming.

THIS IS NOT A SERMON

Rosalie tells the driver to wait for her in front of the sprawling Claremont Hotel. She signs herself in, pockets the room key, and then asks to be driven to the address she has kept folded on a piece of paper for all these years: 23 Rose Terrace.

The driver drops her off at the crest of a hill, where she spots a deer sauntering through nearby woods, a hawk circling above. Rosalie clutches her bag and smiles. The studio matches Walter's description: the black-framed picture windows that resemble a pair of eyeglasses, the bougainvillea that reminds her of Madame Sylvie's courtyard. Walter's entire home could fit inside their garage.

A peacock brushes past her and she shrieks.

"Shoo, Adelaide," says Walter. "Rosalie is our honored guest." He takes her bag.

"My new friends," he says. "They escaped from an upscale restaurant and settled up here. The pretty one is Liberace. He has no idea that his beautiful gown of feathers sweeps the sidewalk, sparing me the trouble."

"I never thought you would have house pets," says Rosalie.

"They are free to come and go."

"Of course they are."

Rosalie marches into the studio and collapses onto a chair.

"I'm here to work," she says. "We have a mission and not much time."

"Sol called with specific instructions. Twelve sermons, at least."

"At least."

"My words and yours. A partnership."

"Did Sol call it that?"

"He said we are to collaborate; let ourselves become true chavrusas."

Rosalie scans the studio. A futon piled high with pillows lines one wall; a long workbench stretches opposite; pencil cans are jumbled together with jars of coriander, garam masala, cumin, and cinnamon. She spots his sil batta. The spice man is still in his garden, she thinks, dipping her fingers into a jar of turmeric.

"Love or Torah, what comes first, rebbetzin?"

Rosalie shrugs. She is here to complete a writing assignment, preserve her husband's job, and save her family. They have to smear words of wisdom on paper, imagine the longings of every congregant's soul and pitch their message just right. Twelve speeches. Two days away from her husband and children. A holy mission.

"Torah! We barely have time, and so much to accomplish—"

"Be honest with me, Rosalie. Would you have come out here without Sol's misguided prompt?"

"Do you think I would have dared?"

"You could have gotten away anytime. You could have pretended to visit Madeline and flown out to see me. This was always possible."

"But I didn't, Walter. And here I am now. Stuck inside this crazy riddle."

"It seems that way, doesn't it? Look—you have turmeric on your fingers."

She'elah: In the world of men and women, which is stronger: Love or Torah?

Teshuvah: As it is written, *many waters cannot extinguish love.* Human love is bounded by choice; Torah is unbounded by interpretation. Love can birth generations, while Torah breeds infinite words that contradict each other for generations.

Rosalie is scheduled to fly home on Sunday night. She and Walter wait until Sunday morning to attack their assignment; they write as if they share one mind, finishing each other's sentences. Rosalie thinks of the congregants' geometry of faith and she makes up a story about a hardened man who sheds a tear made of light that saves an entire village from a flood. She sets the scene in prewar Poland and calls it a Hasidic tale. The words of the Ishbitzer that Rosalie learned from her father court Walter's theories of the eternal return. Together they invent little astonishments as if Madame Sylvie is in the studio with them. As they write,

Walter and Rosalie sniff palmfuls of turmeric root. They travel the world with real and fictional spiritual masters whose words will allow Sol to linger a while longer in the holy paneled sanctuary of Temple Briar Wood.

Once the sermons are drafted, they embellish them with lines from Thoreau, Emerson, Rilke, Rumi, and Native American lore. Walter offers phrases from Tagore's poetry and Rosalie stuffs the words into the near-finished sermons as if she is arranging raisins in a babka. Aphorisms fly out of their mouths like fireworks and Rosalie jots them in the margins. *God cannot be pinned down but peeks about in the shadows between one person and another. We are fully alive when we embrace our potential to be transformed. The meaning of a single human life cannot be decoded, only reinterpreted. The body teaches the soul its necessity. May the garden path of your life be rimmed with fresh growth! Find your boundaries, push apart their seams, and morph into butterflies!*

Walter places the pages in a purple binder and labels it SOL'S WISDOM.

"We now have a book of our own," he says. "To prove that the body does not tell our entire story."

Rosalie arrives home six days before the Selichot service, when the first prayers of forgiveness and redemption are chanted at midnight as a prelude to Rosh Hashanah. She hands her husband the purple binder, its pages darkened with typescript and ink. Sol opens to a random page, holds it to his nose, and sniffs.

"I'm grateful," he says. "In more ways than I can explain."

When Sol delivers his first speech from the binder, the words tumble from his lips with ease. He feels lighter, younger, beloved. Congregants gaze at him, surprised at first, and then attentive. After the first speech Missy Samuels says to Rosalie, "What have you done to him? He's come alive."

At night Sol sits at his desk and pores over the words in the purple binder. The first page is labeled THIS IS NOT A SERMON and contains a single, typed paragraph.

For rabbis, words are tools, as ordinary as dinner utensils. Metaphors are knives that need to be sharpened when they become blunt; words of commentary are ladled out with serving pieces that extract meaning with precision and grace. The entire biblical canon is a stew that can be stirred again and again, flavors adjusted for taste, spices added for new effect. Let the words of this binder inspire you to reach for new sensations and glorious delights.

Just when Sol thinks he has found all the aphorisms Walter and Rosalie stuffed into the sermons, he uncovers random jottings in the margins. *Unfulfilled longings become an altar for faith. Empty days are eyelashes that fall to the earth with God's tears. Our lives are the storybooks and God is the Eternal Reader. We wrap our faith around a yearning for God, and this human yearning forms a silken pillow where God rests on Shabbat and dreams of us.* Sol reads interpretations and stories that he never could have conjured himself. In one, the gleanings of the field in the Book of Ruth are not made of barley, but symbolize the small courtesies of human discourse— *please, thank you, excuse me*—that we toss around like leftover sheaves of grain. In another, a village baker and his wife long for a baby. As the baker's wife prays, her tears fall into a bowl of yeast that bubbles like a small geyser, and she forms this mixture into a dough that pulses like a heartbeat. A woman passes through town, buys challah baked from this brew and nine months later gives birth to Elijah the prophet. When Elijah is an old man, he meets the elderly village bakers and blesses them with eternal life. Sol wonders if Rosalie learned this story from her father or if Walter translated it from a Hindu legend and replaced chapatti with challah.

When Sol delivers the words from the purple binder the syllables roll off his tongue and he feels as if he is soaring beyond the confines of his body. The lines make him feel endowed, charged, replenished. *Such meaningful sermons*, says Missy Samuels. *I've never been so moved.* With the help of the words in the binder and a psychiatrist who prescribes Elavil for his depression, Sol tells Rosalie that at last he is healed, thank God, just in time for his contract to be renewed.

At the end of October, Sol asks Rosalie for another round of material.

"But you're better now. You don't need help. And the holidays are finished. Such a relief, isn't it?"

"I have too many regulars now. They are in love with the words you wrote, Rosalie. God knows their affection is not directed toward me."

"I'm not going back to Berkeley," says Rosalie. "It's too hard."

"But you must, sweetheart. Do you realize what's happening here? The two of you are making me into a rabbi again!"

"I can't explain this, Sol. It's complicated and I'm so confused—"

"Trust me. Once more. For me. For us. For all of us."

Rosalie believes that if she visits Walter now, she will never return. She wants to vanish into his studio and move her body across the futon like a snake in the desert. She wants to stand under a rain of turmeric and dye her limbs yellow. She wants to feed Adelaide and Liberace peanuts from her hands. She wants not to drive her children anywhere, not to be asked what she plans to cook for Shabbat, not to dress in a skirt and pretend to pray in a synagogue.

But when she is alone with Walter, she feels as if she has departed this world and inhabits a distant planet. She misses the antics of her sons, and the synagogue seems like a forgotten dream. When she lies in his arms, she often thinks about the congregants, these intimate strangers who make her feel tethered to something outside of her own confusion, and she relaxes. She likes to ponder their delicate geometry of faith, and consider what they truly need: Serena needs a little astonishment that speaks to the body, something that will bite her behind the knees when she least expects it. Nadine needs to know that the politician she loves will find another woman and she will survive the loss. Delia needs a prayer of healing that she can repeat like a mantra during chemotherapy. Marv needs to marry his son's teacher. And Missy Samuels needs to wear less makeup and quit her job as a Weight Watchers group leader.

Rosalie knows more about these people than Sol ever could. When Delia began chemo, Rosalie delivered casseroles to her house. When Bev's father collapsed for the last time, Sol sent Rosalie to accompany Bev to the hospital so she would not be alone when he died. *He was the love of my life*, said Bev. *My only family*. When Serena sat shiva for her mother, Rosalie delivered the cold cuts and searched Serena's kitchen drawers for the meat silverware, the Saran wrap, and the garbage bags. Know where a woman stores her Jell-O molds, thinks Rosalie, and you will understand the contours of her heart.

If she is away, Rosalie won't be around to take the pulse of the congregants, look out for their well-being. The loyalists of Temple Briar Wood would be alone with their Elavilled rabbi who would be mute to their longings. They would come to shul and wait for Sol to speak, hoping for a word or a phrase they could grasp tightly when they woke up in a sweat in the middle of the night, wondering how and who and why this life instead of all the other possibilities.

"I will go," she says. "For two nights."

"Ten speeches."

"No promises."

This time Rosalie takes a taxi directly to Walter's studio, where Liberace and Adelaide greet her like an old friend.

"We work first," says Rosalie. Books are scattered all over the floor: Rumi, Tagore, Heschel, anthologies of American poetry, Hindu scriptures, Kabbalah, Hasidic tales, and world mythology. Rosalie takes a seat and eagerly digs in. Together she and Walter move their fingers across the pages like pianists, lingering on the phrases that could possibly resonate in the paneled sanctuary.

"Here is one from the Chandogya Upanishad," says Walter.

"I first read this in Shantiniketan. *Wind has no body. Clouds, thunder, and lightening have no body. But we are all gods, all fixed in a single self.*"

"That won't play in Westchester. How about Rumi? We used one of his lines in the purple binder and they went wild for it."

What is the body? Endurance.

What is love? Gratitude.

What is hidden in our chests? Laughter.

What else? Compassion.

"Yes," says Rosalie. "Rumi is good for my Jews."

"Here's another," says Walter. "*The soul should always stand ajar, ready to welcome the ecstatic experience.*"

"Emily Dickinson! I learned that as a girl."

"And another: *Just to be is a blessing. Just to live is holy.*"

"Who wrote that?"

"Abraham Joshua Heschel."

"My matchmaker," says Rosalie. "When he lectured at YIVO, I sat between Sol and a man who reeked of sauerkraut. And everything began."

"My rebbetzin of the between places."

Rosalie smiles. "So it seems."

"I would have liked to meet Professor Heschel," says Walter.

"I believe we were otherwise occupied."

He places his hand on Rosalie's neck and leans in for a kiss.

"Not yet," she says.

"When?"

"Let's finish. Please."

Walter opens another book. "*When a man and a woman*

unite, and their thought joins the beyond, that thought draws down the upper light."

"Iggeret ha-Kodesh. Thirteenth century. A steamy time, obviously."

"You didn't learn that from your father."

"Nope."

Rosalie holds out her hand. *"The rebbetzin's learning comes from fountains the eye cannot discern."*

Walter runs his finger along the rivers at the center of her palm.

"My unwritten tractate," she says.

He licks her hand, lightly bites the tips of her fingers.

"I want what you hold in here," he says.

Rosalie sighs. "I want and I want and I want—"

For two days they move between the pages of the books, the sentences they compose, and the pages of their bodies, opening and closing and opening again on the studio floor. Just before her taxi arrives, Rosalie begins to cry.

"I feel as if I've been dropped inside a riddle that's impossible to solve," she says.

"One day it will make sense."

"You and your damn karma," says Rosalie. "Just keep kissing me so I don't think about how tawdry our little affair has become."

"You don't believe that, do you?"

"I don't know what I believe," she says.

From his perch behind the lectern, Sol peers down at Rosalie in her front-row seat. He raises an eyebrow and delivers the words

written for him, because of him, and despite him. When he needs
to conjure an impromptu comment, Sol tosses his head, and Rosalie meets him at the steps to the bima and whispers words into
his good ear.

Rosalie gives Sol an explanation for everything. She invents
proverbs and interpretations with the ease of Madame Sylvie dispensing little astonishments. She doesn't need Walter to invoke
pockets of wisdom. After he runs through the contents of the
binder, Sol asks Rosalie to deliver a sermon of her own. She talks
about the true meaning of their congregation, and she refers to
the Briar Wood loyalists as her extended family, joined together
in prayers and in hope. She asks them to look around the paneled sanctuary and behold one another. "Every one of you is a
perfect work of nature," she says. "Together we create a magnifi-
cent garden of dignity and courage. Together we will bravely strip
away what clouds our inner joy. We will stand beside each other
in this modest holy space, allow our time together to wipe away
every pinch of sadness, every fleck of confusion."

The local Jewish weekly runs a story about the charismatic
Kerems who have brought a synagogue to life through their
teachings. A single photograph takes up a double-page spread: Sol
sitting behind his desk, Rosalie in a slinky wrap dress, perched
cross-legged at the edge, both of them beaming at the camera. She
mails a copy of the article to Walter and he responds with a postcard: *My work is complete then. The two of you have found your calling.*

Rosalie writes back: *Don't ever say that again.*

NEW SHANTINIKETAN

July 1971

Walter runs his fingers over the stamped cover of his latest book: *Religious Themes in Tagore's Poetry*, Paul Richardson and Walter Westhaus, coeditors. He leafs through the pages he and Paul wrestled over for years. When Paul had translated a line from *Gitanjali* to read: "*Thou art the sky and Thou art also the nest*," Walter changed it to read: "*You are the heavens and You are the home*." *Our partnership is impossible*, Paul had said to him. *I understand Bengali better than you ever will and I can't revise your work. You are closer to the source than I am.* Walter believes that he will always be Paul's lost man, the refugee who followed him off the ship, the Jew who accepted an offer in India that was better than no offer at all.

When he finishes reading Walter calls Paul.

"Namaste." The lilt of a sitar plays in the background.

"I was rereading our Tagore," says Walter. "We created something wonderful, didn't we?"

"That we did."

"I want to thank you for everything—"

"Enough with the propriety, Walter! When are you coming to the ranch? Be my scholar in residence, comfort my more intellectual students with your prowess and reputation." Walter doesn't want to be Paul's sidekick, but he is grateful for the offer. Since Rosalie's last visit to Berkeley, Walter has felt bereft. He needs to get away from the confines of the studio that he now thinks of as their lovers' den, their beit midrash, their hideaway sanctioned by the peacocks that now annoy Walter with their night cries and putrid droppings.

"Think of Eden Ranch as a new Shantiniketan," says Paul. "You can lie under a tree and dream your life into possibility."

The ranch is a seventy-acre desert wilderness overlooking a canyon, dotted with a single house, several tents, outhouses, and a trailer. Paul has set a circle of stones in a clearing and he calls this the amphitheater, the place where his students gather and listen to him speak about the power of juice fasting and the teachings of a Baba he met on his last trip to India. Over the years, Paul has morphed from a scholar into a guru. He has grown his hair long and after years of meditation practice, his left eye no longer twitches. His students call him a maharishi, and he lays marigold garlands at their necks.

At dawn Paul and Walter patrol the perimeter of the ranch.

"I don't get it," says Paul. "All these years later and your head is still in that spice sack. You've built an illustrious life and you're still the vagabond I found in Bombay. There are ways to work through trauma, my friend."

"That was a long time ago," says Walter.

"Then why do you remain so disconnected? You carry on with models in your little studio and do nothing to secure your future."

"I wrote five books," shouts Walter. "One of them with you! Find a tenured professor who's published five books in ten years and still sketches and makes love to women with generosity and care and—"

Paul laughs. "You don't need to tell me the details of your prowess."

"That's not the point."

"You have scattered yourself. Nothing perpetuated from those bones." Paul stops walking and strokes Walter's cheek. "I have always loved you," he says.

"I know," says Walter.

"And I saved you."

"In a way, yes. I'm grateful."

"We go back a long way. Longer than you may even realize. And when you are gone from this world, the university will keep your name alive in an archive and the library will stock your books, but you pass nothing down. It's such a loss."

"Where is this coming from, Paul? What happened to your karmic perspective?"

"Giselle is pregnant."

"Giselle?"

"A student. Like you were once. I found her in India."

"Another stray you adopted?"

"Giselle is my life, Walter. As are you. And yes, our child is my future."

Sol's contract has been renewed. Nathan tells him that he has become a good enough rabbi and that the congregants will fill in the gaps between what he provides and what they need. *It's not perfect, you're not perfect, but we have a history together and we'll work it out.* Sol wakes early and jogs through the streets of Briar Wood before morning services. As he runs Sol tests his memory of the words in the purple binder: *What is the body? Endurance. What is love? Gratitude.* He laces the invented Hasidic stories with his own proverbs and tries his hand at writing little astonishments.

Sol imagines Walter beside him, playing a round of she'elah and teshuvah.

Who is an inadequate rabbi?

An illusion cannot be measured. There is only inadequate faith.

Is there any illusion greater than faith?

One cannot ask this of a rabbi. The rabbi will say, "Yes, of course faith is an illusion." But no one will believe him.

Can a man love a woman and a man?

Only a fool would ask to measure the depths of a human heart.

Many nights after Sol and the children are asleep, Rosalie sits alone in the dark kitchen, but instead of calling Walter, she waits until it is late enough for Madeline to be waking up in London. She speaks to Madeline in a rush of words and emotions, telling her everything about Walter and the sermons, about the congregation, and about Sol and the state of her marriage. If she holds back, Madeline says, "I want the full report, pussycat. Tell me more." As Rosalie delivers the details to her best friend, she talks faster and faster, the story of her life bubbling to the surface like the froth in a Champagne flute. Since they met in Jerusalem, Madeline has divorced her husband; she tells Rosalie that if she had a Walter of her own, perhaps her marriage would have survived. *It takes three, sweet pea,* she said. *A man and a woman and a living spark that keeps all the desire in motion.*

It has been almost two years since Rosalie's last trip to Berkeley. When she phones Walter, she doesn't speak with the same emotional rush that she reserves for her calls with Madeline. Walter believes Rosalie is holding back. Their ghostwriting project was too much of a success; the sermons saved Sol's pulpit and preserved their marriage too. The Kerems are complete, he thinks; the inner circle of their family is nestled safely within the orbit of their congregation. Rosalie yammers on about the exploits of her children. *Charlie this, Philip yesterday, and Lenny, oh Lenny. He is the one who breaks me to pieces, who asks me to linger in his room and read every volume of Tintin's antics until he is fast asleep and dreaming himself into the story.*

"And the fruits of our little project?" asks Walter.

"At times I see the synagogue as a holding place for tenderness. A random group of Jews pausing together, engaging in an orchestrated conversation about the meaning of life."

Walter wonders if her gauzy remarks are a mask, a way to render their affair into a continuous conversation about religion. In the past year she has mailed him sporadic postcards with quips that read like outtakes from the purple binder.

Holiness is another word for dignity; dignity is a synonym for presence.

In the World to Come, each of us will wear a coat sewn from the days we lived on earth. The brightest threads of this coat are woven from love.

Faith is the trump card in the deck of life.

If a student had written these, Walter would have called her into his office and cautioned her against writing soft-brained cupcake theology. But he and Rosalie created this project together and the words she writes belong to both of them.

The desert air and canopy of stars coax Walter into a long, deep sleep and he wakes at dawn with a start, reviewing the filmstrip of their reunions: their rendezvous in the American Colony Hotel, their visit to Madame Sylvie's courtyard, and her visits to Berkeley. The last astonishment Sylvie dispensed for him was about Sonia, of course, but his fiancée has become a distant ghost over the years; she no longer hovers at the edge of his thoughts, waiting for attention. And Rosalie—when will he see her again? Paul is right; his head is forever mired in a barrel of spices in a foreign land. He may have become a well-published tenured professor but he is a man without a future.

Walter phones Rosalie on a Sunday morning and she picks up on the first ring.

"You came to Berkeley twice because Sol sent you. And now it's my turn to ask you for something. The first time and the last."

"Hold on, Walter. I was just making sandwiches—" She rests the handset on her shoulder and counts the slices of bread lined up on the counter waiting to receive slabs of peanut butter. Ten slices, five hikers, one hour left, not enough time to buy ice for the cooler, pick up Sol's tallit from the dry cleaners, wake the boys—

"Come to Eden Ranch."

Rosalie glances at the clock.

"Are you there?"

"It's been too long, Walter. And I can't get away now: the shul, the children, Sol, who is actually well—*more or less*—and can you believe the five of us actually go hiking on Sunday afternoons? And Charlie, Charlie is applying to college—"

"Stop hiding behind your family. I need to see you."

Rosalie is silent.

"Are you there?"

"Yes, Walter. I'm here, always here. It's a big life. More than I ever imagined. I don't expect you to understand."

"Don't mock me. Your playboy refugee understands the power of the tribe."

"I'm sorry."

"Look. Paul has a following here and he's brought me in as a guest teacher. You could work with me; we can teach together. You might even like it."

Rosalie laughs. "I'll be a guru!"

"I'm here all summer. Waiting."

She sends Walter a postcard:

> *Four days. Our last time.*
>
> R.

Rosalie is the last passenger left in the airport van. She wishes she had gotten off at the Lawrence Welk Resort with its uniformed doorman in nearby Escondido, rather than barreling up this mountain road with a driver who tells her that the area is saturated with Western diamondbacks and that she needs to carry a big stick to scare them off. She rubs her ankle, trying to imagine the icy sting of a snakebite, the cold poison coursing slowly up her leg. She could ask the driver to turn around, take her back to the airport. Sol didn't ask her to see Walter this time, and she could have refused the invitation. This visit belongs to her alone.

Rosalie drops her bag at the gate and finds Walter standing in the middle of a circle of stones, addressing a motley group of students who look like teenage runaways. A girl taps her on the shoulder and hands her a copy of *Be Here Now* and she thinks of Nathan's line, *be less remote*. Except for Walter, everyone's hair looks unwashed and Rosalie thinks about buying a family-sized bottle of shampoo. Paul sits beside his pregnant girlfriend and massages her filthy neck. Rosalie shudders and focuses her gaze on Walter.

"In Varanasi," he says, "people use their bodies to understand life and death; they immerse in the ghats of the river that bear the ashes of their loved ones. In the West, we use words to understand life and death and our language is imprecise, distancing. This affects our karmic balance." Rosalie stares at Walter and smiles. She hasn't heard him lecture before and she follows the stream of his words as if she is listening to a symphony. How did he learn all this and how can he teach some of it to her?

At the end of his talk Walter takes questions. Rosalie moves closer to the group and raises her hand.

"Do you think karmic balance can be achieved in one's lifetime?"

"Ah! Excellent question!" He smiles. "Many spiritual teachings are rooted in this inquiry. Karmic balance cannot be achieved, only readjusted on a cosmic plane. And even if one lives an examined life, the ultimate meaning of the journey may not be obvious."

"So it is impossible to know if your answer is correct," she says.

Walter leads Rosalie to his tent and they make love with a level of deliberation and care that feels new to both of them. This tenderness, thinks Rosalie, marks the end. From the geniza to Eden Ranch, a perfect arc from youth to middle age. Our swan song to savor for the rest of our days.

She tells him this is the last time.

"I didn't expect you to come," he says. "We completed our assignment, accomplished our mission, and saved your husband."

"You pleaded with me to meet you here. What choice did I have?"

"Everything we've done together has been your choice," he says.

Meals at the ranch are eaten in silence; Paul calls this the practice of meditative digestion. "The holiness of food," he says, "cannot be experienced through the cacophony of conversation." The students eat sparingly at long tables and then gather outside in the circle of stones where Paul delivers lectures and Giselle crouches before him, her belly dragging on the ground like a giant gourd. Walter and Rosalie teach a class together on Hindu and Hasidic parables. The students ask them for a blessing and Walter says, "Paul Richardson is your holy man; we have no power to bless anyone."

The night before Rosalie is to leave, they lie in the middle of a field, staring up at the stars. Walter asks if she remembers the last line of the Song of Songs.

"*Quick my love over the mountain of spices,*" says Rosalie. "Not an exact translation, but it's mine."

"Sonia loved the Song," says Walter.

"The woman in your astonishment."

"My fiancée. Before India. Before you."

Rosalie turns on her side and faces him.

"My father wouldn't leave. Those last weeks Sonia and I were always together in my bed, fucking like bunnies, drunk on vodka, making plans. She only wanted to go to Palestine. Sure, she was a Zionist, but she also loved the poetry of the Bible. The Song of Songs. The Prophets. She was a singer."

"And she loved you."

"She had a curtain of long blond hair that smelled like cardamom. Made me swoon."

Rosalie smiles.

"We hadn't eaten and she went out to look for crackers," he says. "She was barely dressed. An inconsequential moment."

"She was murdered."

"Everyone at the Seminary knew that part of the story. Shot. Along with my father. His flute fell to the floor with their bodies."

"Walter."

"The bullet—"

Rosalie rests her head on his chest.

"She took the bullet for me, Rosalie. My father was a target, and I was his son. But Sonia had a chance of survival."

"How can you blame yourself?"

Walter begins to sob. "I hid under the bed. They were shot in the next room and I made myself disappear."

Rosalie runs her fingers through his hair, pulls him close.

"You had no choice."

"Sonia took the fall so I could live."

"It was so hopeless, Walter. You all would have been killed anyway. Then, or eventually. You don't know."

"At Shantiniketan I would lie under the date palm trees and imagine that I was in the afterlife and Sonia was on her way to Palestine. I would close my eyes and allow time to disappear, a night and a day and another night until someone came outside to offer me food and tea."

Paul and Giselle walk by, holding hands. Walter stops talking and waits for them to pass.

"I deserved none of it. I was not meant to be saved."

"You deserved me," says Rosalie.

Walter laughs. "That's rather pitiful. I stole you from my first American friend. First I stole Sonia's life, then I stole yours."

"You did not, Walter. This—*everything*—has been my choice. You said so yourself."

"Sonia was so much better than we will ever be."

"She was young, Walter. She was in the process of becoming."

"And what have we become?"

Rosalie turns away, wraps her arms around herself, and begins to cry. "Why is this so sacred to me?" she asks.

"I don't know, darling. Ask my friend who lectures in the circle of stones. He will tell you all about karma. Paul and I have words for everything, just like you and Sol. Is this beautiful or is this an ugly betrayal? Roll the dice and let me know what you come up with, rebbetzin."

Rosalie pictures the congregants looking up at her when she gave her speech, hanging on every word that crossed her lips. They were hungry for the syllables that stumbled out of her mouth, as if she were a mother bird parceling out worms: Feed us. Teach us. Awaken our sleepy lives. And that's what she and Walter did, with their purple binder overflowing with attempts at wisdom, a line here, a story there. Mazel tov, rabbi. You delivered the goods. Our love, your words. Our stained bodies, your sacred mission.

"Shameless and wrong and confounding and beautiful," says Rosalie. "Everything at the same time."

"We never should have met," says Walter. He reaches for her and she shrugs him off.

"Sometimes I wonder if Sol and I would still be married if we didn't have you. But what about you, Walter? You can criss-cross the globe, gaze upon Brahmins immersing in the ghats, then return to your hillside idyll graced with young women and flanked by peacocks. Your life is so big! So why us? Why me?"

"My heart is not aligned to reason, Rosalie. And neither is yours."

Just before dawn Paul and Giselle's voices ring outside the tent. Through a crack in the siding, Rosalie spies a bright red splotch and rising smoke. She turns to Walter and shakes his shoulders but he doesn't wake up.

"Evacuate!" shouts Paul.

Rosalie shakes Walter harder. "Wake up!"

Paul storms into the tent and screams into Walter's face. "Wake the fuck up! There's a fire on the other side of the hill!"

Rosalie shakes him again and Paul screams louder. "Get your head out of the spice sack, Walter! We're evacuating! Get on the truck with the others!"

Rosalie pulls Walter to stand, hands him a shirt and pants, and leads him outside. The corner of the canyon glows orange and the radius of the light spreads down the surrounding hills like lava. The guests pile into the truck and Rosalie runs toward it. Walter grabs her arm.

"There's no immediate danger."

"It's dry as bone here. The chaparral will go up in flames in minutes."

"This is nothing, darling. We have the place to ourselves—"

"Is this some kind of death wish? You can escape only once."

"I know what danger smells like," he says. "This is a trifle."

"You're crazy."

Walter cups her face in his hands.

"Trust me," he says.

Rosalie spies the truck heading down the mountain, chases after it for a minute, and then gives up.

The sky is dark; they have no kerosene and no flashlights. Walter leads Rosalie to the circle of stones and they sit on a single rock. She wraps her arms tightly around herself.

It's three hours later in New York, she thinks. Wednesday. Lenny has a trumpet lesson and Sol doesn't know where he keeps his music. Philip won't do his homework if she's not in the house. The jar of peanut butter is almost empty, not enough for Charlie's sandwiches, and where are her children while she stands on this mountain in the middle of Gehenna? Rosalie stares at Walter in the dark and for a moment he appears to be a complete stranger.

"Who are you?"

She clenches her hands into fists and pounds his chest.

"I am the biggest fool for carrying on with you, ever," she cries. "I have a family. I have children. Boys who need me. Who always need me."

Walter looks stern, professorial. "This is nothing to be afraid of," he says in a guarded voice. She once loved his accent and now she wants to break it apart, shatter his inflections until he talks like she does. Like Sol does.

"Look," he says, suddenly. "Over there."

A family of deer, scattered foxes and rabbits step out of the woods one by one and stand on the path, transfixed by the light in the distance. Squirrels and a single quail appear. Another deer. A lone turkey. The animals pause where they stand, all of them. Rosalie stands. Walter stands.

Rosalie looks into the eyes of the deer emerging from the woods. A family of quail flow onto the road. The rabbits stand frozen; one hops close to Walter's feet. Rosalie gazes at the animals and pictures her children in their beds and Sol at his lectern and her father surrounded by his books and her mother in the kitchen. The animals stare, waiting for her to make the first move. She reaches for Walter and touches his face. He begins to cry and then speaks softly, "Sonia, Josef—" He recites a litany of names and words in German that she doesn't understand.

Rosalie watches the animals who stand frozen in the clearing. She listens to the inflection of Walter's voice as if she is listening to a strange symphonic poem. This is, she thinks, the last time. Walter continues to speak in German and then begins to sob. She takes his face in her hands and they kiss in the smoke that swirls around them.

The fire stops on the other side of the canyon.

STEAL THIS BOOK

July 1973

Sol and Rosalie are lost on a dark road in the Berkshires. Rain batters the car windows and Sol leans his head past the steering wheel, hoping the angle will lend him visibility.

"It won't help," says Rosalie. "We can't see through this torrent."

"I'll pull over," says Sol. "We can wait it out."

"Keep driving."

"Ten minutes won't make a difference."

Rosalie shouts, "Have you grown deaf in both ears? We were expected two hours ago."

Sol continues to drive and Rosalie reads the directions to Lenny's summer camp.

"The roads aren't marked. We were supposed to turn right at a gas station."

"I don't see a gas station," says Sol.

"Keep going." She stares straight ahead, her eyes following the hurried blink of the wipers that are useless in the storm.

"I need your help," he says suddenly. "I can't remember the names of the first-timers who came to shul last week. There was a woman named Natalie, I recall. She stood next to our Bev, the lady with frizzy hair and flip-flops. Was Natalie the redhead or the one who wore a doily on her head? And she brought along a friend: a Sue, a Beth, maybe a Linda. What's with these names that all seem the same to me?"

"Lenny is lying in a camp infirmary with a fever and you want to talk about some lady named Natalie or Linda or Beth or Sue? Who the hell cares?"

"It's a camp infirmary, Rosalie. And Lenny is fine. He wanted to come home anyway."

Rosalie sighs. Lenny is twelve, away at camp for the first time. His brothers had outgrown Camp Herzl, staffed with muscular Israeli counselors who supervised endless games of Gaga, built campfires by the lake, and danced in the baseball field every Friday night, greeting Shabbat like the ancient mystics of Safad. Lenny had begged Rosalie to let him try it out. She questioned his stamina for being away from home, but sewed labels and packed a trunk anyway. At the end of the first week he sent home a postcard: I *hate it here. Too many rules, too many sports. Pick me up.*

When Rosalie called the camp director, she was told that Lenny was beginning to make friends and she should give it another week before speaking to him directly. The director called a few days later and calmly stated that Lenny was running a fever that spiked from 101 to 104.

"Your son is very sick," he said. "How soon can you get him?"

"Turn here," says Rosalie. "This is the road."

Sol asks her again about Natalie, and then says he remembers—*all of a sudden! a miracle!*—that Beth is the one who walks with a cane.

We are trapped, thinks Rosalie. In this car, in this synagogue, in this box of a life. If only. If only she and Sol could start all over with new lives. She would be the rabbi. A rabbi without a pulpit. She would be the kind of rabbi who could receive the questions: *What language does God speak in my ear when I kneel over a bathtub to scour it clean? What story does God tell when I unload sacks of groceries from the station wagon and my life feels so narrow?* Rosalie would be good at answering these; she would have no need to conjure up metaphors that could serve as guideposts for what she knew in her heart. And if she were the rabbi, Sol would be no rabbi at all. He would wake up, daven, put away his tefillin and drive to the hardware store, where he could talk about kitchen faucets with earned authority. *Brushed nickel coordinates with any backsplash* would be his holy motto, his proclamation of faith. And with another kind of life she would not have had to leave Walter behind at Eden Ranch. She would be a rabbi and she would be married to Sol and married, quite differently, to Walter. There would be no need to ever say goodbye.

The camp director is waiting in the parking lot. He hands Sol a clipboard, asks him to sign release papers for his son.

"If he were my kid, I'd go directly to a hospital."

"Why didn't you—" shouts Sol.

"Never mind," says Rosalie. A counselor brings Lenny to the car; he shivers beneath a gray camp blanket.

"Thank God you came," Lenny says. "I can't get warm."

Sol helps Lenny into the backseat and Rosalie sits beside him, offering her lap as a pillow.

They drive in silence and Rosalie lays her hand on Lenny's forehead.

"Is he asleep?" asks Sol.

"Yes. A bit cooler now too. Let's get him home."

Sol peers into the rearview mirror. Rosalie's eyes are closed.

"Are you awake, Rosalie?"

"Of course."

"I've been wondering about Walter," says Sol.

"Uh-huh."

"I think of him often. Did I ever thank you for saving me with that material? The purple binder."

Rosalie looks out the window. The rain has stopped completely.

"You don't need to thank me."

"But I didn't thank Walter."

"No need to, Sol. He knows."

Sol peers into the rearview again and bites his lip. "I think about him more than I let on," he says.

Don't encroach on my story, thinks Rosalie. The place in the Venn diagram where Walter touches you is not the place where he touches me. She imagines Walter's hand between her legs, then blocks the memory. Don't go there, she thinks. Not now, with Lenny, with *this*. Sol can have his little fantasy of the storybook man who showed up at the Seminary so many years ago with his sil batta, but you, Rosalie Kerem, are played out. No more illusions. No more Walter.

She holds Lenny tighter.

Lenny's pediatrician orders a biopsy and arranges for him to be admitted to the hospital. A new doctor invites them into his office and rambles through phrases that are as coded and incomprehensible as Pig Latin. *Cells are out of control. Hodgkin's lymphoma. No longer treatable. The troops will be home in a month, maybe two. Keep him comfortable. Normalize. The best we can do will have to be enough. I'm only saying this because you are a religious family but God has designs on him.*

"I'm the rabbi here!" Sol shouts. "You're a fucking MD. Don't bring God into this!"

Rosalie places her hands over her eyes and begins to heave.

Sol mutters something under his breath in Hebrew. He reaches for Rosalie and she pulls away.

"Rosalie. God is challenging us—"

"Don't touch me and don't say a word to me," she shouts. "Not about God and not about what you think and not about anything I don't want to hear. Don't ever talk to me again, Sol. Never. Again. Ever."

The next day Sol breaks into a tirade about how Camp Herzl made his son sick and he phones an attorney. Rosalie stays in the hospital with Lenny and returns home for a few hours at a time. When she decides it's time to break the news, she dials Charlie, hollers for Philip to pick up the phone in another room and for

Sol to pick up the phone in the study, linking them around the impossible words that Sol mutters to all of them.

After his initial horror Charlie says he's not surprised.

"Based on what information?" asks Rosalie.

"We had that clubhouse out back when Lenny was about five, remember? Gosh, I loved that place. I lorded over my brothers, we pummeled Philip, we mocked Lenny for being such a mama's boy."

"It was the Wild West back there."

"You don't know the half of it," says Charlie. "And you never will. But one Shabbat afternoon Philip shared a cigarette butt he found in the house."

Rosalie sighs. She would occasionally smoke when she spoke to Walter or Madeline late at night, and she sometimes forgot to empty the ashtrays.

"It was Philip's first toke and Lenny asked to try it also and I told him he could die if he smokes tobacco and he turned to me and said, 'I will die before both of you, Charlie.' I told him to stop being an idiot and he just walked away and we never talked about it again."

"That doesn't mean anything," says Rosalie, wishing it were so. "Lenny has always been a dreamy boy. That's all."

Rosalie is an agent of efficiency and detail. She clutches a datebook whose pages are black with doctors' names and a maze of schedules. When she's not at the hospital, she scours medical journals and loads a file cabinet with articles about treatments and medication trials. Sol asks the congregants to pray for Lenny, and Rosalie asks Nathan Samuels to send a note to the congregation, asking that they be left alone. No unsolicited advice. No alternative therapies. It is too late.

Rosalie moves into Lenny's hospital room and sleeps on a chair beside his bed. Sol delivers corned beef sandwiches that no one bothers to eat. Charlie takes a leave of absence from college and moves back home. He and Philip embark on a mission to teach Lenny all the things he will miss in his abbreviated life. Every afternoon they coax Rosalie to leave Lenny's room for an hour and demand that the nurses keep the door shut. Philip steals a steering wheel from his driver's ed class and shows Lenny how to drive. Charlie unpacks a collection of *Penthouse* magazines and talks to Lenny about sex, and then hands him a cheeseburger. "You've got to taste some *trayf*," shouts Charlie. "Transgression is delicious."

"No appetite. What else do you have for me?"

Charlie reaches into his knapsack.

"Everyone is reading this up at school." He reads aloud from Abbie Hoffman's *Steal This Book*: "*Become an internationalist and learn to respect all life. Make war on machines. And in particular the sterile machines of corporate death and the robots that guard them. The duty of a revolutionary is to make love and that means staying alive and free.*"

"Sounds exhausting," says Lenny.

Charlie tells Lenny that most of what Sol taught them about Judaism is a myth. "We were never in Egypt," he says.

"I don't believe you," says Lenny.

"There is no proof," says Charlie.

"This is proof enough," says Lenny. "My suffering is Egypt. It's a metaphor, like Mom always says."

"Even the metaphors are lies," says Charlie.

"But they told us—"

"You really believe everything they taught you?"

"Abba is a rabbi and Mom knows so much," says Lenny.

"That doesn't mean they always speak the truth."

"And does your Abbie Hoffman do any better?"

Later that night Lenny tells Rosalie she fell asleep in her bedside chair and called out a man's name.

"Whose name, sweetheart?"

"Walter. You called out the name Walter and you were crying."

"I'm sorry, Lenny. You don't need to be burdened with my problems." She forces a smile.

"Who is Walter?"

"A friend," says Rosalie. "Your father and I had a good friend."

"And?"

"There's nothing to say. It's over now."

"He's dead?"

"No. Just out of touch."

"That's sad. You could use more friends in your life. Those congregants are so fake."

"They leave messages on our answering machine every day. Those fake congregants care about you, sweetheart."

"It makes them feel better to pretend to care," says Lenny. "Part of the unwritten contract in our shul. How many of them ever talked to me? Serena once asked me if I got good grades in school. Missy and Nathan used to pinch my cheeks. These people saw me every Shabbat for my whole life—*they watched me grow up!*—and all along I was just their scenery."

"So are we," says Rosalie, her voice drifting.

"Charlie is teaching me about sex," says Lenny. "And about *trayf*—at least he's trying to. And about Abbie Hoffman. Charlie is joining the revolution, Mom. He's keeping a running list for me that he calls 'Lies and Illusions that Abba Delivers from the Bima.'"

"It must be a long list."

"It's Charlie's list, not mine," says Lenny.

"And what's on your list, sunshine?"

"I used to wish you were the rabbi. The words Abba spoke would have sounded so much better coming from you. When he was good he reminded me of you."

Two days later Lenny develops an infection and slips into a coma. Rosalie rests her head close to his, warming his cheeks with her breath. Sol stands by the window and davens, and Charlie and Philip sit cross-legged on the floor, squinting away tears. The sun sets that evening and the sun rises the next day and the Kerems stay in Lenny's room just like this, no longer hoping, no longer waiting.

Years later, when Rosalie reflects on Lenny's last months, she realizes that the fog of memory has obliterated the sharp edges, smoothed the jagged stones into a forgiving blur. She cringes when she recalls the Hallmark words that served as ciphers—*comfort, hope, memory, eternity*—words they dispensed like the aspirin that proved to be futile in lowering Lenny's fever, words they reached for as children grasp soap bubbles at a summer picnic, words that evaporated in the air. The empty words floated through Rosalie's brain those last months, days that held beauty because Lenny was still here and days that held sadness because Lenny was gone.

She'elah: Who comforts the clergy who mourn?

Sol's teshuvah: The Holy One whose comfort eludes me.

Rosalie's teshuvah: Abbie Hoffman. Rabindranath Tagore. Frank Sinatra. Missy Samuels. Steal this book. Return my son. No more questions.

The congregants deliver shiva food—whitefish platters with a dozen varieties of bagels—and reach their arms into eager hugs and cry onto each other's shirts. The men arrive for the evening service and stand in the den with Rosalie, Sol, Charlie, and Philip. The boys stand on either side of their father and recite the Mourner's Kaddish, their square shoulders holding him upright; Rosalie mouths the words from a distance. After the week of shiva the platters are replaced with casseroles dropped at the front door and Rosalie can tell who baked the lasagna by how tightly the foil is pulled across the top of the pan. Every comforting gesture feels insincere yet necessary; every dish dropped at their doorstep curses their home.

Rosalie hates Missy and Nathan and Bev and Serena and Delia and Marv and all the others who surround her with gestures of comfort, but when she sees them at the post office or the mall she tugs on their coats to draw them close. Words are wrong.

Silence is worse. Sol spends his days curled up in a ball, first on the floor of his synagogue office, then at home, on the living room carpet. "There is no medication for grief," says Sol's doctor. "When he is ready the rabbi will pull himself out." Charlie returns to college and Philip is the only child left at home. He keeps stashes of weed in his back pocket and Rosalie does not notice that his eyes are always red and he never does schoolwork, never cracks a book. When Sol, Philip, and Rosalie pass each other in the kitchen no one touches. Many nights Rosalie sleeps in Lenny's bed, wrapped in the sleeping bag that held his sweat when he first got sick at Camp Herzl.

She'elah: How?
Teshuvah:
She'elah: Why?
Teshuvah:
Teshuvah:
Teshuvah.

Months pass. In the house of the rabbi the meaningful mourning rituals are as useless as weak tea. Sol's daily recitations of the Mourner's Kaddish do not connect him to Lenny and his prayers are empty and rote. The women of Briar Wood surround Rosalie with affection but the words they speak linger on her skin like cheap perfume and she wants to rub them off with a scouring pad. No atheist is ever found in a foxhole; no believer is ever found in a child's empty bedroom. The sunlight streams into the house during the long afternoons and mocks their brave, sad lives. Termites parade into the kitchen; the exterminator overcharges for treatment. Sol cries to the exterminator, to the gardener, to the handyman, to the floor waxer. Every service man who walks into their house utters the same syllables: *Rabbi, I heard. I'm sorry.* I'm sorry, as if Jeff, who makes a living by carrying a can of pesticide on his back, had stolen Lenny from the Kerems. *I'm sorry,* as if Glen the gardener had swept Lenny into a sewer with autumn leaves and gum wrappers. *I'm sorry,* they all say, bearing words that slash like razors.

You shouldn't have named your son after the West Side Story composer, rabbi. I remember that sermon you gave, how music inspired your child's name. That was a huge error in judgment, thinking you could attach your son's life to art.

You didn't pray enough; better you should be Orthodox and you would be a real rabbi.

Your wife is so aloof. Something is not right in your lives. Rabbi, I'm only telling you this because I care.

Your son was never yours. God lent him to you and then broke the terms of the lease.

Rosalie cannot breathe in the house, cannot breathe in the shul. She cannot bring herself to go anywhere except to the mall where she meanders into stores, and caresses expensive dresses that she has no intention of buying. At the same time every night, Madeline phones Rosalie from London and listens to her cry into the phone. After a few weeks of these sessions, Madeline interrupts Rosalie's sobs.

"Have you told him, Rosalie?"

"No, and I don't intend to. Don't you think my distraction cost me my child? What if I was missing cues about Lenny while

I was running off to California? Even Charlie knew something wasn't right with Lenny's health. How did I miss it?"

"Children are aware of things that adults can't pick up," says Madeline. "You could not have known. And anyway, your visits to Walter allowed Sol to keep his job."

"Those visits allowed me to step backwards into a hornet's nest of youthful desire. I had no business—"

"Jerusalem. Madame Sylvie. You were so hungry with longing and you weren't wrong to follow it."

"Easy for you to say, Madeline. Easy for you to hold your friend's hand while she walks through fire. Safe from a distance."

"Don't judge my life," says Madeline. "I love you."

"I'm sorry," says Rosalie.

Nathan Samuels has granted Sol bereavement leave. After he recites Kaddish at morning services, Sol is free to go home. No sermons to prepare, nothing for him to do. A student rabbi fills in for the holidays. On Kol Nidre night, Sol waits at the door with Philip and Charlie, and turns to Rosalie.

"I presume you won't be joining us."

"As usual," she says.

"This time I won't even try."

After they leave, Rosalie stands on the porch and waits for the first notes of the prayer to pull her away from her house, her body, her life. Walter is far away now, a figment from another time. She wraps her arms around herself and when she hears the first words of Kol Nidre she goes back inside the house, sits down at the dining room table, and wets the white holiday tablecloth with her tears.

PART THREE

All the poems of our lives are not yet made.

—MURIEL RUKEYSER

THERE IS A BOAT

January 1974

Walter takes a hit of cardamom mixed with ginger and mace, places his palms flat on the floor, and springs his body into a headstand. Fluid as paint, he thinks. Still in the game. He lands on his feet and considers the drawing he wants to finish before the new semester begins. Walter is sketching Sonia as he remembers her, but he has no photograph to work from and his memory is vague. He has found the shape of her cheeks, her eyes, her cascading hair— certainly not a true representation, but he captured something.

When he returned home from Eden Ranch that last time Sonia began appearing in his dreams and she has become a frequent guest. She doesn't speak, just stands before him in the slip and sweater she was wearing when she was shot, and stares at him with cool indifference. At first Walter wasn't taunted by her appearance but the regularity of the dream seemed to him like a request, and he picked up a piece of charcoal and began. His studio has become a tangle of sketchbooks and ungraded papers; the books he and Rosalie tore through for their project are stacked in a corner, exactly where they left them.

The door has shut, he thinks. Eden Ranch was the ending, sealed by the fire. May life be sweet for the rebbetzin and her rabbi. May they grow old together in the place where their words bloom, where their Torah flowers and bears fruit. May they teach others. May they prosper without me.

Walter groans and shouts: No! He takes another hit of the spice and sorts through his pile of unopened mail. No papers; just a few journals and a letter postmarked from London.

January 4, 1974

Dear Walter,

You may remember me from the American Colony Hotel—I am Rosalie's friend. I don't think she has any intention of telling you directly, but she and Sol lost their son Lenny to Hodgkin's. As you can probably imagine, they are not shouldering this tragedy very well. I don't want to intrude but I believe Rosalie would like you to know what has befallen them.

Madeline Rosenblum

Walter phones Rosalie and insists she fly out to see him; Rosalie tells Sol that Madeline has invited her to London. At first Sol grumbles about the cost of the ticket and then asks how long she plans to be away. Rosalie arrives at Walter's empty studio on a

Monday afternoon. She lets herself in, lies down on her coat, and sleeps on the floor. When Walter arrives he lies beside her, rests his hand on her hair, and asks for nothing. He cancels classes and meetings for the rest of the week and he stays with Rosalie and offers no words. When they finally make love they become swimmers in a familiar ocean. Time loses its context and the dimensions of the studio become meaningless. Walter passes spices over Rosalie's body as he once did, and they kindle a hunger that rivals their days in the upper geniza and the lower geniza, only this time with a slow passion that carries its own language. They barely speak. They allow the peacocks to wander inside and scatter droppings and feathers. They forget to buy food and consume only what Walter has on hand in the studio: peanuts dipped in cumin, pickles and chopped herring from a jar, a bottle of Champagne, stale Saltines laced with cardamom and garlic.

The studio is their deserted mountain cabin, their geniza, their cave in the snow, every hidden place in the world and no place at all. It is the most ugly slum on earth and the most heavenly palace. At night Rosalie lifts her head from the futon and gazes at the city lights surrounding the East Bay. She believes the lights are stars and she is floating in the sky. Only their bodies are real. Rosalie is forty-six years old. Walter is fifty-four. They are alone for four days and their recognizable lives become obliterated, irrelevant. For both of them, this time is not joyful, but necessary.

Rosalie is scheduled to be picked up in two hours to make her flight home. She has not unpacked her bag, showered, or combed her hair since she arrived. Walter holds up a mirror so she can see how her hair is knotted into haphazard dreadlocks, her face parched and sallow.

"You were making love to a witch," she says.

"A goddess," says Walter. "My holy rebbetzin."

"What does that make you?"

"Not a rabbi."

"Thank God," says Rosalie.

"We are the excommunicated; free to live our prayers out of bounds."

"I thought you don't pray."

"My whole life is a prayer," says Walter. "So is yours."

"You sound like a rabbi."

Walter laughs. "Our transcendent trifecta."

"Don't bring Sol into this," says Rosalie.

"There is always a third," says Walter.

"What I felt for you was always separate from my marriage; it still is—"

"The third is not always a person."

"Oh. God in the room. The three under the wedding canopy. Pulpit words. Convenient lies. Take them and parade them before your students, Walter. They are free for the asking. I'm finished with all that."

She reaches for the bottle of Champagne and takes a swig. "No more lies," she says. "No more dried flowers falling out of a book in a geniza. No more holy rebbetzin channeling some precious wisdom. I fell into this world; an accident of lineage. The rabbi's daughter marries a rabbi. But it didn't have to be this way.

I could have become an archaeologist and my Torah would have been a threshing bowl I unearthed in Indonesia. I could have become a cellist and my Torah would have been Bach. The celestial answer would be unspoken; I'd have no use for these misleading words, this constant attempt at awkward metaphors. What a life that would be!"

"We traveled the route of words, darling. Both of us."

"Years ago I would have conjured some lovely quip to suggest a hidden truth. Such fun I had! But I'm too old to dredge up meanings. And yes, I love you. And I'm tired of this. And Sol—"

"You saved him."

"The purple binder, placed into the rabbi's hands by his loyal wife. Such a bullshit artist. And these congregants, dumb and hungry and needy, they hang on to my words, our words, his words. I despise them for it. Even now they expect us to show up and say, *Oh, we learned from our loss, oh, God took Lenny for a reason, oh, it all makes sense in some kabbalistic terrain.*"

"The myth of the eternal—"

"At least you don't pretend, Walter. Your God has no name. You don't parade your spiritual life in front of an eager audience."

"Saved by indirection and distance. Wise me."

"I used to envy you. I would picture you looking out over the Pacific, free to think your own unmollified, uncorrupted thoughts. I wanted to live in your brain, not this Shabbat-addled Torah-true fiction that I can't escape."

"It was your illusion to live, just like my illusion belongs to me. Does anyone live without some veneer of faith? Even the so-called faithless are circling a great mystery. No one is immune."

"We wanted it both ways, Walter. Spices for the body and poetic words about the soul to satisfy ourselves beyond the body. A seesaw of meaning."

"Wanted? Past tense, Rosalie?"

"Wanted. Want. But it's not only you that I want; there's something else I have no words for. Oh, Walter. Don't let me stop talking. I can't stop—"

Walter kisses Rosalie, and the sky darkens around them. The only place they can travel now is where their bodies take them and they travel there together all night.

Rosalie misses her plane.

Six weeks later Sol and Rosalie lie in bed. The sun has not yet risen but Sol kicks off the blanket and reaches for his tallit and tefillin. Rosalie grabs his hand, pulls him toward her, and whispers in his good ear.

"Is this some kind of biblical joke? You're on the pill!"

"I stopped taking it when Lenny got sick. What was the point? I was getting older and we barely bothered."

"Barely is not never and forty-six is not too old," says Sol. His eyes mist. "This is a blessing."

"Yes it is."

"We will have to tell Walter."

"What does he have to do with it?"

"He called me. Oh, Rosalie. I didn't tell you."

"You're telling me now."

"It was almost one in the morning, about six weeks ago, when you were in London. You had missed your flight and rescheduled for the next day, and I was up late, reading. I didn't even real-ize Walter knew about Lenny. When I heard his voice I started crying, and I cried and cried while he just listened on the other end of the phone. Hours of this, Rosalie, hours. And just before sunrise, I asked him if he was still listening. He was. And then he said to me—at least what I heard him say—*maybe you will be blessed with another child.*"

Rosalie closes her eyes. "We need to tell the boys."

"Yes," says Sol. "And Walter."

"You said that already."

"He wished it for us, Rosalie." He pulls her close and lifts her nightgown.

"You'll miss services."

"This is my prayer today," he says. "This, this, and oh, yes, this."

Three times in her life Rosalie leaned into the arms of a nurse and waited for an anesthesiologist to deliver an epidural into her lower spine to obliterate the pain of contractions. Three times she would wait for the needle that numbed her legs into tree trunks. Three times she would sit up in a hospital bed, Sol beside her, and watch the peaks on the monitor register the pain she did not feel, as if she were witnessing another woman's birth drama. Three times Stu Katz would mosey in and out of the room, nod, touch her shoul-der, and look at his watch. Now, in her eighth month, Rosalie lies back on the familiar exam table in Stu Katz's office, her belly cov-ered in goo, and listens to the *whosh-whosh* of the baby's heartbeat.

"Sounds good, rebbetzin," says Stu. "We're in the home stretch, no pun intended."

"Excellent," says Rosalie. "I'm pushing out this baby without any drugs."

"Are you out of your mind? I already scheduled a C-section. You're too old for a natural delivery."

"I was young enough to get pregnant! No C. And no drugs. It's my last chance to experience what I missed with the other three."

"You can read about it," he says. "We have advanced technology now, rebbetzin. The only women who aren't delighted by this are either shamefully primitive or emotionally unstable. You've been through this three times. This one will be no different, only surgical."

"No surgery. No epidural."

Rosalie thinks of Giselle at Eden Ranch, how she crouched on the ground and let her belly rest there like a pumpkin in a patch. She is certain that Giselle delivered in a squatting position, with Paul standing close by, ready to catch the baby.

"I must insist," says Stu.

"Are you telling me how to give birth to my own child?"

"This birth is more risky than I can explain."

"Try."

"I would need a medical dictionary and I'm sure the details would either bore or frighten you. Look, rebbetzin. You trusted me before, and my hands delivered your three boys into this world. I loved Lenny the most, and I will mourn with you and Rabbi Kerem for the rest of my life. Just trust me once more."

Rosalie glances at Stu's hands and realizes that he touched her children before she did. She notices the age spots on his knuckles and begins to feel nauseated.

"Give me my records," she says.

"What?"

Rosalie adjusts her bulk and rolls off the examining table.

"The folder with my charts. Every recorded heart beat, every added pound, every notch of blood pressure. Every damn detail."

"That's for me—"

She reaches to the counter and snatches the folder.

"Where are you taking that?"

"To a midwife," she says.

Stu laughs. "Good luck with that! And even if you find a misguided midwife who wants to stand in harm's way and risk a lawsuit, no one will treat you in your eighth month, not in your condition."

When she returns home Sol is standing in front of the garage, his hands on his hips.

"What do you think you're doing, Rosalie?"

"I'm going inside. I have to make some calls."

"Are you out of your mind? Stu Katz just phoned and told me what you're up to."

"What we are up to, Sol. We. Together."

"Are you risking my baby's life?"

"This is my baby, Sol. The last one."

"Our baby."

"Yes. And so will you help me find a midwife in this backwater suburb or are you going to wring hands with Stu Katz over my foolishness?"

––––––––––––

In her thirty-fifth week of pregnancy, Rosalie is learning how to breathe. A midwife named Gail instructs her to exhale, and Rosalie opens her mouth, panting like a thirsty dog.

"Natural breath," says Gail.

"You have to treat me like a first-time mother," says Rosalie. "I can't even remember how to exhale."

"You've been breathing all your life. Try it again."

"I have no patience for this." Rosalie bursts into tears. "Can I just have the baby now?"

"You're not in labor, honey. We don't make appointments for giving birth, and you have to learn a few things, be reminded of what your body already knows."

"It's just—"

"This was your choice, Rosalie. If you want to work with someone else I'm sure your doctor will take you back. Are you with me or not?"

"My husband is not the baby's father."

"And are you the mother?"

Rosalie smiles.

"Then look at me and breathe normally."

Rosalie reaches for Gail's hands and holds them tight.

"I'm sorry to blurt. It's so different with this one."

"No more sleepwalking. Now inhale and exhale. When the time is right, we'll see if you are dilated."

When Rosalie's water breaks later that week, Sol picks up the phone to call Stu Katz.

"What are you doing?" Rosalie screams. "If you call that idiot, I will chain myself to our bed and deliver this baby myself."

Sol puts down the phone, sits beside her, and waits. When the contractions begin she pushes her weight against his, then cries into his arms during the endless taxi ride to the birthing center.

Rosalie labors for seven hours. Sol stands in the corner of the room and davens. When she is fully dilated, Rosalie calls out her mother's name and asks Sol to explain why he couldn't be more like her father and why the fuck can't he quit being a lying rabbi and why did she marry him when she had been far too young to be a wife and too young to be a mother and look at them now, just look at this mess of a tribe. And when Rosalie closes her eyes she thinks of Walter at Eden Ranch calling out the names of the dead and she pictures the animals walking out of the forest and feels their eyes holding her in their creaturely gazes. With every contraction she believes her body will split open but then Gail calmly asks her to bring her breath to the center of this moment and they breathe in sync and this goes on for an eternity during which Rosalie trusts Gail's knowing instructions— *what choice does she have?*— but secretly longs for death or deliverance from this body that betrays her, cursing its history, spitting on her divided life, and then she finds a brief moment with the animals in the forest, locking eyes and then losing them again, until, miraculously, Gail shouts, "Push! Now!" and Sol repeats "Now!" Gail and Sol look at each other and reach for Rosalie's armpits. They pull her up to a crouching position and she grinds her feet on the sheet and groans in a voice she does not recognize as her own, and then she hears Gail say, "The baby is crowning," and Rosalie imagines her baby wearing a garland of flowers, and then Gail's hands catch the baby's head and she gently pulls and Sol cries out, "We have a girl, Rosalie. This one is a girl."

Rosalie asks Sol if he wants to choose the first name. "Maya," he says. He explains how the baby connects him to the prayer for rain he recited on Shemini Atzeret. As he stood on the bima in his white robe he glanced at Rosalie's swollen belly and asked God to provide the water—*mayim*—that would repair their broken souls. As the baby suckles from her breast Sol asks Rosalie to choose a middle name.

"Oh, there are so many," says Rosalie.

"We have our grandmothers—"

"No grandmothers."

"What then?"

Rosalie pauses.

"Sonia. I like the name Sonia."

"Significance?" asks Sol.

"It's a lovely name; that's all." She brushes her baby's soft cheeks and smiles. "It suits her, don't you think?"

Walter and Paul have box seats for the San Francisco Orchestra performance of Haydn's "Nelson Mass," a gift from one of Walter's wealthy doctoral students. Before the music begins, Paul peruses the libretto.

"We should write about this outing," he says. "An evening of music with the scholars of religion. Just look at the words of the Mass. Everything beautiful connects to God in some way. I know several editors who would be happy to publish our reveries in their journals."

"A night at the symphony as career promotion," says Walter.

Paul laughs. "It's not self-promotion. It's love. All this wonder, everywhere. Let's create a Music and Awe retreat at the ranch."

"You've been tainted by fatherhood."

Paul pulls a baby picture from his pocket and passes it to Walter.

"Jacob Rabindranath Richardson."

"Such an august name for an ordinary baby."

"My son is anything but ordinary. He's a cathedral of magnificence, Walter! A work of art! As exalted as the music that embraces our longings in this concert hall we share with thousands of strangers. Holiness is everywhere!"

Walter gazes at Paul. His mentor's white hair falls past his shoulders, the creases around his eyes are pronounced, his skin has darkened from the sun. The man with the brown felt hat has morphed himself yet again, while Walter still feels like a lost refugee who wanders around a foreign spice market, looking for the single hit of cardamom that will change his life.

During the Qui Tollis movement, Walter thinks of the daughter who isn't quite his. They named her Maya Sonia Kerem. *Her middle name is the thread that connects us,* Rosalie said to him on the phone. *Our little secret.* The baby belongs to Sol and Rosalie, his gift to them. Given in consolation, conceived with love. He closes his eyes and tries to still his mind by following the line of the chords that resolve and open, invite and sustain and bear so much beauty.

After the performance Paul says, "I listen to this music through my child's ears. I evaluate everything in my path with a single question: Is this worthy of bequeathing to Jacob Rabindranath? Nothing else matters to me now. My tolerance for mediocrity is nil. I want everything to be as transcendent as this Mass."

Walter stares ahead at the empty stage.

"I'm sorry," says Paul. "You have no idea what I'm talking about and I've intruded somehow. I try so hard to be good to you, and often feel as if I'm letting you down. I once promised you everything and look at you now."

"What do you see?"

"You are so very successful and so very alone."

"You made good on your promise," says Walter. "You gave me an American life."

"I hope it's been good for you."

"I have a daughter now," says Walter. "A newborn, a love child. She belongs to another family."

Paul takes Walter's hand and holds it against his wet cheek.

"You're crying," says Walter.

The concert hall empties out and the two of them sit in their seats until an usher asks them to leave.

Maya has colic. She screams more than she sleeps; Rosalie weeps from exhaustion, and longs for the brief spells when the baby gets milk-drunk at her breast and falls into a deep nap. She wonders if the incessant crying is a curse. Her boys were such easy babies, but Maya's face is set in a hard, wizened scowl. But one day, seemingly out of nowhere, Maya quits crying and her features soften. Rosalie gazes at her face with new understanding. The baby does not resemble Walter or Sol; Maya looks just like Rosalie. No one would ask her to explain why she doesn't look like her father, the rabbi. She would go to school and she would go to camp and on Shabbat she would listen to her father deliver words from the bima, and no one would ever doubt that she belonged to him.

After Sol bathes Maya at night, he wraps her in a towel, and sings, *Yessir, that's my baby, no sir I don't mean maybe, yessir that's my baby now—oww.*

On weekday afternoons Walter rushes home from the university and waits for Rosalie to call and tell him when he can come to New York to see Maya. He can't concentrate on grading papers; his class lectures are based on old notes, outdated research. He has abandoned his drawing of Sonia and he no longer invites models to the studio for inspiration or for sex. Weeks go by. Then months. Walter stares at babies in their strollers and asks their mothers and nannies, *How many months old? Why does the baby need a pacifier? Where did you buy such a pretty blanket?*

When Rosalie finally calls, Walter doesn't tell her he has been waiting. Years ago when they used to speak late at night, Rosalie's voice was sultry and the hours unfolded before them like an open field. But now she speaks quickly and her voice is harried.

"Tell me about her," says Walter.

Rosalie rushes through her words. "What's there to say? She's a baby. Delightful, cooing, babbling. A girl who notices everything."

"You talk so fast and say so little. Slow down. I want to hear this again."

"Oh, Walter. I've got six loads of laundry and Sol is at a meeting. There's no time."

"You sound different."

"I'm a new mother. Of course I sound this way."

"This is not new for you."

"But for you it is." Rosalie closes her eyes and waits. She wants to offer him something, but has no idea what to say.

"When, Rosalie?"

Two years later, Walter is invited to speak at a conference in Boston and he arranges for a stopover in New York. Walter and Rosalie sit side by side in a crowded terminal at JFK. They lightly hold hands while Maya runs in circles, pretending to be an airplane, shrieking with pleasure.

"You can play with her," says Rosalie. "Go ahead."

Walter hesitates at first, but then he lopes along, following Maya's stride, waving his arms, tears streaming down his cheeks. Rosalie glances at his face and winces. She remembers the names he called out at Eden Ranch, and how he filled the night air with words she didn't understand. She had never known anyone so very alone, and now he seemed more alone then ever.

Just before they part, Walter tells Rosalie that in Sanskrit, the word *maya* means illusion.

"Our daughter is no illusion," she says.

"I get it now."

"Get what?"

"Everything."

"It's about time—"

"—that I've become like the rest of you?" asks Walter. "Well, yes. I've arrived."

"Welcome to the aching world of ordinary mortals. Join our little party. Joy in one corner, heartbreak in another. Now help me trim the crust off their sandwiches and watch where you dribble peanut butter because half the children are allergic to it, and give me the back of your hand to wipe up their snot."

"Do you disdain me?"

Rosalie bursts into tears and Walter wraps his arms around her. He reaches for Maya, places her awkwardly between their bodies for a moment, kisses the top of her head, and then turns away.

Charlie and Philip live in Manhattan and only return to the house for holidays and an occasional Friday night dinner. To Charlie, Rosalie no longer seems like the same mother who raised them; he can barely remember the clothes she wore when he was Maya's age. Philip believes Maya is the replacement child for Lenny, and looking at her prompts old sadness. Maya's presence in the house makes her brothers feel as if the door to their childhood has been closed a second time; first when Lenny died, and now with this new addition.

At shul, Maya is everyone's child, passed from shoulder to shoulder, lap to lap. During services congregants reach out their hands to touch her. When she jumps on her lap, Missy shouts, "Oh, lucky me!" Bev calls her *my girl, my* maidele, *my Maya*.

On a Shabbat morning in the middle of winter, the synagogue is packed with bar mitzvah guests. While the boy gives his speech, Sol peers down from his velvet chair, Rosalie sits in the front row, and Maya loiters in the aisle, smiling at the congregants. Rosalie turns around to beckon Maya back to her seat, and she sees him in the very back of the sanctuary, wearing a suit, leaning against the doorframe. She looks again. A man in a suit, yes. But Walter? Rosalie rises and walks to the door but when she gets there the man is gone.

She never asks Walter if he passed through town that morning to have a glimpse of his little girl, but Rosalie believes that he did.

A year later Sol and Rosalie arrive in Jerusalem for the wedding of Missy and Nathan's son. Maya sits between her parents in the back of a taxi that races through traffic.

"Where are we staying?" asks Rosalie.

"The American Colony," says Sol. "Right near the wedding venue."

"Find another hotel. Please."

The driver glances at them in the rearview mirror.

"But we already have a reservation."

Rosalie stares out the window. She can't go back to the American Colony with her husband. That hotel belonged to Walter, not Sol. It was impossible to trespass from one life to another, as if she could put on a different skin. And yet she did it again and again, made the interweave of three strands possible and beautiful and wrong all at the same time. Those three words were her braid: *possible wrong beautiful, wrong possible beautiful, beautiful possible—*

"Not that hotel," says Rosalie.

"I thought you'd be pleased. Walter stayed there, as you recall. Anyway, the Samuels arranged everything; we're their honored guests."

"Of course we are. Nathan kept you employed so you could one day officiate at his kid's wedding, pro bono."

"They mean well, Rosalie; don't mock them."

Maya listens to her parents banter. The driver mutters something about the congested streets, takes a detour through Old Katamon and speeds through the narrow alleys, calling it a shortcut.

"Stop the car," says Rosalie. "Let me off here."

"Are you carsick?" asks Sol.

"No. I'll meet you later. The American Colony will do. Whatever. Just let me out."

"Mommy! I'm coming with you!" calls Maya.

"Rosalie—"

She leans into the window. "It's okay, Sol. I just need time to walk." Maya runs after Rosalie and asks where they are going.

"To visit an old friend."

Rosalie steps through the familiar blue door framed with bougainvillea. The courtyard is empty, and at first Rosalie doesn't notice Madame Sylvie sitting in a corner, shaded by a tree.

"That old lady scares me," whispers Maya.

Madame Sylvie approaches and kisses Rosalie on both cheeks.

"*Asseyez-vous.*" She turns to Maya and asks if she would like some cake. Maya nods. Her eyes follow the ancient woman as she disappears into the house and returns with a slice of lemon cake.

She takes a bite and tries to make out what Madame Sylvie says to her mother.

"I have thought of you often. I regret that I couldn't offer you an astonishment back then, nothing beyond a strange braid. You have suffered a great loss, *n'est-ce pas?*" Sylvie taps Rosalie's chin with her wrinkled hand, coaxing her to meet her eyes. "You lost a child; it is written on your face."

"Yes. A son. This is Maya, my little girl."

"This one is a great blessing."

Rosalie's body shakes and she begins to sob. Madame Sylvie leads her into a corner.

"*Ma chère,*" says Madame Sylvie. "A woman with two men has an impossible life. Better to suffer with one."

"It's too late."

"Close your eyes."

"I didn't come for an astonishment today."

"*Ça ne fait rien.* You will take what I have to offer."

"I don't want anything now."

"You walked through this door for a reason. Now shut your eyes. You and your daughter are alone in a dark cavern. You look around for one of your men but the darkness overwhelms you. You call their names but the sound of your own voice echoes off the cavern walls. Birds fly out. Your daughter holds your hand tightly. You keep walking until you find the opening to daylight."

"That's it? After all this time?"

"What do you expect?"

"I was hoping for guidance, for comfort."

"Then why did you come to me?"

After the wedding, Rosalie walks alone to the Western Wall and tucks a note between the stones: Ani Ma'amin. I believe. With all my strength I believe that the man I saw in the back of the sanctuary was Walter and he will always find his way to Maya. And one day she will understand.

Rosalie sits cross-legged in front of the Religion shelves at the new bookstore in town. She scans the books that bear Walter's name and reads sentences at random. She skips from page to page and book to book, listening for the cadence of his words, hoping to find him in the prose. But his books don't bear a trace of his voice, his touch. The purple binder was their secret project, separate from the books that define his career. She wishes his words would help her understand the shul she has grown to love, but she can't find the connection between Walter's temple of religious scholarship and her Temple Briar Wood. Walter held every religion in his brain and what does Rosalie hold? A paneled room filled with Jews who bring themselves inside every seventh day (a selected few, barely) and three times a year (a selected many, barely) whose yearnings and voices have become her entire geography. Walter's flights take him to New Delhi and Istanbul and Oxford and Paris for conferences and book parties, with stopovers in New York so he can appear like a ghost at the back of the sanctuary, behold the sight of his daughter, and then disappear. He lives with his peacocks in a studio where no one cooks a meal or shuckles in prayer or pours her little-girl body into his arms.

Rosalie's trajectory is limited to the cubits of a prescribed life that seems very small and quite vast. She sits on the floor of the bookstore and ponders this until closing time. She drives home, kisses her sleeping daughter, and slips into bed alongside her husband.

Every night after her bath, Maya runs into Sol's study and climbs onto his lap. He takes his tallit out of its bag and wraps it around both of them. Sol opens a volume of Talmud to a random page and points out the words to Maya. He lays his hand over hers and leads her fingers around the black letters, the two of them exploring where black ink meets white paper. Rosalie watches them from the corner of the room. Maya concentrates on the words and twirls her hair in ringlets just as Rosalie did when she learned with her father.

She'elah: How is the world passed down?

Teshuvah: Only the days can answer this question.

THE FOURTH NIGHT

December 1985

Time bites all of them. Years back, if Rosalie skipped Shabbat services for a few weeks, she would have missed the sight of a woman in the first blush of pregnancy, a baby taking its first steps at the edges of the sanctuary. Now she notices other passages of time—reading glasses, receding hairlines, the swell of congregants who rise to recite the Mourner's Kaddish for a parent, a sibling, a spouse. When she stands in the back and notices the slight insults of age that form on their skins—tiny brown spots on Missy's hands, the gradual sprawl of Serena's hips, the bulges that puff beneath Nathan's eyes—Rosalie realizes that time is biting her too. Her periods have eclipsed, her ankles have widened, the skin on her knuckles has thinned. Her own mother died two years ago, and Sol's mother soon after. She never arranged another rendezvous with Walter because Maya was getting older and she did not want to invite the inevitable query.

She sends Walter a postcard:

We were able to build a bridge for ourselves but
we cannot build one for her. She doesn't know
you. How I wish this were otherwise.

R.

At Maya's birthday parties, Rosalie invites her to make a wish before blowing out the candles. Every year, Maya closes her eyes and tries to envision something she wants, but she can only imagine things that defy ownership. *I wish for white flowers. I wish for an arched doorway. I wish for a footpath that crosses a river.* She once wished she could meet Lenny, but she realized that was impossible and cancelled the wish.

After one of her parties, Sol asked Maya what she wished for. She didn't think he would understand the flower, the doorway, and the footpath, so she said, *to hear a great symphony.* The next week Maya sat sandwiched between Sol and Rosalie at a New York Philharmonic performance of Mahler's Ninth, which felt unbearably long and made her restless. When Sol asked if she liked the music, Maya said, *I'd like it better if the music were made of words.* Sol smiled and turned to Rosalie. *She is ready to study Talmud. Our little girl is just like me.*

When Maya is eleven she overhears her mother talking on the phone late at night. "Maya will know everything. We will figure this out." When Rosalie hangs up, Maya asks why she was talking about her and why she looks so sad.

"That was an old friend, buttercup. Someone far away," says Rosalie.

"Madeline from London?"

"Yes, honeybunch. You guessed it."

Maya knows her mother is not telling the truth. She can hear it in her voice. When she talks to Madeline, her mother seems to be unloading secrets. When she talked to this friend, her mother sounded sultry; her voice seemed to caress the words as if she didn't want to let them go. This friend was not Madeline.

She often spies on her parents at night, sneaking up on them in every room except their bedroom. She watches her mother join her father in his study, wrap her arms around his neck and plant a kiss on his good ear. She watches them dance to Frank crooning "Fly Me to the Moon," Leonard smoking "Dance Me to the End of Love," Dionne singing "I Say a Little Prayer." After, they sit side by side on the sofa and study the liner notes to their favorite albums, reading the lyrics to each song as if they are studying a sacred text together. One day she saw her mother pick up an unopened letter with a postmark from India and her father snatched it out of her hands. *The letter is for me, Rosalie. This one is mine.*

Rosalie tells Sol she wants to offer a class on Hasidic thought, spin out the teachings from the Ishbitzer she learned from her father. She has three students: Missy, Serena, and Bev, and she sets out a plate of homemade cookies, along with a source sheet. While Rosalie is teaching her class, Sol sits in his study and retrieves a letter he received from Walter a few months back. He holds the thin paper to his nose, sniffing the chalky aroma of onionskin and dried ink. The letter is tinged with words of affection: *How we are woven together, I have not forgotten the geniza, I love you both always.* He reads it again and again, permitting himself to feel a semblance of joy at their rekindled friendship. Now it is possible, he thinks. He picks up the phone and dials Walter's number.

"Thank you," says Sol.

"For what?"

"For your letter from Varanasi. For the sermons. For letting me cry on the phone for hours and hours after Lenny died."

Walter laughs. "That's a long list!"

"*Dayenu!*" says Sol. "Any one of those would have been more than enough." His voice breaks.

"How is your messy brew these days?"

"Sometimes I feel as if I'm racketeering; other times I feel as if I'm doing holy work. I marvel at the rabbis who are good at this—their sincerity is completely aligned with their intent and they become masters of spiritual leadership. But I'm not one of them; I'm the other kind."

"Then why bother?"

"What else would I do now? It's a soft job. I'm supporting my family, my commute is a few steps across a parking lot, and my president leaves me alone. I have time to study now and I'm finally dipping into the Zohar!"

"You? Mysticism?"

"Yes!" Sol reaches for a book, opens it to a flagged page. "Listen to this. *This mystery is that the flowing, gushing river never ceases; therefore, a human should never cease his river and source in this world, so that he grasp it in the world that is coming.*"

"You're practically quoting Tagore! From *Gitanjali*. Listen: *All things rush on, they don't stop, they don't look behind, no power can hold them back, they rush on.*"

"Remarkable," says Sol, beaming. He rises from his desk chair and spins in a circle. Their minds are in sync again, he thinks, just like when they were young.

"You seem much better now," says Walter.

"I owe it to my daughter," says Sol. "Maya brings us such joy. When she learns Talmud with me I feel utterly complete. For a preteen, she discerns startling patterns in the text."

Walter doesn't respond.

"Are you still there?"

"Of course," says Walter. "I'm always here for you."

"When will I see you again?"

"I don't know."

"So find a way to know. Make time for your old chavrusa."

"Look. I have a two-day conference in New Haven next week, and plan to spend a night at a colleague's place in Manhattan. I was hoping to see——"

"Perfect! Next week is Hanukkah. I'll take you to the symphony. My treat!"

"We don't have to go out——"

"Of course we don't. It's better that way."

"Next Tuesday night, then. West End Avenue at 71st. I'll call you with the exact address."

"Rosalie teaches on Tuesday night."

"I know——"

Their wires have gotten crossed, thinks Walter, and he blames this on the Ishbitzer. He had spoken to Rosalie only an hour ago, told her how he had arranged to give a paper at Yale as an excuse to pass through New York for a single night. *But I can't cancel my class,* she had said. *I need to teach my students about Ha-nukkah. I prepared such a great source shet on the hidden light. Oh, I'm sorry. I wish I could see you.* And now Walter would have Sol, who would be eager to resume their Zohar-Tagore riff, and share some jazzy theological be-bop.

If back at the Seminary, someone had played a reel of their future lives, would he have believed that Sol would carry the whole messy braid of them in his arms? Walter sometimes thinks of Sol as Sisyphus, lugging a heavy sack up a steep, rocky incline. He has bouts of relief—*the Zohar! Maya!*—but inevitably the load overtakes him. Walter wants to see Sol, but he had earmarked this single night in town for Rosalie. He hadn't seen her in so long and he wanted to ask if Maya laughed like she did, or if the swell of his daughter's cheekbones resembled his own.

Maya is learning to sing. She lip-syncs to Linda Ronstadt and Phoebe Snow, belts show tunes in the shower, and occasionally joins her father on the bima, leading the congregation in a folksy rendition of Adon Olam. Every Tuesday afternoon she has a voice lesson with Lucie Morgan, who specializes in training the vocal chords of young singers. Maya doesn't care about the hour she spends running through arpeggios with the legendary Miss Morgan, but she relishes the forty-seven-minute train ride from the leafy platform of the Briar Wood station to Grand Central, where she delights in the smells of diesel, pretzel salt, and the cologne of the men who take the train to work. Her own father's commute is a brief meander across a parking lot, and he never wears cologne.

On the fourth night of Hanukkah, a Tuesday, Sol offers to drive Maya to her lesson. "My old chavrusa is passing through town," he says. "And he's staying only a block away from Miss Morgan's studio. So close!"

"I can take the train, Abba."

"I'd like you to meet him, even for a second. We'll light candles when we get home."

She pouts.

"Please, sweetheart. I ask you for so little. And I often get bored in the car without company."

Maya never thinks of her father as bored. For as long as she can remember, he has carried a volume of Talmud in his arms, opening it to a random page and running a finger across the trail of letters. Sometimes she catches him looking forlorn. When she was small she would climb onto his lap and nestle herself under his chin until he would wrap his arms around her and soften.

At times, her father seems to be weighed down by sorrow. Even though the sad story of her dead brother lingers in their house—old family photos and sports trophies line the shelves—her mother seems too busy and distracted to let loss pull her down. But Sol swims in a moody haze that sometimes surfaces as deep misery, other times as a frisson of worry. And yet, when he stands on the bima and gazes at her and Rosalie, he seems tethered to happiness, at least for a moment. The rabbi needs his girls, Maya thinks. We save him from himself.

"Okay, Abba. I'll go. For you."

As they cruise down the Hutchinson Parkway Sol turns to her.

"Do I look old to you, sweetheart? My friend hasn't seen me in so long. Tell me, how do I look? Younger than Nathan? How about Marv?" He smoothes his hair, glances at himself in the rearview mirror.

"Younger than your congregants, for sure. But older than Mom."

"Everyone looks older than your mother."

Maya laughs. "Sometimes I think even I look older than Mom!"

"That's because you have an old soul, sweetheart."

When they pull up to Lucie Morgan's building, Sol hands Maya a slip of paper with an address. "Meet me after your lesson and I'll introduce you."

She steps out of the car and then turns back and smiles. "You look good, Abba. Young. Like a rabbinical student."

He winks.

After forty-five minutes of deep breathing and an exhausting arpeggio practice that makes Maya wish she had cancelled her lesson, she walks down the block and waits for the doorman to buzz her up to the apartment where she is to meet her father.

"No answer," says the doorman, "but you may as well go up."

Maya hesitates outside the apartment and listens to the voices on the other side of the door.

"I missed you terribly. Who we once were. More than I can ever explain—"

"I remember everything, Sol."

"My God! Look at you!"

Maya knocks gently. Sol opens the door, and a barefoot man wearing a brocade Indian tunic and tailored pants stands before her. Maya notices his high cheekbones, then glances down at his feet. So familiar, she thinks. Famous? Ballet famous? The choreographer from the PBS special she watched? She stares at his bare feet. He can't possibly be a dancer because his feet are not worn and calloused, but smooth. Is this her father's study partner? Someone he knew in rabbinical school? *Him*?

"You must be Maya. I'm Walter. We met when you were small—"

"My father talks about you all the time."

"Actually, we haven't met," stammers Walter. "Not exactly."

"And not approximately either." She turns to Sol. "We should go, Abba. Mom's class will be over soon and we have to light—"

Sol turns to Walter. "Hanukkah."

"I'm aware of it," says Walter.

Sol excuses himself to go to the bathroom, and Walter and Maya are alone. Walter stares intently at her face, as if she is a statue in a museum. His hands are clasped behind his back and a faint smile softens his mouth. Maya gazes straight ahead and holds herself perfectly still. He is just like a strange congregant, she thinks, only he is wearing a costume and resembles that choreographer from the PBS special.

Walter angles his face close to the ends of her hair and inhales, as if trying to pick up the scent of her shampoo. Uh-uh. Too close, too weird, too costumey, she thinks, flinching.

She hears the sound of the toilet flush and sighs. Sol emerges and clears his throat.

Thank God, she thinks. Both she and Walter turn to face Sol. "We should go, Abba," she says. "It's late."

Silence.

Sol is staring at her and at Walter. He squints, takes a step back, and then squints again. His eyes are fixed on Walter's face and hers. He bites his lip, then audibly exhales and sighs.

"Earth to Abba," says Maya.

Sol wipes his eyes and Maya can't tell if he is wiping away tears or sweat.

"Abba!"

"Yes—"

"We need to go—"

Silence.

Now, she mouths.

Silence.

Maya rolls her eyes. "I'll be waiting outside." She turns to Walter and waves. "Nice to meet you."

"Wait, Maya!" calls Sol.

She lets herself out and then lingers for a moment, picking up fragments of the muffled conversation on the other side of the door.

"Go home and light your candles. Maya is waiting for you."

"My daughter—"

"Of course, Sol. Yours and—"

"Rosalie's and—"

"Yes. Now take her home and make your holiday."

The door opens and Sol walks out, his face streaming with tears.

The car is thick with silence.

"Earth to Abba!" calls Maya.

Sol turns to her and faintly smiles.

"Your friend is an interesting dresser," she says.

Sol stares at the road and doesn't respond. Here comes his haze of moodiness, she thinks. The capsule of sadness that she can't identify or name. She begins to say something and then stops herself. She reaches into her bag for headphones, clasps them on her ears, and leans her head against the window.

After they pull into the driveway, Sol turns to Maya. He tenderly takes her cheeks in his hands and lays a kiss on her forehead.

Rosalie sits at the kitchen counter, the phone cord wrapped around her arm, wincing as she listens to Walter sob. He had phoned right after Sol left the apartment. "I wasn't prepared to meet her today. All these years I longed to see Maya again, with you. Sol didn't tell me she would be stopping by, and then she arrived and I said the wrong thing and I couldn't take my eyes off her and stood too close, and now I feel so empty—"

Rosalie gasps. "I'm so sorry. Sol has no idea—"

"Past tense."

"Are you sure?"

"Your husband isn't blind. Stop underestimating him."

"But—"

"He and I go back a long way, Rosalie."

"But you can't be sure."

"Oh, Rosalie. Our daughter is so lovely. I only wish—"

"Please don't, Walter. Please—"

Maya unpacks her book bag, sings a brief arpeggio, glances at the clock. Can't they light already, get this little ritual over with so she can do her homework and listen to her new Flora Purim record? Her parents occupy opposite ends of the house: Rosalie at the kitchen counter, holding the phone in her hand; her father sitting in his study, hunched over a book.

She sits on the top stair and calls out, "It's late! We have to light! Abba? Mom?"

No one answers.

"Mom? Abba?"

I can light without them, she thinks. I can make myself a dismal little Hanukkah party, and then get down to finishing my homework.

Sol emerges and rests a hand on Maya's shoulder. "It's time," he says.

Rosalie walks toward Maya, her eyes puffy and red. The three of them face the clay family menorah. Maya places the pastel candles in their holders, carefully arranging the colors in a patterned sequence. She stands between her parents and begins to recite the blessings and then her father joins in quietly, and then her mother. Sol lights the *shamash*, the server candle, and then uses it to kindle the others. They stand in silence and watch the candles burn down, each adrift in separate glimmering thoughts. Maya tries to guess what her parents could be thinking, what sparks they see in these delicate flames. Sol once taught her that Hanukkah symbolizes the infinite potential of the human spirit, but she has no idea how the three of them connect to anything beyond this small, sad moment.

She'elah: What binds a constellation of stars?

Teshuvah: An astronomer explains the properties of shared light. A poet ponders the revealed and the concealed. A child dreams of a path she cannot yet see.

THE BRACELET

January 1987

Sol praises Rosalie for her ongoing class on Hasidic thought, then asks if she can teach something with broader appeal, like tennis.

"After teaching them about the *Mei HaShiloach*, you want me to play tennis with them? I've never even held a racket! Don't you know me anymore?"

"How about a cooking class? You can teach them how to use a wok. Or play cards! Make friends with them somehow. Nathan wants us to become more of a community, raise the bar for membership. Think we're up to it?"

Rosalie scowls. "Why can't I teach a real class again?"

"To the same three students? No, sweetheart. That's not enough."

Rosalie hosts a weekly mah-jongg game for the Sisterhood, and serves coffee and fresh strawberries because all the women are dieting. As their long nails click against the tea-stained tiles the women tell Rosalie about impending divorces, ailing parents, wayward children who marry out of the faith. Over the months these talks become laden with details that are conveyed with furtive glances and Rosalie listens to every story, offering bits of practical guidance and occasional Hasidic sayings.

Maya joins her mother and the women at these confessional mah-jongg games. As they talk she folds empty Sweet'N Low packets into perfect squares and builds tiny pink paper houses on the table. Maya ponders what these women seem to be looking for. Serena needs to apply for a passport and move far away from Briar Wood. *She is eager to embrace the world,* Maya thinks. Missy Samuels no longer sleeps with Nathan. *She needs to find surprise in her life and teach it back to him.* Beth, Natalie, and Sue repeat the gossip they overhead at the Cosmos Diner. *They need to feed their hungry imaginations with art.* These women want Rosalie to wake them up, tell them she understands, that she believes—with absolute certainty—that everything in their lives will turn out all right. Maya thinks her mother is too reticent with them, that she could provide more than strawberries, coffee, and an occasional proverb, but she holds back.

At times the house seems to Maya like a palace of countless stories—the ancient ones from the Bible and Talmud that she learns with her father—and the stories the women share over mah-jongg and strawberries. The stories that her mother whispers into the telephone late at night, either to Madeline or to someone else. The love stories in the songs that her parents play—each one a tale of desire set to music. Sometimes Maya drifts off to sleep and imagines that all the yearnings and all the stories that course through the walls of the house are one single story, and no matter how much she listens, she will never know everything.

Walter calls Rosalie and announces he is going to Bombay on a two-year research grant.

"That's good," she says. "I feel less confused when you're stuck on the other side of the world."

"It's better for me too," he says. "Time passes differently in India."

"She is growing up so fast."

"Once I had less sadness," he says. "Before her."

Rosalie closes her eyes and imagines Walter in his studio, holding the phone, a sketchbook resting near his bare feet, the sil batta and spice jars lined up like silent witnesses to his youth. His daughter would always be an abstraction to him; he had missed out on all the ordinary moments that marked her childhood—ripped tights and car rides, nut-free cakes and inside jokes, report cards and leaky pens, and at night, the remains of her half-finished milk souring at the bottom of a jelly glass. When Rosalie would drive Maya to her voice lessons in the city, Maya would sing "The Song that Never Ends" in a continuous tedious loop, and just when Rosalie thought she would go mad, Maya was old enough to take the train to her lessons, and Rosalie was alone in the car without the song and without Maya, and she hummed that ridiculous song and made herself weep with longing. Walter had missed out on holding the pudgy fingers that began so tiny and so eager, their potential hushed inside invisible molecules, until one day Rosalie looked at Maya's hands and noticed how her small wrists bore the long fingers of a young woman, and she wondered how that happened while the song that never ends never quite ended, until it did.

"Do you have any idea what I used to find at the bottom of her knapsack, Walter?"

"Tell me."

"Tic Tacs, paper clips, pretzel crumbs, an Origami fortune teller, a troll with pink hair, a stale wad of Silly-Putty, and a barrette made of silver glitter."

"Significance?"

"Nothing that would seem to matter. Just the details. All the good parts."

Walter's voice becomes professorial. "The years tumble for all of us. Those of us who remain."

"Walter?"

"Yes, darling?"

"I want to make it right for you. Arrange a stopover in New York on your way back from India. Day or night—whenever. I'll find a way to bring her to the airport. She's grown taller since you saw her. So lovely, so assured. She's transcended us in some way. You'll see soon enough."

Walter dreads the long flights and hopscotch layovers, yet every time he travels to India he feels as if he is returning to his true home. When he and Paul published their translations of Tagore's poetry, they co-taught a seminar at Shantiniketan and lectured in New Delhi. His research on cremation introduced him to Varanasi, a city he has grown to love. But this is Walter's first return to Bombay. When he walks past the spice markets he looks for a glimpse of his younger self among the throng of tourists. These well-fed Westerners wear saris and kurtas with cameras dangling from their necks. The sound of Hebrew is everywhere; young Israelis storm the markets.

At a silversmith's stall, Walter sorts through a pile of bracelets and tries to picture Maya's wrists—how small they seemed. He wonders if her hands would have grown bigger in two years, and what size bracelet would fit her now. He stops a girl who seems to be Maya's age and asks, How old are you? Can I see your hands? Do you like silver? He chooses a small bracelet and mails it to Rosalie with a note: Please give this to her at the right time.

A week before Passover Rosalie is alone in the house, taping paper to the cabinet shelves. Her forearm is ringed with a roll of masking tape, the unofficial ornament she wears to prepare her kitchen for the ritual reenactment of the Exodus. Each year she explains to the Sisterhood women that it's best not to ask too many questions about Passover preparation, but rather meditate on every meaningless tear of the masking tape that is not prescribed by law but seems driven by the body's understanding of tradition.

The phone rings but Rosalie doesn't pick up. Just before Passover the congregants call with their picayune questions about how to kasher the handle of a pot and if wine glasses should be soaked in cold water for three days or in warm water for two. They crawl out of the sidewalk with their questions—those who never inquired about a single aspect of Jewish law, and those who slammed the door in Sol's face when he would try to gather a minyan on Shabbat morning. Rosalie listens to the sequence of rings and finally answers.

"Rabbi Central, rebbetzin speaking."

"Is that you, Rosalie? It's Paul Richardson, Walter's friend. From the ranch."

"Paul! Of course. How is your family?"

"Our son Jacob is a father now."

Rosalie doesn't respond. She twirls her masking-tape bracelet and glances at the rolls of shelf paper scattered on the floor. This holiday is beyond ridiculous, she thinks. Maybe Paul can invite them to Eden Ranch; the Kerems can hold a karmic seder in the circle of stones they called the amphitheater.

"Listen to me, Rosalie. Last month Walter was hit by a car in Bombay. He was biking on a crowded road and probably sniffed something in the distance and got mired in his thoughts. There were witnesses but no single story."

Rosalie moans.

"I handled the cremation."

She slams her arm on the counter, crushing the roll of tape.

"No, Paul. It can't be—"

"I'm so sorry. I loved him more than I can say."

"You have no idea——"

"It was way too soon. He crossed over before his time."

Rosalie drops the phone, lays her head on the countertop and screams into the granite.

"Are you still there, Rosalie?"

She stiffens up, holds the handset to her mouth, and whispers. "He has a daughter."

"Yes," says Paul. "I know."

Rosalie winds the phone cord tightly around her arm until it bites into her skin, and then loosens it. Why now, when she had finally figured it out? He would have returned from India via New York; she and Maya would have met him at the airport, just as before. But this time Rosalie would tell Maya that this man was important to their family in so many ways. Simple as that. And Maya, such a wise girl, would look at the man she had already met and everything would become perfectly clear.

Rosalie finds a napkin and a pen, and writes: *Walter is gone.* She reads the word *gone*, then x's out the line, and replaces it with the words he would have used: *Walter has crossed over.* She folds the napkin in half and writes SOL on the flap.

She grabs the car keys and without putting on her shoes, drives down the Hutchinson and the Henry Hudson, and parks outside the Seminary building. She sits behind the wheel and sobs, and when she catches her breath she looks up, hoping to see Walter walk out of the building, wearing a green kurta and cloth shoes. *I've been waiting, Rosalie. Lower geniza or upper. Both, Walter. I want both. Sol and Walter. Milk and meat. Always both. No limits.*

Sol arrives home from a meeting and notices the car is gone. Out shopping, he thinks. A dress for the seder or something new for Maya to wear to all those bat mitzvah parties. Sol would never admit this to Maya or to Rosalie, but compared to other girls her age, Maya appears dowdy in the calico dresses and chukka boots she wears; she dresses like an Orthodox girl, all buttoned up. Well, he thinks, her time will come.

His enterprising wife left the rolls of shelf paper scattered on the floor, God bless her. The shelves are almost lined, all dressed up for the holiday. The preparations will be finished just in time, as always; the miracle of Passover will be complete. He finds the napkin note on the counter. At first he doesn't allow himself to recognize the name Walter and then he doesn't understand why Rosalie wrote *crossed over*—a phrase she never used. But then Sol reads again, quite soberly, and lets the words sink in. He sits on the bottom stair, waiting for tears to come.

The rest of the day and evening Sol drives around Briar Wood, looking for his wife. After a few hours of circling the dark streets, Sol returns home and walks up to Maya's room. He gazes at his sleeping daughter, kisses her forehead, and leaves. Sol spends the rest of the night weeping silently on the sofa, waiting for Rosalie to return.

Just before dawn, he rises and crosses the parking lot to the shul. He enters the sanctuary and finds Rosalie in a middle row, slightly disheveled, sitting perfectly still. Sol takes the seat directly behind hers and she reaches her hand toward his. When the men arrive for morning services, they linger in the back of the sanctuary, unsure if they should disturb the rabbi and his wife. After a few moments, Rosalie and Sol rise together and walk home, hand in hand.

Later that morning Rosalie marches into the office of Maya's school.

"I'm signing out my daughter, Maya Kerem."

"Doctor's appointment? Death in the family?" asks the secretary.

"No. Yes. Sort of," mutters Rosalie.

"I'm so sorry."

Maya trudges in. "Who died? What? Are you serious, Mom?"

"Please come with me, Maya."

"I can't. I have chorus practice today and it's my turn to present my book report and it's Deena's birthday and—"

"I signed you out already."

"Who died?"

"Everyone you know is fine."

"Then go home. I'll see you later."

"I need to be with you."

"Are you pulling me out of school just because—"

"Yes, Maya. Just because."

"I used to wish you would pick me up for no reason at all. I once would have wanted this," she says. "But not today."

"Please."

"Where are we going?"

Rosalie drives and Maya fumes silently in the passenger seat. "Can we at least spend our little date at the mall? I need a dress for Deena's bat mitzvah."

"Who?"

"Wake up, Mom. Deena. My best friend since second grade. And stop looking at me like that."

"Like what?"

"You keep staring at me."

The darkened store reeks of overly spiced teen perfume and Led Zeppelin blasts from the sound system. Maya searches for dresses to try on and Rosalie sits in a leather chair, waiting to say what she has no words for. Her head pounds and she shuts her eyes to block out the throbbing music and then opens them to block out the pain. She pushes her fingers onto her eyelids and presses, sealing her eyes shut.

Maya is alone in the dressing room and she feels bereft. Her mother usually follows her inside and replaces the clothes on their hangers. Maya tries on a simple flowered dress, looks in the mirror, and pouts. Too childish. She wore a calico dress to her own bat mitzvah and to every party since, but Deena is her best friend and she wants to look more sophisticated this time— elegant, fancy. *Dressed*, as her mother would say. *You should look put together. Like a young lady.*

She tries on a black cocktail dress with spaghetti straps and rubs her hands over her hips. Her father would never approve of her wearing this to her best friend's bat mitzvah. It's about time, she thinks, admiring her reflection in the mirror. Her friends wear slinky dresses and heels to these parties and Maya has been slow to catch on. Enough, she thinks. Her mother is too distracted to refuse her and her father would never say no to her. He never does. She is his best girl, his occasional chavrusa. *Don't you want to learn Talmud with someone your own age?* she once asked him. *You get this*, he said. *Learning with you makes me feel young again, like everything is possible because we can interpret these ancient words together. We are creating a bridge, Maya. One day you will understand.*

When Rosalie opens her eyes, Maya is standing before her, modeling a black silk cocktail dress that makes her look like a woman. Rosalie shakes her head.

"It's too revealing."

"But how do I look?"

"Turn."

Maya spins around slowly and then faces her mother again.

"You hold his beauty," says Rosalie.

"Whose?"

"Your father's."

Maya rolls her eyes.

"Whatever."

"You want it?"

"I do, but it's expensive."

"What is?"

"The dress, Mom!"

"Yes, of course." Rosalie stammers. "I have something for you to wear with it, sweetheart." She reaches into her pocketbook and pulls out a silver bracelet nestled in tissue paper. She hesitates and then places it in Maya's hand.

"It matches nicely, don't you think?"

Maya unwraps the paper and slips it on.

Days later, at their family seder, Rosalie stares at Maya's bracelet. It fits her perfectly, neither too loose or too snug. Walter had noticed her small wrists; a random observation on a misbegotten

Hanukkah night. She gazes at Maya, sandwiched between Charlie and Philip, her voice rising boisterously with every verse of Dayenu, her brothers banging their hands on the table. *She will know and she won't know*, thinks Rosalie. *Both at the same time.*

When Maya stops singing for a moment she realizes that her father isn't singing, and he barely claps his hands. She looks at Rosalie and notices that she too has dropped out of singing the endless refrains of this melodic thank-you note to God—freedom from slavery, manna in the desert, Shabbat and Torah and the Land of Israel—every gift bearing just one more and then one more. Maya tries to meet her mother's eyes and invite her back to this moment, but Rosalie gazes out toward the window, lost in a private dream.

Months later Rosalie stands in the back of the paneled sanctuary on a Shabbat morning, looks at the faces in the room, and reflects on the narrowing field of her life. This place is her ashram, her Shantiniketan, the place to consider what she does not think of as God but rather as Desire—the desire that sets all things in motion. She stares at these people with whom she has walked through the chapters of her life, each of them aging in sync with one another and yet—despite the mah-jongg confessions and shared life-cycle events—she barely knows them.

Prayer is impossible for Rosalie, but she sees now that it is impossible for all of them, impossible for anyone. Her daughter and her friends use this room as a showcase for their blooming bodies. If her grown sons were home for a holiday (they rarely are) they would roll their eyes at the modest gathering and they would think, *such sad lives.* Why do these people come here to listen to Rabbi Sol Kerem preach about God when the world is so vast with possibility?

It's inexplicable to her, even after all these years. Faith becomes a habit that cannot be explained. A few of the congregants practice it like a musical instrument; they open the black prayer book and shuckle from side to side as someone once taught them. They place themselves in this paneled room once a week, take the same seats. Bev sits to the right of Serena; Missy and Nathan Samuels claim the second row. One Shabbat after another, these people show up at the shul for reasons that cannot be explained in words and if Rosalie would ask, *Why are you here?,* Bev would laugh and say, I *come because I used to bring my father, may he rest in peace.* And Serena would say, I *come to see you, of course, now turn around, I love that dress.* And Missy would strike a pose because she needs to be seen, and the more she is seen the more proof she has that she is alive, truly alive. The great mystery is played out in Temple Briar Wood week after week, year after year. The pulsing heart of theology drums its beat in this paneled room. Missy and Nathan and Serena and Bev—who now sits in the row that was once designated for her father's wheelchair—are to Rosalie a sampling of souls that express the unquenchable thirst of humanity.

Walter wrote about this in the introduction to one of his books; Rosalie remembers when he told her the story.

On a research trip to Varanasi I approached a man who was bathing in the Ganges, the ashes of the freshly cremated bodies floating around his legs. He was wearing a Western suit and tie and I was surprised to see him standing in the water with the legs of his pants rolled up. When I asked him why he said, "My father bathed in the Ganges and called it holy. So at first I came here for my father, to understand the heart of the man who raised me. And then I came back again and looked at the people who were lifting their tunics and walking into the filthy river and I admired their faces. And then I realized I was one of them. A cesspool became love became dignity became everything that mattered. Love in this dirty holy water. Love on my body. Love on the faces of the people who are doing this with me, who are me, who could be me, and the dead who once loved this world too, who once stood in this water, just like me."

By the time she turns fifteen, Maya has colonized all the upstairs bedrooms. When she wants to write in her journal she encamps in Lenny's old room and burns white musk. When she wants to listen to music and burn sandalwood, she stretches out on the butterfly chair in Charlie and Philip's room. The entire second floor of the Kerem house smells of the incense Maya buys off the street in Greenwich Village on Sundays. She no longer takes voice lessons with Lucie Morgan but spends every Sunday carousing Manhattan record stores, spending her babysitting earnings on albums by Flora Purim, Nina Simone, Miriam Makeba, the Bulgarian Women's Chorus. After, she rides the subway simply to look at the people who surround her in the crowded cars and test out her theory of Everyone-Is-Beautiful-on-This-Train.

Maya holds a book in front of her nose, gazes up, and glances from face to face she alights on someone who seems wounded in some harsh way. Then she stares, trying to locate what shines from within. An inkling of longing. Someone turning the page of a book, yearning to find out what happens next. A harried woman who combs the knots from her hair, a student who pinches the pleats of his jeans, a homeless man who wipes crumbs off his beard and then sniffs his palm, looking for the remnants of the roll he ate for breakfast. Every Sunday Maya rides the #1 local from 14th Street up to the Bronx, gazing at the faces of strangers until she finds some degree of beauty underneath what seems so broken, so lost, so unbearably sad. She thinks of the congregants and their brave lives in Briar Wood, dressing up for shul every Shabbat morning and listening to her father reach for a bit of wisdom that could wake them up in some way. They were also a little bit broken and a little bit radiant—often both at the same time. Just like her parents. Just like everyone.

One night after she finishes her homework, Maya joins her father in the study.

"Pull up a chair," he says. "I miss learning with you."

"Okay. One for old times, Abba."

"She'elah," says Sol. "Why do we count the days of the Omer between Passover and Shavuot?"

Maya answers, "Teshuvah: We measure days to fathom the mysteries of time. We throw ourselves against the truth of numbers to block out the unforgiving light."

Sol looks at Maya and thinks of the contents of the purple binder, the frolic of words that saved him and his rabbinate.

"Did you come up with that idea yourself or did you read it somewhere?"

Maya smiles. "All mine."

Sol kisses the top of her head. "You're so much like him."

"Who?"

"Walter. The man you met. Always full of surprises. When we were young he and I traveled through the texts—"

Maya thinks of the strange barefoot man who gazed at her, and how she heard words spoken on the other side of a door, words she vaguely remembers but didn't understand.

She wraps her arms around his neck. "Just like we do," she says.

Rosalie phones Madeline every week. She sits at the kitchen counter late at night and winds the cord around her arm as she once did when she talked to Walter. Sometimes Madeline asks Rosalie how she copes in the wake of so much loss. Rosalie gives the same answer every time: *If I asked myself such a question I would not survive my life. I just keep going.* But she doesn't tell Madeline how grief ripples through her body and surprises her at least once a day. When she walks past Lenny's old bedroom she feels a great weight in her belly that she recognizes as the immovable ballast of sorrow. It never dissipates and makes her feel old and heavy, like an ancient hag. When she thinks of Walter—*of course I do, Madeline*—she is overcome by a floating sensation and she needs to shut her eyes, reclaim her balance, and go on. Before she falls asleep at night Rosalie indulges in recollection, hoping that the thought of Walter will invite him to enter her dreams, but he never appears.

On Maya's last night in the house before she leaves for college, she pulls a volume of Mishnah from her father's bookshelf. She often scans the Mishnah at random, but always returns to her favorite seder, Zeraim ("Seeds"). She alights on the description of how the figs grown during the sabbatical year may not be cut with a fig-cutter but with a knife, and how many cubits render a vineyard authentic enough to grow grapes for wine. Know the dimensions of a vineyard and you can grow grapes for the wine that you will one day bless. Know how to cut a fig with the proper knife and you will understand how to tell a story and make it bear fruit. Maya is in love with these laws, with this obscure book she thinks of as an ancient Farmers' Almanac. If she knew how to sketch, she would create a series of drawings based on these figs and these grapes, breathing new life into their ancient skins.

THE KISS

When Sol is just shy of seventy-two Rosalie drives him to the same hospital where she gave birth to her sons in the maternity wing decorated with balloons and flowers, and where Lenny died in a room along the corridor decorated with aquarium-themed wallpaper. Sol has lung cancer, the non-smoker's kind. Lungs poisoned from simply breathing, and in Sol's case—so he believes—inhaling the dry ink from the pages of the Talmud he loved.

During Sol's last weeks Charlie and Philip keep an around-the-clock vigil with Rosalie, and Maya flies home from Los Angeles, where she attends rabbinical school. When Maya arrives in his room, Sol sits up in bed and asks her to play the she'elah-teshuvah game with him.

"Sure, Abba," she says. "Ask me anything. You go first."

"She'elah: Where does God live?"

"Teshuvah: Within the seeds."

"That's it, Maya? You sound like some kind of enigmatic rabbi. Too much subtlety and you won't have a following."

"I'm not sure I want one."

"Do yourself a favor and stay away," says Sol. "It's a terrible profession."

"Stay away from what?" asks Rosalie.

"The rabbinate. Let her love the Torah in complete freedom."

"She's doing what she wants, Sol." Rosalie smiles at Maya. "And in her own way."

Maya excuses herself to get some water and bursts into tears. Charlie meets her in the hallway.

"It's awful to see him like this," says Charlie.

"It's not that," says Maya. "Abba spent his whole life trying to solve a riddle he could never understand."

"I have no idea what you're talking about."

"He was never meant to be a rabbi."

"Welcome to the world, Maya."

"It can be a beautiful life. And it doesn't have to be so confining."

"You'd better be right, or you'll wind up like him."

Maya wipes her tears. "There's practically a revolution in rabbinic creativity out there. It's intoxicating. I've signed up for a social action project in Ghana, and I'm translating—"

She notices Charlie's smirk and lets her voice trail off. Her brother grew up in the same house as she did and he would never understand why she wakes at dawn to translate excerpts from the Ishbitzer's work—Rosalie's suggestion—so she can build a bridge between her Jewish meditation practice and the Hasidic rebbe whose understanding of the human heart was once considered so radical.

"I always thought you were the milkman's daughter," says Charlie.

"You're the foreigner, Charlie. You're too cynical to understand your own parents and you miss out."

"I'll suffer my losses," he says. "You look good, Maya. And despite the circumstances, you seem happy. Mom told me about your wilderness rabbi." He begins to hum "The Hills are Alive" from *The Sound of Music*.

Maya chuckles.

"Do the two of you pray aloud in the open fields of Rockland County?"

"I won't judge your approach to spirituality if you don't criticize mine."

"What approach to spirituality?"

"Exactly, Charlie. That's the point."

"I'm sorry, Maya. We had different versions of the same parents. I'm not talking about the generational gap, though that's part of it. Philip and I missed out on your childhood. You were an adorable baby and you made everything better for them. And that made life better for all of us."

Maya leans her head on Charlie's shoulder. "Thanks for saying that. And yes, I inherited the crazy religion gene. My friends used to play school and pretend to be teachers; I would pretend to be a rabbi. I would put on Abba's tallit, stand on a chair, and recite the Shema to my dolls."

Charlie laughs.

"Temple Briar Wood was my childhood intoxication. Even the smell of the stairwell was delicious to me."

"That stairwell! Those bathrooms! Philip and I used to stash our weed inside the sanitary napkin box in the girl's bathroom."

"No wonder that thing never worked."

"We stole the custodian's key and rigged it, and no one ever bothered to fix it."

Maya remembers how she and Deena invented stories about the failed sanitary napkin box. It became the place where Missy Samuels stored her breath mints, where the custodian lost his toupee, where the golem of Briar Wood would one day be born.

"That explains everything." Maya wipes her nose. "Charlie?"

"Mmm?"

"What was going on with them? I used to eavesdrop when Mom talked on the phone to her supposed best friend in London that I never met, and I just couldn't figure out what secret thing consumed them. I would sometimes imagine that an abandoned suitcase had been dropped in the middle of our house and no one knew what to do with it."

"Something seemed strange, but I never gave it much thought. I suppose they did the best they could. If anyone can understand that, it would be you, Little Miss Everyone-Is-Beautiful-on-This-Train."

"Wait! I told you about that?"

Charlie smiles.

"My ancient brother. I used to think you held a secret code I needed to crack."

"The enigmatic Kerems, the riddle at the center of Temple Briar Wood."

She'elah: Why did her family seem so fucked-up half the time and so enlightened the other half?

Teshuvah: The human heart is not a mystery to be solved.

Rosalie closes the door and checks on Sol's IV. The doctor said he wouldn't linger much longer and Rosalie has avoided being alone with him until now. After a lifetime of negotiating secrets, she doesn't know what she should reveal, and what should be left unspoken.

"Morris phoned you yesterday."

"Morris? From the Seminary?"

"He said he was praying for your recovery."

"It's too late for that."

"Then he started to reminisce about Professor Heschel and how he wished he had appreciated him because now he quotes his work all the time."

"Who doesn't? You can't be a good American rabbi without quoting Heschel."

"Then he mentioned Walter, told me that he borrowed his books from the library and—get this—he was actually impressed."

Sol closes his eyes. Rosalie lies down next to him and rests her hand on his chest.

"There was an attic, Rosalie. Walter brought me up there and something happened. Between us. He and I."

"What?"

"It was nothing to him—a little kiss from a chavrusa. A gesture of friendship, a moment of affinity. But then I couldn't shake it." He begins to drift off, then mumbles, "I held him all my life."

Walter was mine, thinks Rosalie. What kind of little kiss?

Sol is short of breath and a nurse lets herself into the room, silently adjusts his IV.

"Are you comfortable, rabbi?"

Sol nods and closes his eyes, waiting for her to leave.

"God is in the morphine drip," he says.

Rosalie lays her hand on Sol's cheek and he covers it with his.

"I lived with shame, Rosalie. So much shame. Working a job that asked me to turn myself inside out, reveal my soul, explain my passion—all in the service of the tribe. And the clapping, the cheerleading, trying to make people sing when they didn't feel like singing. *Feel the love! Feel the love!* What an awful burden. Better to be a spiritual civilian than a spiritual leader."

"You're finally catching on," she says. "A little late, but—"

"Thank you for the binder," says Sol. "For all those words."

Rosalie smiles. "Did I tell you that Bev called?"

"I can't recall a Bev. Hat? Doily?"

"Frizzy hair. Flip-flops."

"I remember now."

"She told me to thank you."

"You're welcome. Whatever."

"No, Sol. For something you did many years ago. After Bev got up from sitting shiva for her father, you stopped by her house and offered to drive her to the supermarket. And then you took her to the Cosmos Diner and bought her a plate of scrambled eggs."

"So?"

"You sat across from her in a booth and she told you stories about her father's tailor shop, how she would draw pictures on the backs of the yardsticks and eat pastrami sandwiches while his customers came in for a fitting. And you listened to every little story about her father and his customers, all afternoon, until the sun began to set."

"Not such a big deal."

"But it was."

Rosalie shuts her eyes and remembers the night Sol introduced Maya to Walter. *Your husband isn't blind,* Walter had said. *Our daughter is so lovely.* After she listened to him cry on the phone for a long time, she lay her head on the granite countertop, and let her own tears come. And then Maya called out, *It's late! We have to light!* and the three of them stood before their clay menorah, this remnant of a family cobbled from grief and desire, and they recited the blessing and stood together silently as the candles burned down.

Sol summons the strength to grab Rosalie's hand. He winces.

"Did I bless the children?"

Rosalie begins to cry.

"When I blessed them did I seem like an overblown rabbi or did I seem like a normal father? Was I authentic?"

"You blessed them as a father would."

"Tenderly?"

"Quite."

Sol closes his eyes, winces, and then opens them again.

"I wish Maya wasn't going ahead with this."

"This is what she wants, Sol."

"It's a terrible profession for someone with imagination. She will always feel let down. As soon as the words leave her mouth she will wonder what gave her the nerve to speak about what's unknowable and parade it as truth."

"But the Bevs of the world need their rabbis."

"If she finds herself a Bev maybe it will be okay."

"The two of you are cut from the same cloth."

"*Yessir, that's my baby, no sir—*"

"*Don't mean maybe,*" whispers Rosalie.

"*A three-way cord is not readily broken,*" says Sol. He closes his eyes and winces again. "Has Walter come to see me yet?"

"He's gone from this world, sweetheart."

"Come and gone," whispers Sol.

"Yes," says Rosalie.

Sol sighs. God flows into his veins and he can breathe again. He feels his own lips soften around Walter's. They sit in the geniza, Walter in his cotton tunic and Sol in his wedding suit. They are surrounded by the books each of them has ever read—multitudes of volumes in Hebrew and Aramaic and English and Sanskrit and Bengali and German—a repository of infinite words and endless silence. The books jumble together in ragged piles and the words seep from one volume to another, flowing like a river, as Walter allows Sol to kiss him and Sol allows Walter the same. They kiss and taste each other and drown out the laughter and loud footsteps of the students on the floors below. Daylight fades and night comes and still they kiss.

When old rabbis die, new rabbis arrive, take their seats on the bima, move into their offices, occupy their homes. These young replacements show up with their hopeful wives and their small children, eager to install a new countertop, paint the bookshelves, replace the aluminum siding. The synagogue board offers Rosalie an apartment in town but she declines. Madeline has moved from London to San Miguel de Allende and Rosalie wants to join her in Mexico. The children protest—Charlie is to be married, Philip has a stepdaughter who calls her bubbie, Maya is still in rabbinical school in Los Angeles and wants Rosalie to keep a home base for her in New York—but Rosalie knows their pleas have nothing to do with her.

The children return to the house to help Rosalie sort through the rooms. Their work is an elaborate choreography of nostalgia and efficiency. They fill black garbage bags with the clothes and shoes that one of the Kerems wore at some moment in their lives and never discarded. Charlie overturns the file that held articles about clinical trials that should have saved Lenny, and Philip shreds the tax returns that were filed along with Sol's synagogue contracts. Rosalie gathers memorabilia to donate to the shul. Maya sorts the books, and boxes up her grandfather's set of Mishnah and her father's volumes of commentary for her own growing library. And Philip sweeps up scattered socks, paper clips, coins, and dried-up etrogim. The children take turns tossing stuffed garbage bags from the top stairs and Rosalie watches the bags tumble down to the landing like boulders falling from a hill.

Rosalie saves Sol's desk for last and opens the overstuffed drawers. In the bottom file she finds a folder of sermons: Sol's original work, and those she wrote with Walter, preserved in the purple binder. In the same folder, behind some bank statements, the childrens' class pictures, the *yahrzeit* calendar for Lenny so they would know what date to light a candle and recite the Mourner's Kaddish projected fifty years into the future—an envelope, opened and then closed, postmarked from India.

October 27, 1985

Dear Sol,

I write you from Varanasi, where I am doing research on cremation. I feel very far from home, yet somehow close to you and Rosalie. I often think about how the three of us are woven together in a way that feels sacred to me. I believe we created something that we may not comprehend in this lifetime.

I am no longer the chavrusa you once desired, and I have not forgotten how I disappointed you in the geniza— but how we lived tells a story that is bigger than what the two of us could have told by ourselves.

Herzlich,
Walter

P.S. I love you both, always.

CASA ROSALIE

Rosalie stands on her balcony and peers down at the street. A parade of white-haired expatriates gambol down the cobbled walkways, the choicest mangoes weighing down their straw market bags. By day San Miguel de Allende is a tourist paradise of cafés and English speakers who roam the art galleries and tour the gardens where the wealthiest gringos live. But at night, Rosalie lies awake and listens to gunshots in the surrounding hills, the howling of a coyote that prowls for leftovers in the alley behind a cantina. She falls asleep to the sound of rats outside her casa, rats larger than the raccoons that once rummaged through her yard in Briar Wood.

When Rosalie first moved here she felt homesick and questioned her choice to live so far away. She didn't unpack for a year, and spent long hours sorting through boxes of memorabilia. On the days following 9/11 she practically lived at the Internet café, checking names and scanning photographs, scouring for anyone who may have passed through Temple Briar Wood. And then one day she just stopped looking. Let others check the lists. Let others send the condolences, sign the cards, give the donations. She could not look back when she needed to look forward; San Miguel de Allende was her new home.

Just as she began to settle in, Rosalie went to a clinic for a routine test and was diagnosed with stage-three pancreatic cancer. Harvey Berger, expatriate internist and leader of the San Miguel Torah study group, told her what to expect, and that in time, she would have trouble sleeping, not because of discomfort but because she would be preoccupied with remembering the details of her life.

Rosalie is still strong and coltish; she scurries up the hills without losing her breath. She has let her hair go gray and wears flowing embroidered dresses that she purchased in the tourist boutiques when she first arrived. Harvey calls her his young *rabbanit*. "Do not tell anyone your age," he says. "Your illness will be our little secret." The two of them smoke weed together and conspire to create a little Jerusalem in San Miguel, radiating out from the Torah study group they lead every Saturday morning in the lobby of the El Norte Hotel. "Without us the little study group would be reading selections from Kahlil Gibran and performing *alef-bet* yoga," says Harvey. "We are their living Torah."

Harvey leads an abbreviated prayer and meditation service, and Rosalie presents one-minute sermons she calls frissons of Torah. Her fellow expats ask her questions that they never broached to a real rabbi: *If I'm cremated, will my children sit shiva for me? Is there an afterlife? Do Jews believe in angels? Does the soul survive?* Instead of answering their questions, Rosalie offers brief Hasidic stories, and then asks if anyone wants to join her on the San Miguel House and Garden Tour, or meet up after her yoga class, or sit with her in the *jardín* at sunset.

When she passes the *mercado* in town and wakes up to the smell of burning cornhusks and *chile rellenos*, she tries to imagine Walter's Bombay. The city where he woke up to the smell of spices connects Rosalie to the town where she will use spices to stay awake. His holy city of spices; her hilly town of scented candles and cornhusks smoldering in the street vendors' tiny grills. His land between two worlds; her country between one life and the next. To Maya she writes: *I'm so sorry, my sweet girl. I moved far away from you but I knew I could not leave this world without starting over, this time for myself. One day you will understand. And you, Maya, will be the child of mine who understands everything.*

Over tea one afternoon, Madeline asks Rosalie why she won't return to the states for treatment. "I sit under the skylight in my bathroom," says Rosalie, "and I am surrounded by blue tiles. Even the inside of my toilet bowl is a work of art. During the day the light pours in and there is no place I would rather be. And that's only my bathroom. I am in the perfect spot to conclude my life. I don't need to create an ugly chapter."

"You will have to bring your children down," says Madeline.

"I will," says Rosalie. "Soon enough."

"You plan to tell Maya, don't you?"

Rosalie plays with her sugar packet, folds it into tiny squares. "Maybe she senses it."

"Be honest," says Madeline.

"Not everything has to be spelled out. Maya understands subtlety. I'm sure she can figure this out on her own. She's a rabbi, for God's sake."

Madeline laughs. "You realize your contradiction."

"I sometimes think Sol knew more than he let on," says Rosalie.

"Everyone has their blind spots," says Madeline.

"Maybe Maya will do better. She's the real deal now. A newly minted, honest-to-God unemployed rabbi who lives in Morningside Heights."

"Men? Women?"

"Off and on with a wilderness rabbi named Jase. He leads retreats in the mountains." Rosalie laughs.

"Why the derision? Didn't you spend time at Eden Ranch?"

Rosalie tries to remember what happened there but she can't place all the details. She can picture Paul walking with a very pregnant Giselle, and she can recall the litany of names that Walter called out during the fire. His sobs and her fear. Had she told Madeline everything? Even that? At least she kept some of the details to herself: the way the sound of Walter's voice made her body soften, the perfume of cardamom on his palms, the swirl of desire that flowed and flows still—

"I suppose Maya will be just fine," says Rosalie.

"Were we any less confused? Madame Sylvie and her little astonishments! We bought it all, didn't we?"

"Sometimes I wonder if I was up for the challenge of my own life."

"You pulled it off with style, pussycat. You carried this crazy bundle in your arms as if you were born for the task."

"Did you ever worry about me, Madeline? All those conversations, our long nights on the phone. Why didn't you wake me from my convoluted dream?"

"I wasn't going to sever you from your life, sweet pea."

Rosalie smiles. "My savior."

"What about your children?"

"They are my own business," says Rosalie. "And yes, I will sit them down and tell them. And I'll start at the beginning. How we met. Our first time. All our first times, until the last times."

"Have you invited them yet?"

"Not yet. Soon."

After Passover, the San Miguel Torah study group recites an English translation of the Song of Songs. When they come to the last verse Harvey turns to Rosalie and asks why the lovers are always running on the mountain of spices, and why the book is filled with so much unrequited love. Rosalie shrugs.

"I once loved to look for interpretations, Harvey. I could unravel meaning out of a pie crust if I wanted to. But no more. You met me too late."

The children have been summoned. Rosalie phoned each of them and explained the details of her diagnosis and how she feels mostly okay, and not to worry because she treasures her life in

Mexico and has everything she wants. Charlie, Philip, and Maya fly to Mexico City together and rent a car from the airport. A sudden rainstorm delays their nighttime arrival until dawn and Rosalie spends the evening anticipating and dreading their visit. She wants to tell them everything. She wants to talk about Lenny, about Sol, and most of all, she wants to tell them about Walter. And after everything is hashed over, revealed, and reviewed, Rosalie wants to top it all off with a coda: a little astonishment for each child—*dream beyond your marriage*—just as her father once gave to her.

As she waits for their arrival, she imagines them in their rented car: Charlie examining a map, squinting because he won't buy the reading glasses he desperately needs. Philip, driving through the rain, rubbing his sleeve against the windshield because even if the car has a dehumidifier he won't know how to turn it on. And Maya in the backseat, taking in the sights of a country she has never seen, forcing her eyes open even when she is too tired to stay awake.

Years back, when she was alone in the house, Rosalie would sometimes wrap herself in Sol's tallit. She would pull it over her head, drape it on her shoulders, carefully fold the sides, and then immediately yank it off. The white wool was heavy and dank with her husband's dried sweat, and the black stripes against her skin felt to her like bars of a cage. When Rosalie turned seventy Maya gave her a royal blue tallit made of diaphanous silk. She wears it around her casa and loves how the shade of blue matches Liberace's plume and reminds her of Walter's studio. In the predawn hours before her children arrive Rosalie sits on the floor of her bathroom, rubs her bare feet on the blue tiles, lights a joint, and wraps the tallit around her shoulders.

For every telling there is a story, a narrator, and a listener. Rosalie can sum up the story in a single word—Walter. And just as she would read a K'tonton story to them when they were small, she would tell them this one. She would begin simply, with a refugee who followed a man wearing a brown felt hat. But does the story really begin with Walter? What about Sonia who was murdered? Maybe the story begins on the day Sonia and Walter set eyes on each other in Berlin. They were so young! It all began with their first kiss. Or it began the first time she kissed Sol. Or the first time her parents kissed each other, or their parents, or their grandparents, or theirs. Trace any love story back to its origins and you will find yourself in the Garden of Eden itself.

Living far away in Mexico Rosalie spends hours considering the tributaries of choices that flowed from a single river. If Sol. If Walter. If her father. When Maya was small she would say *feewee* instead of *if*, and so Rosalie thinks *feewee* Sol or *feewee* Walter, *feewee* a mango or *feewee* a peach. All those choices, all those details swimming back to her in a refracted jumble of time. So much is in order and yet so much is confused. The other day she ordered dessert in a restaurant and said to the waiter, "Apple cake and flan, please. My mother and I like to share something sweet." She had no idea what she had said until the waiter asked Rosalie if her mother needed a menu.

And who would listen to her story anyway? Why would her grown children want to know of her love for Walter, and what would it mean to them after all these years? Her children have lives of their own, their own tributaries of impossible choices. Why ask them to gather the discarded threads of a previous generation? Sol had introduced Maya to Walter, and she briefly encountered a stranger who seemed to have no consequence in her sweet life. When Rosalie reached into her pocketbook to give her the silver bracelet, she thought, *Let her know this matters, let her know this will one day hold meaning, let her know, somehow, of him.* And then she handed Maya the bracelet as if it were a random dollar bill, a candy bar, a tube of lipstick. *Here. This will look nice with the dress.*

Charlie and Philip, of course, don't seem remotely interested in imagining the underside of her life. To them, she would always be the mother of the original Kerem boys, the woman who raised them, then shouldered impossible grief, and when they were just about grown up, she held a baby girl in her arms and said, *Meet your sister.*

But Maya is another story. In the deepest part of herself, maybe she knows about Walter. Even if Rosalie leaves out the details once again, Maya will find a way to live between the dual cracks of uncertainty and truth, just as she had. Rosalie lights another joint and lays her head on the cool blue tiles of her bathroom floor. She allows herself to think of nothing for a while, nothing at all.

Charlie and Philip enter first and embrace Rosalie in their big arms. She has forgotten that her sons have grey in their hair, that their bodies have grown paunchy with age. Charlie brushes tears from his eyes and Philip holds Rosalie's arm as if she is frail. Maya takes Rosalie's face in her hands and stares into her mother's eyes. Rosalie wonders if her daughter learned this gesture in rabbinical school, where they teach pastoral skills just as they once taught the intricacies of Talmudic thought. After drinking a cup of tea, Maya softens. She rests her head on Rosalie's shoulder and plays with her mother's fingers as she did as a child, only now she measures her mother's fingers against her memory of how they were once not so frail.

Maya insists on serving breakfast. She finds her way around her mother's kitchen, notices how Rosalie stores her teacups and mugs on a low shelf just like she did in the Briar Wood house. The same pots and pans. Here is her mother's favorite whisk and carrot peeler, ensconced in this new drawer. *We have to convince her to come home for treatment,* Philip had said in the car. *She can't be so sick,* said Charlie. *Just be in the moment with her,* Maya said to her brothers. *Both of you.* Maya whisks the eggs and wipes tears from her eyes. *Such a bullshit rabbi, dispensing wisdom about being in the fucking moment. This is impossible.*

Maya tosses the eggs into a skillet and scrambles them. One day soon, she thinks, my mother will be gone and I will long to recover this time. This kitchen, these eggs, these plates, my brothers yammering away about nothing important. She slices mango and lays the uneven pieces on a plate, places fresh rolls in a basket, and gathers the food onto a tray.

Words fly all morning. Charlie and Philip pass around the latest photos of their children: Charlie's son Sivan, named for Sol (*Don't you think he looks more and more like Abba? Look at this one from the preschool play; he's a miniature Rabbi Kerem!*), Philip's adopted stepdaughter Kayla (*Look, Mom, she drew this picture for you!*) The children offer summaries that are already familiar to her: Charlie has a job as a public defender, Philip teaches high school history, Maya needs to find work but she doesn't want a pulpit job and she is off and on with her wilderness rabbi. Their words alternate in a stream of loud and soft syllables, humming like chords in a great symphony. And then Charlie says, *Remember how Lenny wrestled us to the ground and how Abba gave those unbearable sermons when we were small and won't you come home, Mom, just for awhile, or better yet, let's go to Hawaii together, we can schedule a time that works for all of us. Philip—see what you can find online, I heard about some specials. Oh, what a fabulous idea, don't you think, Mom?*

Rosalie follows the sequence of their words, alights on some details, and lets others slip through. She is weary now—too much weed and too little sleep. They have turned out decently, she thinks. Charlie and Philip are kind; Maya is radiant. Despite it all, she passed down the generational gift and kept the story alive. This fact fills her with solace. The pleasure she feels as her children surround her is enough for now, more than she could ever want. In their company Rosalie forgets that there may have been something more she had intended to say. Charlie's, Philip's, and Maya's voices fill the rooms of her casa and she bursts with joy. Everything she wanted to give her children has been received; everything she had intended to say is already known.

AWE AND WONDER

Maya opens her eyes in the chilly tent before dawn. She and Jase are in Fahnstock State Park on a Wednesday morning, testing out an overnight retreat program that Jase calls The Wonderful and Wild Weekday Shabbat. She rests her cheek on Jase's back, sniffs the curls that cascade down his neck, basks in his radiant warmth. So sweet, she thinks. Leave it to Jase to suggest a weeknight camping trip because he dreamt of waking up in a field of morning dew.

Jase reaches for her hand. He is wide awake, beaming his flashlight on the last pages of Heschel's *Man Is Not Alone*. Maya wraps her arms around his torso.

"A little awe and wonder before breakfast?"

"It's always time for awe and wonder."

Maya smiles. "How could anyone become a rabbi without a little Heschel in his book bag?"

"It's great stuff. The deepest of the deep." He closes the book and pulls her close.

"Talk to me," she says.

"About what?"

"Give me something fun to chew on. A line of poetry. Or make up a she'elah and I'll answer with a teshuvah. It can be about anything; it can be about sex! I speak the same language as you, Rabbi Jase! Different school, same books, same crazy-holy-weird thing that most of the world won't ever understand. So give me your best."

"That I can do." He cradles her hip.

"With words, sweetie."

He begins to hum a wordless Hasidic melody.

"I'm not in the mood for a *niggun*," she says. "Not when I want to have a conversation. Why on earth did you become a rabbi if you don't love to talk?"

Maya ruffles Jase's hair. How did she land the least intellectual rabbi of her generation? They met at a Jewish food conference, flirted over lentil soup and torn chunks of spelt challah, cracked jokes about eating cholent cooked with organically grown meat. After the other guests retired to their rooms, she and Jase strolled the perimeter of a mountain lake, kissed in the faint glow of tea lights scattered around a bench. If her father knew Jase, he would be incredulous; he would have wanted Maya to find a mate who could be a true chavrusa, a co-traveler in the galaxy of texts. A chavrusa like his. A strange man full of surprises. The barefoot man in the apartment. Someone like that. Where had their flights taken them, and why was her Jase so flat, so sweet, so unstrange and so unsurprising?

"We should study together," she says. "I'll help you out. When we get back to New York, okay?"

Jase kisses her, rubs his hand down the length of her torso, circles, hovers. Why does she even care that he can't talk philosophy? What use are all those words anyway? He is so good to her, his touch so perfect: not strange, not surprising, yet always just right.

"You spoil me," she says.

"I intend to."

"What time is it? Shit. I'll miss the Mourner's Kaddish."

"We can still make it, Maya. I ran MapQuest and there's a shul about ten miles from here."

"Never mind. I can miss it for once."

"Are you sure?"

"Of course I'm sure. I'll be mourning my mother all my life. And she wouldn't want me to leave your toasty sleeping bag to find a shul where I could race through the Mourner's Kaddish, which has nothing to do with her anyway." Maya laughs.

"What's so funny?"

"My mother wouldn't have cared if I recited Kaddish."

"But it matters to you. We can make it in time."

Maya shakes her head. "I'll meditate instead. A good sit in the woods to honor her memory." She smiles.

"So we're staying."

"Yes. For now."

"I was hoping you'd say that." He kisses her belly, dives his face between her thighs.

Is this what Rosalie would have wanted for her? Maya wishes she could meet her mother at a nearby diner for breakfast, share a plate of pancakes, tell her how her wilderness rabbi is excellent in bed but she's just not sure she wants him on the other side of her Shabbat table when she is forty and fifty and sixty, the two of them dissecting the flavors of the latest artisinal kosher cheeses at the farmer's market.

Be careful, Maya, her mother would have said. *Listen to your heart.*

She begins to cry.

"Maya?"

"It's too much for me now. I can't—"

"But last night—"

"We were stoned last night, Jase. And it was great. With you it's always great. Unconditionally. I just don't know—"

"It's okay."

Jase turns, clutches his book in his arms as if he is a small boy and *Man Is Not Alone* is his teddy bear.

"Can we go now?"

"You just said you wanted to stay, meditate in the woods. A gentle, mindful practice will center you—"

"Of course it will, Jase. But I don't want to get centered or be mindful or get in touch with my feelings or find my soul or travel the holy path to some sustainable future. I just want to go home. I want to check my email and call my brothers and think about my mother and sleep in my own bed."

Maya looks at Jase and takes in his stubble, his elegant nose, his gracious lips, the way he wants to absorb the words he reads without having to interpret them for himself. So earnest. So sincere. So wrong for her. She just buried her mother and he keeps asking if she can join him in Jerusalem when he begins his year-long fellowship in Jewish leadership. *No,* she says. *Not yet. Maybe one day. Or maybe not.*

And Maya doesn't know. She buried her mother only four months ago, back in Briar Wood, as Rosalie had specified. She stood in the cemetery, right next to her father's grave, and delivered a eulogy that seemed so flawed and so sketchy, so distant from the way she understood her mother. After the service, a well-preserved Missy Samuels embraced Maya and thanked her for speaking so truthfully. "Your mother was my role model, my inspiration." Bev leaned on her walker and wept. "The shul was my home," she said. "Your parents made my life complete." Maya and her brothers lingered at the graves and the three of them lay pebbles on top of Sol's and Lenny's headstones, and she stayed behind for an extra moment and kissed the headstones too.

"It's okay," says Jase. "I get it."

Maya grabs a sweater and pants and rolls up their single sleeping bag.

"Maybe you met me at the wrong time."

"After my year in Jerusalem we'll see. Maybe that will be the right time."

"For what, Jase?"

"We could live together. Or get married."

"I adore you, sweetie," she says. "And I don't want to marry anyone."

Jase packs up his clothes, his volume of Heschel, the banjo he is teaching himself to play. He takes out the embroidered bag that holds his tallit and tefillin, and steps outside the tent to face east. Maya leans on her elbow and peeks out, watching him drape his rainbow-striped tallit over his shoulders with surgical precision. He wraps the tefillin on his left arm, tight enough to leave indentations that will linger on his skin all morning. She stares at him as she once stared at her father when he davened. Just like Sol, Jase doesn't need a prayer book because he knows the morning prayers by heart. He glances back at her and smiles, just as her father smiled at her mother. *You get me. You get this. We are in this together. Stay with me.*

She closes her eyes and imagines the house in Briar Wood when she was small, how her parents lived in separate universes in the big house—her father leaning over the Talmud, her mother whispering into the telephone—and came together at night to listen to their favorite records. *Fly me to the moon. Dance me to the end of love. I say a little prayer for you.* She would spy them from the doorway and smile at the sight of them, yet her parents seemed to live behind a veil. So much was inaccessible to her, just like she would always be inaccessible to Jase. He would assume that the crazy-holy-weird thing they shared would make them true soul mates, but it would only be an illusion. He would never understand the depths of her imagination, and in time their delicious, organic Shabbat meals would be tinged with sadness. He would sustain her with good sex for a while, and then she would feel alone.

I'm a piece of work, Jase, she thinks. You deserve a sweet rabbi-loving girl, a hippie chick who wants to fuck you in mountain huts and whose brain does not careen into imaginative overdrive. A girl who will sit beside you at Jewish food conferences and laugh at your cholent jokes. A girl who won't mind that you never talk about books, that you can't play the she'elah-teshuvah game. Not a woman who wants to create something bigger than a rabbinate, more encompassing than a single marriage—whatever that might look like. *It sounds like a recipe for being a lost soul,* her mother would have said. *Better you should stay with the sweet rabbi who pleases you in some way, at least for a while.*

They drive home in silence, listening to NPR and old Dylan CDs. When they pull up in front of her building, Maya hesitates.

"I'll call you," she says. "Promise."

She lets herself into the apartment, hops into bed, and falls into a long dreamless sleep. When she wakes up the next afternoon she feels as if she has been hibernating for a year. She brushes her teeth and plays her messages: three from Jase and one from Madeline in San Miguel, insisting she come down to visit. All her life Maya had imagined Madeline as a tiny British elf who lived inside a telephone wire, accessible only to her mother. And now.

Just for a few days, pussycat. Tell me when you're free and I'll book the flight. My treat.

ALL THE WALTERS

June 2003

Maya rests her head against the window of the Flecha Amarilla bus that careens out of Mexico City. She listens to the tourists chatter about San Miguel de Allende's art galleries and she envies their allegiance to the town where her mother took her last breaths, a town that Maya identifies with grief. The man sitting next to her reeks of tequila and has fallen asleep on her arm. This is her mother's bus, the one that brought Rosalie to the last home she would have.

She tries out her game: Everyone-Is-Beautiful-on-This-Bus. *This man who drools on my arm.* The chicken that escapes from a girl's hands. The gringo who won't stop talking about the first-run films he just viewed in New York. The gringa with the Texas accent who won't stop talking about the gardener who peed into her fountain. Did her mother lean her head against this same window and did this same drooling man lean against her mother's arm? Maya wants to feel her mother again, touch everything she touched, without Madeline intruding on her private sorrow.

The bus enters the town and parks in front of a cantina. Maya nudges the sleeping man off her arm, retrieves her bag from the shelf overhead. She wishes she could unspool time and this moment could be the same moment of arrival she shared with her brothers only a year ago, just before breakfast. Wasn't there a theory of time somewhere that allowed for this? Go to the same place and fold yourself back into a scene that has already ended?

Maya steps off the bus and spots a tall, wrinkled woman with cropped white hair and cat-eye glasses waving in the distance.

"Yoo-hoo! Maya Kerem!"

Maya winces. No one has ever shouted her name quite this loud. Her mother's best friend sounds like a British cheerleader. Madeline wipes away a tear, then folds Maya into her arms. "You look so much like her," she says.

"I know."

Madeline picks up Maya's bag. "Let me carry that. We'll have lunch and then you'll go to your hotel."

Maya only wants to visit her mother's casa—now rented to another expat—and summon the sound of her mother's voice. She would ask to go inside and stand at the kitchen sink but this time she would not cry with the anticipation of loss; she would listen closely for an echo.

Madeline leads Maya through the jardín, stopping to greet every white-haired gringa who carries a basket filled with fresh fruit and books checked out from the town's English library. They could be in Briar Wood, thinks Maya. They could be in Jerusalem. These people could be living anywhere, only they chose Mexico, which allows them to retire on social security, bask in the dry heat, and gather for afternoon mojitos at the local art galleries. No Spanish required.

"Don't you love it here?"

"It has its appeal," says Maya.

"I have an extra room if you'd like to hang out for awhile," says Madeline. "You could help me run my little press, join the Torah study group. Harvey would be honored to have a real rabbi as his partner."

"Thanks anyway, but no. I have a lot of decisions to make and I can't figure it all out from here."

"Indecision is the privilege of youth. You eat vegetarian, right?"

"Sure."

"I found a new place. El Colibri. Plenty for you to eat."

Before they open their menus a flamenco guitarist approaches their table and begins to play. Madeline gives him a few pesos and shoos him off. "*Mas tarde,*" she mutters and her eyes follow him until he leaves the dining room.

"The water's purified, Maya. Perfectly safe to drink."

Maya raises her glass and takes a sip.

"Tell me, sweet pea. What's going on with you now?"

"I'm not exactly working and I'm not sure about my boyfriend, not sure if he's right for me. I'm not sure about anything. A common rabbinic dilemma."

Maya wishes the guitarist would return to their table, divert them with a flamenco.

"Your mother and I knew a French kabbalist in Jerusalem

named Madame Sylvie. She parceled out little astonishments, direction signals for understanding the soul. Sometimes they were direct and other times obtuse."

Maya squints, vaguely recalling the old woman in a Jerusalem courtyard who gave her lemon cake. "I'll figure things out on my own," she says.

Madeline glances at the menu. "I always order the vegetable enchilada with brown rice."

"I'm not hungry."

"You'll pick and save the rest for later, sweet pea."

Maya listens to Madeline place the order in perfect Spanish. She is good at this, she thinks. I feel as if I'm five years old again.

"Truths are skittish," blurts Madeline, suddenly.

"Huh?"

"I had great love for your mother."

"Thank you for taking such good care of her at the end."

"She was my best friend."

"That's why I'm here," says Maya.

Madeline folds her napkin into tiny squares, then unfolds it and folds it back.

"His name was Walter Westhaus."

Madeline's voice is barely audible.

"Excuse me?"

"Wal-ter West-haus." Madeline draws out the syllables.

"A friend of yours?"

"Not *my* friend. Not exactly."

"Wait! Westhaus wrote *Ordinary Sacred*. I own that book."

"It's a classic."

Maya pictures the dog-eared copy she kept on her bookshelf when she was in rabbinical school, her random marginal jottings, the blurry postage-stamp photograph of its author on the back. That book was once so important to her and now she can't remember a single line of it.

"An important work in the field."

Maya closes her eyes and waits.

"They were in love."

"Who was?"

"Rosalie and Walter. Your mother and—"

"My Rosalie? When? With *him*? You can't be—"

Madeline lowers her voice. "Yes. Rosalie. Your mother."

"Before my father?"

Madeline bites her lip, fidgets with her fork.

"At the same time as. For a long time. It was complicated and I don't know everything."

"Obviously you know quite a bit." Maya inhales deeply and pulls up air from the bottom of her lungs. Daughters are deprived of so much but friends like Madeline know everything. When did her mother see him? Was this Walter the barefoot man in the apartment? Or was Walter the person on the other end of the phone when Rosalie said, *Maya will know everything. We will figure this out.*

"He's gone now."

"Who?"

"Walter. Hit by a car in Bombay in 1987."

Maya sighs. Walter was her father's chavrusa. And her mother loved him. He had smooth feet. And then he died. It was complicated. Of course it was. They were all human. Now where is that guitar player and how about we ask for the check and call it a day—

"Walter was your father, Maya."

"Sol Kerem was my father."

"I'm sorry to be the one to tell you, sweet pea."

"Don't tell me who my father was."

Maya's eyes fill with tears. *Who died? Anyone I know?* The day she bought that black dress. Her mother sitting in the big leather chair, crying for a reason she did not understand. *You hold his beauty. Your father's.* Him? The barefoot man in the brocade tunic who looked at her too long? *Him?*

"Let it go, Madeline. I've heard enough."

"You have a lot to process, pussycat."

"I have nothing to process. I prefer my family history to your fictive tale. Besides, you are intruding on my parents, my real mother and father. They don't deserve you clouding up the past with your lies."

"Do you think I'm lying to you?"

Maya looks up at Madeline's cat-eye glasses. She was the best friend from London who was always on the other end of the phone, but not always—

"No," she says. "You're not making this up."

"I begged her to tell you herself."

"My mother had her shortcomings."

"We can talk about that if you'd like."

Maya grimaces. "We have nothing to discuss, Madeline. You are not my therapist, you are not my friend, and my family is really none of your business."

"I'm sorry, then," says Madeline.

"You didn't have to tell me."

"Do you truly believe that?"

Maya shakes her head. The waiter approaches with their food and Madeline begins to eat.

"Why do you care so much? My parents are gone."

"Your mother was my best friend."

"I get it. But why?"

"Why? You are a rabbi, Maya! Don't you realize that my best friend's life became intertwined with mine? In some small way, we bear each other's burdens, carry each other's stories—"

"That would sound good in a sermon, Madeline, but we're sitting in a restaurant in San Miguel de Allende, I have no idea why I've come, and frankly, it's time for me to leave. Let's call this a very short stay."

"Sweet pea."

"Stop calling me names," says Maya.

"Your mother never minded."

"I'm not my mother."

"Look. Many years ago in Jerusalem, I watched her stand on a folding chair, clutching her little folded note, and she looked too sophisticated to play the part of a superstitious Jew who believes in a God who reads mail. I muttered something that probably sounded too rational for her to hear, and then I helped her down, and the words flowed from our mouths and we kept the conversation alive until she died. And I begged her to tell you."

"Well, she didn't. For whatever reason. And if this story is true, it's my choice to unravel it or keep it spooled up tight. I'm pretty good with silences, with uncertainties, and unlike you, not everything is my business."

"Your mother's story enlarged my life."

"How convenient for you. A friend who lent you great fodder. I'm sure you enjoyed that."

"Please don't be cruel. I understand that you may hate me for this. I had no choice."

"Of course you had a choice."

Maya picks up her fork, tears apart the enchilada and mashes it up.

"I cleaned out your mother's place. Boxed up everything for you. Letters, mostly. Some clippings, writings, sermons—"

"And I presume you combed through every scrap."

"That's your job."

Maya closes her eyes and opens them again. "It's hard to breathe in here."

"I can't imagine what this is like for you," says Madeline.

"You've imagined quite a lot so far. You didn't have to do this to us."

"I believe I did," says Madeline. "Maybe one day—"

"The nerve of you to crack open my family as if we are playthings for you. My mother didn't want me to know, okay? I trusted her, I trust her still, and who the hell are you to violate us?"

"I know," says Madeline.

"You know shit." Maya runs out of the restaurant and down the cobbled street. "Intruder!" she shouts to no one. "Trespasser!"

The street is slippery and Maya trips and falls. She limps to her hotel, checks in, and collapses on the floor of her room, blood trickling down her leg.

Maya cleans herself up in the bathroom sink and then leaves the hotel, runs up to the casa where her mother lived, and sits on the curb. She stays there until the sun sets, waiting for her mother to slip out of the Mexican night, unlock the door, and invite Maya in. Rosalie would wrap herself in the tallit Maya bought for her and she would tell Maya everything. *There was a Walter. Yes, that Walter. Your father's chavrusa. The man you met. He was your father. And Sol was your father in all the ways that matter.* And then she would say, *I'm sorry. I can't spell it out for you. It was my life and everything happened as it did.*

When the box arrives later that night Maya brings it up to her room, places it on the bed, and stares at it. She wonders why the ancient rabbis didn't create a prayer for setting eyes on something that had been previously hidden. She would have to create that prayer herself; she would add it to the list of new liturgies that awaited her. A prayer for finding out your father is not your father. A prayer for forgiving the woman who told you. A prayer for being confused and tired and curious and thirsty for water that doesn't need to be purified. A prayer to understand her and him and him and why.

Maya washes her hands and pulls the tape off the box. The tallit she bought for Rosalie rests on the top layer and Maya wraps it around her shoulders and begins to read.

INSIDE THE WEB

August 2003

The Lawrence Welk Nursing Home is located one strip mall away from Eden Ranch, which is no longer an eden or a ranch, but the site of a Lexus dealership. A social worker leads Maya into a room where a dozen elderly women pour bingo chips into paper bags. A man with a thick mop of white hair sits among them and accuses the women of cheating.

"I saw everything!" he shouts. "Nothing is lost on me."

"That's him," says the social worker. "Such a pity when a brilliant man declines. You should have known him in his prime. A self-proclaimed guru, apparently."

"Does he remember anything?"

"In and out. He's generally quite sharp, but moody. You need to be careful with him." She pushes his wheelchair away from the others. "Let's not start up today, Professor Richardson, okay?"

Paul windmills his arms.

"No punching today either. Agreed?"

Paul notices Maya and stares. He wheels close.

"I know you," he says.

Maya smiles and reaches out her hand. "I'm—"

"No need for formalities. You're Walter's daughter."

"Yes," says Maya. The sound of her own voice seems unnatural to her. "I believe I am."

"Belief is not imperative," he says, "but it's a good place to start." He grabs Maya's hands and kisses them.

"How did you know? When you saw me, I mean—"

"I loved him as a father loves a son."

"Good to meet you," says Maya.

"Let's not waste time being polite, baby girl. Wheel me to my room. We're just down this godforsaken hallway. Do you know this place was once a resort? Now it's a shit farm for old people who wear diapers and dwell in dwindling reality. Welcome to my new Eden Ranch."

Maya wheels Paul down a long hallway and into a small, cluttered room.

"It's right here." Paul reaches into a pile and pulls out a yellowing journal article. "Your father wrote this. The paper that started it all, translated into English. You like the Song of Songs?"

"I'm more of an Ecclesiastes type, actually."

"Ah! Then you're either a religious existentialist or a depressed soul."

"Neither."

"Naturally Walter's daughter won't be pinned down. *Floating in the boat is a person I've never seen, playing the flute*," he recites in a sing-song melody. "That's you."

"I don't understand—"

Paul smiles. "You're so much like him."

Maya glances at the article and reads aloud. "*The words of the texts echo in the lives of the people who read them.*"

"Your father lived those words."

Your father. Which one? The only one Paul knew, of course, but Sol, her father, lived his texts too.

"Take the pile with you. Don't need it anymore. The books also. I'm finished with the detritus of my life."

Maya reads the titles: *Ordinary Sacred; Religious Themes in Tagore's Poetry; Imposed Grace: The Clergy's Dilemma; The Radical Theology of Atheism; Cremation in World Religions.* She opens one and reads the inscription:

> *with love to Paul Richardson who saved me*
> *Herzlich,*
> *Walter*

"I cared for him deeply," says Paul. "More than I can say."

"I don't need all the details," says Maya.

"Then why have you come? I have a kid of my own, grandkids too. I don't need charity visits from strangers. It's bingo time for me. If you don't want details, why bother?"

Maya begins to cry. "I only just found out. Please understand."

Paul shakes his head. "You are just like him, baby girl. You've got your head in some spice sack that smells sweet."

"You don't know me."

Paul pulls Maya close and unbuttons his shirt.

"Look at this scar." He takes her hand. "Touch it. Go ahead. I'm not some old lech."

Maya touches the raised zipper of skin on his chest and flinches.

"Open heart surgery. They cracked open this old salt at eighty years old. So don't tell me what I don't know. Anyone else on this planet understand your father like I did?"

"My mother, apparently." Her eyes focus on the stack of books.

"I loved him more than words can say. He followed me off the *Conte Rosso*, baby girl, but the story didn't start there."

Maya caresses *Religious Themes in Tagore's Poetry*, examines the spine.

"Spice sack like I told you. Put down the damn book. I'm talking to you."

"I've never read Tagore," says Maya.

"Walter's daughter hasn't read Tagore? How old are you?"

"Too old to admit my gaps."

"Pitiful! Who the hell raised you?"

Maya touches his arm. "I'll catch up with Tagore. I promise."

"Suit yourself, baby girl."

"Tell me how it started. Please."

"Not yet." Paul snatches the book from her hands. "Read this one. Aloud." He points to a line.

"*The traveler has to knock on every alien door to come to his own, and one has to wander through all the outer walls to reach the innermost shrine at the end.*"

"I read that sentence aloud when I dumped his ashes."

"Dumped—"

"In the Ganges. He was cremated, of course."

"That was his epitaph," she says.

Paul jabs his finger in Maya's face. "You are his epitaph."

"I'm practically a stranger."

"Then go, baby girl. Like I said, I don't need visitors."

"Please understand how confusing this is. Be patient with me. I'm unenlightened."

"Clearly."

Paul bows his head, rests his chin in his hands.

"Early 1938. I was in Berlin on fellowship, researching common religious themes in Heine's and Tagore's poetry. Heady stuff. Good material for a brash young man. It became the foundation of my career, for all it was worth. And then I heard her sing in a café."

"Who?"

"Sonia. She had an endless mane of blond hair. Down to her waist. And a voice like Billie Holiday. You know Billie Holiday or is she another mystery to you, like Tagore?"

"Don't insult me. My parents listened to her recordings."

"Your parents."

"Yes. Rabbi Sol and Rosalie Kerem."

Paul leans forward in his chair. "Get out, baby girl!"

"But—"

"Your father was a great man. He may have been an appendage to your family but he deserved more."

Maya shudders.

"She sang Brahms. Sonia had the kind of smoky voice you hear once in a lifetime, maybe twice if you're lucky. I waited for her to finish and bought her a drink. She told me she was Jewish, and that she was learning Hebrew, and she had a crazy fascination with the Song of Songs.

"If Billie Holiday sang Brahms she would be you—

"I assume that's a compliment.

"The highest. Come to England with me, and then to America—

"My fiancé and I are going to Palestine.

"Your homeland?

"Yes.

"She got this faraway look in her eyes, as if she were listening to music inside her body. I waited for her to come back to my gaze.

"You are breaking my heart.

"But I am already in love.

"I should have been the first.

"And then we kissed. Spent the night. A single sleepless night. I'll leave the details to your imagination, baby girl. I'll never forget how her long blond hair cascaded down my arm like a curtain, how she winked at me. I wanted to save her, grow old with her. She showed me a photo of Walter and said, One day you'll come to Palestine and I'll introduce you. She told me how they had certificates in hand; they just had to convince his father that his public denouncements of the Nazis had branded him a target, and a new life in Palestine was preferable to no life at all. And then Sonia reached into a bag and handed me a brown felt hat. I was going to give it to my fiancé, she said, but I'd like you to have it. And take this too. She gave me Walter's paper on religious desire in the Song of Songs. He wrote this for me and it's very good. Maybe you can translate it into English."

Maya remembers the time she asked her mother why they chose Sonia for her middle name.

Your father and I liked it, Maya. Not all of our choices are imbued with deep meaning.

"I translated the paper and got it published. She sent me a simple note: *You can't have me but the words you translated for Walter will link us together.* And that was it. She was shot, along with his father. It was all backwards."

Maya reaches for Paul's hands.

"You loved her."

"Were you born yesterday, baby cakes? Of course I loved her. And whomever Sonia loved would connect me to her again. I was due to leave Berlin when a mutual friend told me that Walter was on his way to Trieste. I tracked him down and then shadowed him around the port, like an undercover agent. And when he boarded the *Conte Rosso,* so did I."

"He never made it to Palestine."

"Walter wasn't meant to live there without Sonia, I suppose. Karma, divine providence, the alignment of stars—call it what you like. But throughout his life, your father told all his students how he followed a man off the ship in Bombay. A man who wore a brown felt hat. It became his little mantra."

Your father. She may want to know everything but she can't build a bridge between the barefoot man named Walter and the words *your father.*

"I was the man wearing the brown felt hat."

Maya tries to imagine a younger Paul moving through a ship like a spy, a brown brim shading his eyes.

"Do you still have the hat?"

"You want souvenirs, baby girl? Life isn't a gift shop. I lost the hat a long time ago. I lost everything but my words."

Paul leans in close and grabs Maya's arm, almost twisting it. She winces.

"Will my words be enough for you?"

She nods.

"I boarded the *Conte Rosso* because I wanted to watch over him, coax him into disembarking at Bombay with me. That part was easy; he was eager to follow a man he didn't know. But then he got swallowed up in a crowd, and I lost him. I searched for a few days and was just about to give up when I found him at a market stall, getting high on spices.

"At first I needed to be connected to the man Sonia loved because it was the only way I could keep her alive. Walter was the living link to Sonia, just like I'm the living link to Walter—for you, now. It's why you've come, isn't it? But when I talked to him for the first time I felt that we somehow belonged to each other. I wanted to save him for myself."

"What was he like?"

"A wreck! Your father was a forlorn vagabond from a world that was quickly being destroyed."

Paul coughs.

"I never told him."

"Told him what?"

"That I was in love with his fiancée. I needed to keep it a secret, something for myself. But after a while Sonia didn't matter. Walter needed me to save him and I needed him to love me as a student loves his teacher. We completed each other; we translated Tagore's work as if we shared a brain. We could go to the symphony and hear the music in the same way. We could speak to the students at Eden Ranch about the price of laundry detergent and if we called it dharma they would cry over our words and declare that we changed their lives. Walter didn't need to know how our own story began."

"What about his time at the Seminary?"

"I arranged it through my university connections; an administrator wanted to help a refugee like him. I made the introduction, then let him find his way.

"Your father was a broken man. You should have seen him wearing his green kurta with that black yarmulke they popped on his long greasy hair. He was skinny and handsome and frightened and foolish and so very brilliant. That defined Walter Westhaus: never one thing or another; he was always *all of the above*. When I walked away from the Seminary without him beside me, I wondered how he would make out among those young rabbis, but I had immense faith in him."

"He met my parents there."

"He brought your mother to Eden Ranch." Paul laughs. "She looked so out of place among our disheveled tribe, but I could see how she loved him."

Maya closes her eyes.

"Is this too much for you?"

"As long as you feel up to it," she says. "Please."

"Walter always had women falling at his feet. No one permanent, baby doll. And after you were born he told me he had a secret daughter, a child who belonged to another family."

Maya wipes tears from her face and looks at the pile of books. My father wrote those, she thinks. My sad father. My second sad father.

Paul coughs again and Maya pours him a cup of water. She watches him sip from a straw, one tiny drop at a time.

"Is there anything else?" she asks.

"There are lifetimes of anything elses, baby doll! Infinite realities! Warped memories and flawed interpretations! If this is too much for you, go to a photo booth, sit behind the curtain, and say 'capture.' You'd still be all wrong, but at least you'd have the photo to keep as a souvenir.

"When I found him in Shantiniketan, he was resting in the shade of the date palm trees. We talked, your father and I. He learned English at the ashram and he was eager to try out his new vocabulary words. He told me his dreams. The books he wanted to write. The places he would live, the women he would love, and that one day he would have a daughter who would track me down in a shit factory near the Pacific Ocean and she would—"

Paul's voice booms and he begins to sob.

"He told me that you would come to me near the end of my life and we would hold each other tight and you would save me from the shadows that linger in the bingo parlor where the old broads steal my chips and turn my words into salt and—"

Paul's forehead is beaded with sweat and Maya thinks about calling the social worker but then stops herself and holds both his hands, tightly. Paul lets go, pounds the air with his arms, and then drops them. He leans against her, whimpers for a while, and then stops.

"Better now, baby girl." His chin drops to his neck and he begins to snore.

"I was named for her," Maya whispers. "For your Sonia."

She watches him sleep and thinks about the story that circles around in the past, addled and confused in an old man's mind, yet perfectly clear. Two men had loved Sonia and Sonia chose Walter and then she was killed. Rosalie had loved two men and she chose both; her mother built an entire life around that choice. Maya doesn't know if she loves Jase and what she longs for is greater than what any man can offer. The world is an immense garden of desire, a tangle of muddled love stories that wind around each other in an endless spiral.

She thinks of Paul's story as soft clay between her fingers, history that changes shape under her touch. Where would it end? Touch the web any place and it ripples and flows like an ocean current, beginning with the story of one person who longed for another, body and soul.

Maya tears a page out of a notebook and writes:

> *Thank you for saving my father.*
> *Be well,*
> *Maya Sonia Kerem*

On Maya's flight back to New York, she dreams of Walter in his studio, lean and fit, practicing headstands. He offers her a whiff of sweet coriander and she sniffs. Then she places her palms flat on the floor, steadies herself, and slowly pulls up her legs. Walter grabs Adelaide and Liberace and places them on the soles of her feet and laughs.

Maya wakes up thirsty. She longs to pick up the thread of Walter's life that was torn away by a car on a Bombay road in 1987. Had he lived. Had he made it back to America for an airport rendezvous with her and her mother. *I'd like you to meet an old friend of mine*, Rosalie would have said. *Walter, this is Maya.* I *know*, she would have said. *I met you before.* This time Walter would have been wearing shoes and she would have looked at his face and understood. The dream of their reunion would have been real this time, not like the dreamlike encounter that seems so hazy to her now. And this time Walter would have asked her to read something he had written. *What do you think of my newest work on the sacred?* Or maybe he would have brushed his eyes with the back of his hand because he wouldn't want Rosalie to see that he was crying. Or maybe he would have reached out to touch Maya and she would have flinched and said, *This is awkward, please understand.* Or then. Or then. There were so many routes her imagination could take. She could no more finish their thoughts than she could create a quilt out of the frayed threads of their lives. All she could do was touch the edges and listen.

Maya remembers sitting in her father's study when she was small. He had taught her some Hebrew letters and then she handed him her copy of *The Velveteen Rabbit*. "Read it, Abba," she said. He read to her slowly and when he closed the book she covered the T on *Rabbit* with her little finger.

"That's Velveteen Rabbi," said Sol.

"That's what I'd like to be when I grow up," she said. And Sol looked into her eyes and said, "You will be a very real rabbi,

Maya. But I am the original Velveteen Rabbi. Not real unless loved into existence. I need people to listen to my sermons, purchase my wares, feed my ego. Don't tell this to anyone—let it be our little secret."

And it happened. Maya fell in love with the texts, with every word that began as a seed and then flowered into sentences, paragraphs, tractates, commentaries—infinite interpretations that spiral around each other in a symphonic web. Its authors are long dead but the words in the web are always alive, thriving with possibility, begging for connection. And Maya wasn't velveteen at all; without a congregation, she was free to travel through the web, explore its underbelly, welcome its seductions, dance with its mystery. Free to choose the people whose lives are woven into the filament. Free to unravel the storylines and follow each thread back to its kernel. For her first time out she would begin with her parents. All three of them. A woman and a man and another man, braided together.

Back in New York, Maya keeps the box open at the foot of her bed. She sleeps fitfully and then wakes up with a burning question—*Where was my mother when? And what did Sol know?*—and forages through the box to search for clues. But the box only contains fragments. Maya calls Madeline and asks if she has anything else.

"I have some journals. Quite a few, actually. It's overwhelming."

"I'd love to read what you wrote about them."

Madeline hesitates. "I could make photocopies, but it's just so—"

"Personal?"

"I'm afraid so. I was a shameless diarist in those days. I had a notebook for every occasion; I even wrote when I was sitting on the toilet. Your mother's story claimed my imagination; at times it took over my life."

"Yenta."

"Guilty as charged."

"I'll forgive you on their behalf."

"Are you still furious at me, Maya?"

"The cat's out of the bag, Madeline. At times I wish you'd never told me but now I can't concentrate on anything that isn't about them. I don't return Jase's calls and I forget to buy groceries. I spend entire days in the apartment, unshowered, half-dressed, thinking about Walter and Sonia and how one thing led to another. And yes, I resent this intrusion terribly, but it's too late now."

"What's your address?"

Within a week an envelope arrives from Mexico, stuffed with photocopied pages from Madeline's journals from the '60s and the '70s, the words written out in tiny, perfect script, every detail of *he said, she said* etched on lined paper. She sorts through the unopened boxes of papers that had been stored in Charlie's house and finds more letters between Sol and Walter and Rosalie. Maya pores over the purple binder filled with sermons and marginal aphorisms, and with Madeline's journal as a navigation tool, she deciphers how these words were composed. She reads all of Walter's books and academic papers, and buys her own volume of Tagore's poetry and a translation of Hindu scriptures. And she continues to delve into the *Mei HaShiloach*, trying to understand how the Ishbitzer's teachings wove into her parents' lives.

Philip mails Maya a book he found in their grandparents' kitchen cabinet after Ida moved to a nursing home—a volume of the Song of Songs, translated into Yiddish, inscribed:

> *To my butterfly Ida,*
> *Beloved in touch and in word and in deed. This book*
> *tells the story of how we yearn. There is only one desire,*
> *butterfly, and it begins with our kiss.*
>
> Love,
> Shmuel

Maya calls Philip and asks if he ever told Rosalie about the book he found tucked away behind their grandparents' dairy dishes. "I always meant to tell her," he said. "But I forgot and then it was too late." Was the Song of Songs a love poem for her grandparents, just as it was a love poem for Walter and Sonia? Why did they all get off on this ancient poem when she, an Ecclesiastes girl, never did? Every book, every letter, every piece of paper is a fractal of another story; every crack of light conceals a deeper mystery. Maya fills a notebook with questions and answers, each one labeled she'elah and teshuvah. She lies awake at night and thinks about how her three parents created something together that she could never understand.

In rabbinical school, Maya was taught that if she wanted to fully comprehend the Torah she would need to know seventy languages. But even seventy languages would not be enough to truly comprehend the Torah of her parents. She would need to know how the words they carried and quoted and taught and translated echoed in their lives, just as Walter had written in his paper. She would have to know why her grandmother hid her inscribed copy of the Song of Songs in the kitchen cabinet—was it because of Ida and Shmuel's own intimacy, or was it because Ida didn't want Rosalie to know the language of desire when she was perched on the edge of her married life with Sol?

Maya would need to find Walter and Sonia in a Berlin bedroom—this Sonia whose name she carries, this woman whom Paul loved, this woman who might have lived instead of Walter had she not left the bed to look for crackers. Maya imagines herself walking in Jerusalem on a Shabbat afternoon, an elderly survivor named Sonia holding her arm for balance. The Sonia who would have survived would be wearing a tweed suit that covered the numbers on her arm and she would be on her way to her granddaughter's house for lunch. Survivor Sonia would hold Maya's arm and faintly remember the young man she once loved, how he soothed her with the words of Tagore and Whitman and the Song of Songs, just minutes before he was murdered. *Thank you for walking with me, Rabbi Maya,* survivor Sonia would have said, except that had Sonia lived and not Walter, Maya would be as fictional as survivor Sonia.

The details would matter: How the shade of the date palm trees soothed Walter in Shantiniketan. How the path of his dreams was somehow connected to the astonishments conjured by Madame Sylvie. How the thread woven on one side of the story could surface on the other, peacock blue to the blue of her mother's silk tallit. How a butterfly imagined by Tagore could emerge in Walter's description of a haiku, in her grandmother's pet name, in a style of chair in her brother's room. How the smells of turmeric, coriander, and cardamom wafted through their lives—sometimes hidden, sometimes pungent—just like they filled Kalustyan's Spices and Sweets on Lexington Avenue on the afternoon Maya went there to buy turmeric root so she could understand Walter and how he woke up to life in Bombay.

And Maya would need to understand Sol, how he lost his hearing in one ear when he was a boy—*easy to imagine because he told her the story*—but she would need to imagine—*impossibly*—how he loved Walter and what exactly transpired in the upper geniza and what lay behind the words she could barely make out behind a closed door. She would need to hear the secrets that Charlie and Philip taught Lenny before he died and how they pummeled one another into the grass in the backyard—*easy because they told her*—years before she was born. She would have to understand the ways Rosalie and Sol loved each other, and the ways Rosalie and Walter loved each other, listening to the words they spoke and the silences between the words—*impossible*.

And she would have to find herself in the story too: in the scenes she didn't remember (meeting Walter in the airport lounge when she was two), the scenes that didn't make sense when they happened (Walter, barefoot; the gift of a silver bracelet in the clothing store), and the scenes she could never recover (did she lose that bracelet on the subway, or was it tossed out with the garbage bags when they cleaned out the house?).

No doubt she would make an unsalvageable wreck of things. What kind of daughter would permit herself to imagine her parents' most intimate secrets? What kind of rabbi would trespass in a geniza and sew its scattered scraps into a haphazard crazy quilt? She is the intruder, not Madeline. But it's too late; she is already crawling inside this web, wrapping her fingers around its sticky tendrils. The path is partly illuminated: here is a slice of lemon cake in a Jerusalem courtyard, a sil batta burnished with spices, ash from burning sheet music, a brown felt hat, and scattered around the margins of a girl's birthday wishes and Tagore's poetry: a flower, a doorway, a footpath.

Just like at shul on Kol Nidre night, everyone is here, perched on the edge, waiting. They gather around; their eternal silence prompts her to listen. *It's okay*, they say. *We grant you permission. Our lives are over; we lived as best we could. You own the copyright now. Rearrange the fragments, invent a new art form, compose a song without words. It's your turn to make the beautiful possible. We are your parents and maybe we can show you the way.*

DEAR MADELINE

December 2008

Just the other day a backpacker with a faint Dutch accent knocked on my door and asked me if this was the correct address for an elderly French kabbalist who dispenses astonishments.

"Same address but she's long gone," I said. "The generations come and go."

" . . . but the earth remains forever. Ecclesiastes."

"You're a good student."

"Too bad I missed out on all that kabbalistic magic."

"There are still plenty of astonishments to go around," I said.

Jerusalem is the only place in the world where this can happen. I can pluck fresh dates from a tree that grows in my garden and meet a kid who knows his sources, searching for his place in the order of the universe. Everything here is layered with history and imbued with a challenge. I live in a crazy city where old dreams are translated into new ones— twisted, rerouted, corrupted, and quite often saturated with beauty. I believe Jerusalem has something to teach me, and I'm learning all the time.

I make a living leading meditation retreats that weave together Hasidic texts, world poetry, and my own conjurings. I'm the lead singer of Besamim, an Israeli-Arabic–South Asian fusion band. My boyfriend Gil plays sitar and oud, and Jase—who now lives on a yishuv with his wife and four kids—joins us on banjo when he's not leading American kids on hikes through the Sinai Desert. It's taken us awhile to gel as a band but we have quite a following now and we're about to record our first CD. I'll send you a copy.

Every Rosh Hodesh I join the Women of the Wall and we read Torah at the Western Wall—the Kotel—at the same spot where you first saw my mother slip her note between the stones. We are often harassed for leading our own Torah service and I find it helps to wear a tallit that doesn't remotely resemble the traditional one my father wore. My tallit is sewn out of a cotton batik tablecloth that I bought during a rabbinic service trip to Ghana. The batik is patterned with scrolling vines, textured with a border of blanket stitches I embroidered myself. It's rather immense and I love how it encompasses all of me. When I drape it on my shoulders I feel as if I'm the queen of a vast wadi.

When I was small my mother and I would stay home from shul on Kol Nidre night, just the two of us. She would sit on the chaise lounge on the back porch and hold me on her lap. Together we would listen to the first notes of the prayer wafting from the shul and I would rest my head on her shoulder and close my eyes. What better Kol Nidre could there ever be? If a child is given a complete world, why ask how it was created? And if that world was created on a bedrock of secrecy, who was I to crack it open? I could nibble on hints for the rest of my life and tango with what I knew and what I did not know. And Madeline—that would have been enough for me.

Honest to God, it would have been enough.

But we can't undo the past. I had buried both my parents and made my peace with the closed door of my mother's life. And then you blew it all up when you spoke his name. I hungered for every word you gave me and I sought out every seed of truth I could find. And at the same time I cursed you for leading me down that path. But no worries, Madeline. I'm a rabbi; I try to see life from all sides. You had no right to betray my mother, but you were brave enough to teach me what you believed I needed to learn. I never would have chosen you as a chavrusa, but sometimes our chavrusas choose us.

Once you gave me the bones of the story I had to find my way through it, interpret its code, make it my own. At first I thought I would create a source sheet of their favorite texts and simply meditate on the white space surrounding the words, letting the unspoken patterns speak for themselves. But without a narrative linking the texts, the tesserae would not form a mosaic, the words would be frozen in antiquity, and the story of their lives would be lost forever. My retreat students would show up for a dose of inspiration, but without a good story they wouldn't stick around to find out what happened. The she'elah-teshuvah lines were easy for me to write, just like the contents of the purple binder were an easy assignment for Rosalie and Walter. Wisdom is easy, Madeline. It's actual history that proves to be an unknowable, fugitive dream.

The writing of this half-imagined, half-true book about my three parents has been a comfort of sorts. Like all books, this is an inquiry, a game of blindfold in the dark, a whiff of spice, a forgotten prayer remembered. If I trespassed on their lives, I beg their forgiveness. My inheritance has many layers and unraveling is a messy, dangerous act.

I hope you will consider publishing The Beautiful Possible with your little press. My retreat students are always hungry for another book—a new seed—and our story may interest them in some way. As for my brothers, I haven't decided if I will share this with them just yet, though I suspect they won't be surprised that the milkman's daughter is really the milkman's daughter. I'm sure you know the Yiddish proverb the heart is half a prophet.

But I'm finished now, Madeline. This book is yours. It's time to free myself to remember my mother and my father as I knew them. My father's fingers pointing out the words in the Talmud, my tiny hand resting on top of his knuckles. My father standing on the bima, staring down at my mother and me, unable to hide his smile because we were alive in the world and we belonged to him.

I gave away all my mother's clothes except for her white cotton Shabbat dress patterned with red bricks. I brought it with me to Jerusalem, along with my father's books. At times I reach into the back of my closet and touch the satiny fabric, caress the huge flower-shaped buttons that I played with when I sat beside her in shul. The woman who wore that dress was my real mother. How I know and love her cannot be translated into the pages of any book. I am her daughter and she was my mother and I will miss her always.

On the last day of my retreats I invite my students to meditate on this: Inside every story lies the hidden kernel of an infinite one. We chant it together to a niggun I composed; you can hear a version of it on our CD. I came up with that line after I finished writing this book. I'm not sure I understand the essence of my own words, but I believe you will, Madeline. At least I hope so.

I often think about the day you met my mother at the Kotel, looking on as she tucked her note between the ancient stones. You told her that her words would not find their way to a geniza or to God but now I believe that you contradicted yourself. Her words were being watched over; the story was in your hands. And you carried it for all those years so that one day you could give it to me.

Yours,

Maya

ACKNOWLEDGMENTS

This novel owes its existence to many books, teachers, and conversations. I discuss some of these influences in the "Books Within the Book" essay in the P.S.™ section, and offer particular gratitude to the late Alex Aronson, whose journey inspired Walter's story.

Much appreciation to my insightful and intuitive editor, Jillian Verrillo, for her vision, generous work, and advocacy; to Terry Karten for inviting me on board; and to everyone at HarperCollins, especially Amy Baker, Dori Carlson, Cal Morgan, Kathryn Ratcliffe-Lee, Marry Sasso, Nikki Smith, and Sherry Wasserman; with thanks to Katherine Haigler for her astute copyediting. I am grateful to my dynamic agent, Rena Rossner of the Deborah Harris Agency, and offer special thanks to Ilana Kurshan and Deborah Harris for their comments and support.

Thank you to the scholars who answered my questions: Francis Nicosia (Berlin), Peter Schmitthenner and Stephen Legg (Bombay), and Rabbi Morton Leifman (who shared anecdotes about JTS in the 1940s). My gratitude to readers of early drafts: Richard Greenberg, Sarah Heller, and Lisa Feld, with special thanks to Leah Strigler for her historical lens and multiple readings. I am indebted to my longtime cherished reader, Laura Glen Louis, whose generous and sage advice saved this novel (and me) more than once.

I am grateful to my teachers: Reb Mimi Feigelson, who first introduced me to the teachings of the Ishbitzer Rebbe, and Rute Yair-Nussbaum, whose illuminations helped me understand how Hasidic ideas and literary fiction could share a common language. Thanks to cartoonist Jennifer Berman for permission to use the Velveteen Rabbi, and to Rachel Barenblat for giving the term new life.

Thank you to the Bronx Council on the Arts for generous financial support, to the Drisha Institute for Jewish Education for providing a gracious home for learning, and to my friends at the Rabbinical Assembly and JTS who invited me into their circle and gave me a front-row seat to their scholarship. I am grateful to my chavrusas Susan Kaplow and Jill Minkoff and to my Rosh Hodesh group for conversations about all things Jewish and feminist. And thanks always to Laura Paradise.

This novel owes a debt to the memory of my father, Eli, whose unfinished journey seeded a legacy. Much gratitude and love to my mother, Edie, for providing a house overflowing with stories; to my siblings, Jane and Michael; and to my extended tribe.

Finally, all my love and appreciation to my husband, Ralph—best reader and best friend—and to our sons, Eli and Ezra, for their many kindnesses.

About the author

About the book

Insights,
Interviews
& More . . .

Read on

Meet Amy Gottlieb

AMY GOTTLIEB IS a graduate of Clark University and the University of Chicago. Her fiction and poetry have been published in many literary journals and anthologies, and she is the recipient of fellowships from the Bronx Council on the Arts and the Drisha Institute for Jewish Education. She lives with her family in New York City, where she teaches and writes. *The Beautiful Possible* is her first novel. ✣

The Synagogue at the Edge of Macondo

IN THE LATE 1950S, my parents bought a house in East Meadow, Long Island. There wasn't a synagogue in walking distance, so they joined forces with a handful of neighbors and started one. This fledgling synagogue grew in sync with my childhood: When I was a baby the small congregation gathered in a drab green tent; when I was a kindergartner we assembled in a split-level house; and when I was old enough to attend Hebrew school we had moved into a brick building fronted with glass. Its classrooms were where I first visualized Lot's wife rendered into a pillar of salt and the Israelites dancing around a golden calf. My friends and I would practice our first kisses in the synagogue bathroom, sample our first cigarettes in the stairwell, and spy on our neighbors in intimate moments of prayer—or gossip—in the sanctuary. I often thought of this synagogue as a palace of guarded secrets, but I eventually outgrew its relevance. I wanted to become a writer, and the Judaism of my childhood couldn't compete with my literary aspirations.

As a teenager, I looked to literature to teach me the language of the soul. My dog-eared copy of *The Book of Nightmares* by Galway Kinnell taught me about poetic transcendence in the face of mortality. I turned to Colette's novels to appreciate the vocabulary of physical desire. When I discovered Virginia ▶

3

The Synagogue at the Edge of Macondo
(continued)

Woolf in college, I identified with her stalwart atheism yet held a deep spiritual reverence for her fiction.

When I was in my early twenties, I fell in love with Gabriel García Márquez's *One Hundred Years of Solitude* and enrolled in graduate school, as I somehow believed that studying comparative literature at the University of Chicago would reveal the hidden aspects of Macondo, García Márquez's fictive city of mirrors. (As a naïve and idealistic young writer, I didn't quite get the irony of this scenario.) I wanted only to pave a life that would allow me to worship the books I loved and, in time, write novels of my own.

While dissecting Latin American novels and slaving over critical theory during that cold Chicago winter, I craved a diversion and wandered over to the Divinity School, which housed a glorious labyrinthine bookstore and a decent coffee shop. I was quickly welcomed into juicy discussions about ancient fertility cults, everyday mysticism, and the eroticism of the Song of Songs. (My childhood Hebrew school had obviously left out all the good parts.) I took classes with religious historians Mircea Eliade and Paul Ricouer, and identified with what Thomas Merton referred to as the "ingrained irrelevancy" of monks and hippies and poets—marginal seekers whose lives are defined by a quest for meaning.

I eventually left academia to pursue

fiction writing, and moved to a one-room studio on Manhattan's Upper West Side. It was a magical time: I wrote my first publishable short stories in a single room with a dial-free phone that rang only when my elderly neighbor called to tell me she had laid out tarot cards and had discovered a revelation about my future. (She correctly predicted I would marry my husband.) Without a kitchen, I invited friends for gourmet meals prepared in a single electric pan, and I washed the dishes in the bathtub. One night when I couldn't sleep I examined my bookshelf crammed with literature and criticism, and realized I owned two Jewish books: the small white prayer book I had received for my bat mitzvah and Isaac Bashevis Singer's *Collected Stories*. I had no interest in prayer, so I started reading Singer.

I soon found my way to the writings of Abraham Joshua Heschel, Martin Buber, and other Hasidic masters, and discovered a faith-based language that made sense to me, not as a rabbi or scholar but as an iconoclastic Jewish seeker. From study halls, yeshiva classrooms, and synagogues of many stripes, this quest took over my life, and on the way allowed me to make a living as a Judaica editor.

For fourteen years, I worked as director of publications for the Rabbinical Assembly, the international association of Conservative rabbis. I spent my days in a spacious book-lined office at the Jewish ▶

The Synagogue at the Edge of Macondo
(continued)

Theological Seminary; from my window I would gaze at the statue of Gabriel blowing his trumpet atop Riverside Church. I was immersed in editing liturgy, theology, biblical scholarship, and a palette of spiritual writing, and received an extraordinary education. I had an insider's view of the complex lives of rabbis and their families—in the words of my characters, "the impossible holiness trade." I was also given a glimpse into the Seminary's history and was often regaled with stories about the days when Conservative rabbis referred to one another as "gentlemen and scholars," long before women were permitted to join the rabbinate and the shifts in American Jewish life demanded new paradigms for spiritual leadership. As the consummate outsider—a writer working a day job—I could naturally imagine a stranger like Walter passing through the Seminary and began to ponder the threads of what became *The Beautiful Possible*.

The relationship between an author and her characters is ultimately steeped in mystery, and I am grateful to these fictional beings whose stories allowed me to re-create a fraction of my childhood synagogue and its guarded secrets. In the surreal logic of my literary imagination, my characters brought me to the edge of another Macondo and invited me to pitch a synagogue tent, just like the tent that welcomed Sol and Rosalie to Briar Wood, just like the tent where my own story began. ∾

On Writing Enigma

I WORKED ON THIS NOVEL for well over a decade—with many interruptions—though at a certain point I no longer kept track; I simply kept writing within slices of time carved between the demands of a full-time job and family. For most of those years I would awake at 4 a.m. so I could write before the day began, and those hours passed like a living dream. I had never intended for this intimate story to blossom into a novel filled with historical backstory, large sweeps of time, and a medley of texts. I often felt as if I were trying to build a trapeze sturdy enough to support all this weight yet supple enough to allow my story to fly with a semblance of grace.

Ten years is a long interval, and the labor of writing a novel is at odds with the pace of ordinary time. In the predawn hours, scenes may become more saturated and characters more textured, but a writer's day often begins when she has to abandon the desk, wake her children for school, and leave for work. While I wrote this book, my life had spawned a wealth of responsibilities and many essential joys. I also began to write poetry and explore Hasidic texts, both of which brought me closer to honoring the hidden and the unseen behind the words on the page. The novel demanded that I respect these internal shifts and allow its architecture to make room for theological uncertainty. This proved to be a precarious balancing act, and it sometimes felt as if I were ▶

On Writing Enigma *(continued)*

teetering between poles of subtlety and excess. Just before I dug into a last-ditch attempt at revision, a writer friend sat me down at her kitchen table, reminded me of the central enigma within my novel, and urged me to stay true to my characters' storylines, wherever they led.

Chekhov writes, "Art doesn't provide answers; it can only formulate questions correctly." In many ways, *The Beautiful Possible* is a book of questions. Hidden things—secrets, veiled truths, refractions—dwell at its core. Rosalie, the daughter of an iconoclastic Hasid, accepts that a life of faith is filled with tension and is best lived between the lines. Her unfolding story—from Brooklyn to her blue-tiled bathroom in Mexico—reveals rather than declares. The heart of her belief is not paved by theological certainty but by a desire, in Rilke's words, "to live the questions." Rosalie's truth is expressed in her ambivalence and her yearning, both of which fuel the love story and propel the spiritual flow of the novel.

As the author of the manuscript *The Beautiful Possible*, Maya uses her imagination to navigate the contours of her parents' braided desires. She is the inheritor of a mash-up of influences, stories, and texts; interpretation is her modus operandi. As a rabbi and novelist, she tries to reconcile the rabbinic compulsion to make meaning with the artistic tenet of "negative capability"—

Keats's term for the ability to dwell in uncertainties, mysteries, and doubts. In her closing letter to Madeline, Maya writes, "Every story contains the secret kernel of an infinite one," and then adds that she's not sure she understands the essence of her own words. *Read this as you wish*, she seems to say, *just as I do*. As I grappled with the enigmatic core of my novel, I wanted to leave room for readers to engage with the story and contemplate its questions, just as Maya does.

A traditional Hebrew phrase *l'dor v'dor*, "from generation to generation," often seems cliché, but it feels apt for my novel, which begins with a harrowing trauma and ends with Maya's fulfillment of Sonia's dream. Because Maya lives, Sonia's desire is actualized, at least in a mystical sense. This ending is not meant to be a statement on post-Holocaust continuity per se, but suggests the flaws of history. We don't know what convoluted braid or karmic dance will lead us from the past to the future, but life *is* potential; desire spurs us forward, seeding new stories and fresh questions to ponder and savor. ❧

Books Within the Book

MY CHARACTERS DWELL among books, and I invited several works to become part of my novel's essential conversations. Readers may want an introduction to some of these books and their authors, along with other works that influenced me.

The Ishbitzer school of Hasidism is a radical branch of Hasidic thought that expresses ideas about how to live an authentic life. The Ishbitzer Rebbe, Mordecai Yosef of Ishbitz (1800–1854), was author of the Torah commentary *Mei HaShiloach*, published posthumously by his grandson and later translated into English as *Living Waters: The Mei HaShiloach* by Betsalel Philip Edwards. The Ishbitzer's subversive theology was often invoked by countercultural rabbis Shlomo Carlebach and Zalman Schachter-Shalomi, both of whom contributed to a spiritual revitalization within the contemporary American Jewish community. Zalman Schachter-Shalomi's *Wrapped in a Holy Flame: Teachings and Tales of the Hasidic Masters* is an excellent introduction to the motifs of Hasidism, neo-Hasidism, and Jewish existentialism. His early work, *Spiritual Intimacy: A Study of Counseling in Hasidism*, provided the source for the Radish's interpretation of the bride's seven circles.

This novel owes an immense debt to the legacy of theologian, scholar, and activist Abraham Joshua Heschel (1907–1972), author of *Man Is Not Alone*,

God in Search of Man, *Moral Grandeur and Spiritual Audacity*, *The Prophets*, *The Sabbath*, and more. Heschel's works are marked by a faith-based vocabulary that is honest, challenging, and grounded in poetry. His writings are accessible, but for readers who wish to understand his influence and context I recommend *Abraham Joshua Heschel: The Call of Transcendence* by Shai Held. Heschel's 1945 YIVO speech is recounted and partly quoted in Edward Kaplan's *Holiness in Words: Abraham Joshua Heschel's Poetics of Piety*.

The transcendent poetry of Rabindranath Tagore (1861–1941), India's first Nobel laureate, is connected to Walter's journey and lives at the heart of this novel. The mystical language of his epic poem *Gitanjali* ("Song Offerings") shares some overlaps with images from the Zohar. (Tagore was a beloved and popular Bengali folk poet, making it plausible that Kavita would have been familiar with his songs.) The Zohar quote about the ceaseless river is taken from Daniel Matt's magisterial translation, *The Zohar: Pritzker Edition, Volume 3*.

I originally conceived of *The Beautiful Possible* as a midrash on the Song of Songs. (*The Mountain of Spices* was its working title.) Several of the novel's motifs derive from the Song of Songs, with hints of Ruth, Job, and Ecclesiastes. *The Same Sea*, a lyrical novel by Amos Oz, served as a model of how ancient Jewish texts could wind through a contemporary character-driven story. For a poetic look at the subversive ▶

nature of biblical texts, see *For the Love of God: The Bible as an Open Book* by Alicia Suskin Ostriker.

My love of the Bible is enhanced and renewed by the work of Avivah Gottlieb Zornberg, author of several volumes of biblical commentary, including *Genesis: The Beginning of Desire* and *The Murmuring Deep: Reflections on the Biblical Unconscious*. Her biblical explorations form a tapestry woven from rabbinic midrash, literary criticism, Hasidic thought, and psychoanalytic theory. Her discursive approach is illuminating and often quite moving.

Some of the novel's language of contradiction owes a debt to the poetry of Yehuda Amichai.

Anita Desai's novel *Baumgartner's Bombay* made me aware of Jews who fled Nazi Germany and went to India.

I am indebted to several books that enabled me to imagine Walter's journey. Martin Kämpchen's chapter in *Jewish Exile in India 1933–1945*, edited by Anil Bhatti and Johannes H. Voigt, taught me about Alex Aronson's sojourn at Shantiniketan. Aronson wrote a beautiful account of his stay at the ashram, *Brief Chronicles of the Time*, which was published in India and bound in purple sari cloth. *Rabindranath Tagore: The Myriad-Minded Man* by Krishna Dutta and Andrew Robinson was a source of useful background information, and Helmut Newton's *Autobiography* gave me a window into the 1938 voyage of the *Conte Rosso*. *Zionism and Anti-Semitism in Germany* by Francis Nicosia lent me insights into my characters' circumstances in Germany.

The character of Madame Sylvie owes a debt to the memory of the Jerusalem kabbalist Colette Aboulker-Muscat, whose work has been documented by several of her students, including Rodger Kamenetz in his book *The History of Last Night's Dream: Discovering the Hidden Life of the Soul*.

This novel was influenced by Hasidic thought, which invites enigma, and a radical honesty in the face of the unspoken—essential tools for a writer. For perspectives on embracing literary paradox and uncertainty, I find inspiration in the essays of poets Jane Hirshfield in *Ten Windows: How Great Poems Transform the World* and Mary Ruefle in *Madness, Rack, and Honey*. ◠